"I HAVE SOU."

"Oh?"

"We must do   , everything they woul   ue said.
"We have done   we are ready
but for a few small details."

"Which are?"

"This is one," he said and lifted from a porcelain box
an object that sparkled in the lamplight. "A ring. It was my
mother's."

Marianna blinked and felt her heart constrict. His
mother's ring.

He sat beside her and took her hand in his. His fingers
were warm against hers. She expected him to slide the ring
onto her finger and let go, but he lingered, stroking the
back of her hand with soft, slow circles of his thumb.

"It . . . it is lovely, my lord. Shall I put it on?" she asked,
unable to keep a nervous flutter from her voice. Was he
aware of what he was doing to her hand?

"My mother never took this ring off," he answered without letting go.

Gently, Marianna tried to pull her hand free. "I . . . it . . .
under the circumstances, it seems improper to wear your
mother's ring."

He shook his head. "You must. It is a family heirloom.
Our guests will expect it, and they will think it odd if you
are not wearing it, just as they will think it odd if—"

"If, my lord?"

"If you try to pull your hands away when I touch them,
as you are now."

"Oh!" So he was not caressing her hand to express affection, he was simply making a point. Her cheeks flamed.
She felt foolish for having thought, even for a second, that
he had formed some sort of *tendre* for her.

"Our guests will also think it odd if you balk," he said,
leaning toward her, "when I do"—he took her into his
arms—"this." And then he kissed her. . . .

BOOK YOUR PLACE ON OUR WEBSITE AND MAKE THE READING CONNECTION!

We've created a customized website just for our very special readers, where you can get the inside scoop on everything that's going on with Zebra, Pinnacle and Kensington books.

When you come online, you'll have the exciting opportunity to:

- View covers of upcoming books

- Read sample chapters

- Learn about our future publishing schedule (listed by publication month *and author*)

- Find out when your favorite authors will be visiting a city near you

- Search for and order backlist books from our online catalog

- Check out author bios and background information

- Send e-mail to your favorite authors

- Meet the Kensington staff online

- Join us in weekly chats with authors, readers and other guests

- Get writing guidelines

- AND MUCH MORE!

**Visit our website at
http://www.kensingtonbooks.com**

MISS GRANTHAM'S ONE TRUE SIN

Melynda Beth Skinner

ZEBRA BOOKS
Kensington Publishing Corp.
http://www.kensingtonbooks.com

For anyone who has ever read to a child, especially my own mama, Erma Andrews, who read aloud so often that she had our storybooks memorized. Thank you, Mama.

ACKNOWLEDGMENTS

My novels could not happen without the love and support of many fine people. This time around, I wish to thank my editor, Amy Garvey; my literary agent, Jennifer Jackson; my critique partner Mary Louise Wells; my test readers, Amy Augustine, Cathy Marie Hake, my brother David Andrews, Jane Myers Perrine, my mom, and finally Carrie Ribnikar and Sandi Mozdzierz (whom I left out last time around!). I must also thank my husband, whose flawed eyebrow and devilish ways have always inspired me. Having someone believe in me the way he does is humbling—and essential. Thank you, my love. Thank you, dear reader. Thank you all.

One

His name was True Sin.

At least that's what the ladies of the ton called him behind their fans. They whispered he was sent by Satan to tempt the feminine wary, a great many of whom, by all accounts, hadn't been nearly wary enough. No one seemed to know exactly how many ladies had fallen prey to his charm. Various numbers were bandied about, all of them jaw-droppingly large.

While Miss Marianna Helena Grantham was never one to pair credibility with such gossip, when it came to Truesdale Sinclair, gossip was all she had to rely on, for she'd never set eyes on the man. Still, she was resolved to remain impartial. She would form her own opinion. Logic mandated that she would either find him agreeable or she would not. Logic reasoned that the rumors were false, that no one man could have had so many . . . willing companions.

But, just in case, Marianna would be on her guard. She had no intention of becoming one of the viscount's conquests. She approached his great country house with the caution of a gazelle creeping into a lion's den.

When the oaken doors of his library were thrown open for her, she marched resolutely forward and stood before his desk, where he sat concentrating over a book of accounts. Marianna wasn't even certain the Viscount Trowbridge realized she was there, for he did not look up. She

took the resulting opportunity to scan the room, which was
filled with polished wood, rich leather, sumptuous fabrics,
and what had to be over a thousand fine volumes. Her gaze
landed on touches of silver and gilt, ivory and crystal. If
this well-appointed room were any indication of the quality
of the rest of the viscount's estate, Marianna's parents would
be well satisfied.

If Trowbridge accepted her offer.

And if he did not?

Then she would have to return to London to await the
arrival of her parents. Marianna did not wish to contemplate
their reaction were they to discover what she'd done, what
she'd been doing for the entire year she'd been in London
without them, the lies she'd told in the letters she'd written
them.

She was supposed to have been having a London Season.
She was supposed to be a belle of the *ton,* and she was
supposed to have an understanding with a titled young gentleman even now.

But if she were a belle, then surely she was a blue belle,
for no such understanding existed. She hadn't had the first
offer. In truth, in the entire year she had lived in London,
she hadn't had so much as an offer to dance.

She turned her attention to the large, wide-shouldered
man sitting behind the desk. At nine and twenty, the Viscount Trowbridge wasn't exactly young. Thank goodness
she'd been so vague in her letters to her parents! She wondered if he looked his age, but she could see little more
than the top of his head. Marianna frowned a little. He wore
his dark, wavy hair unfashionably long and looked more
like a pirate than a gentleman. His coat lay carelessly tossed
over a chair by the fire, and there was no cravat in sight.
Before she could stop them, her eyes darted to where his
cravat should have been. His white linen shirt was loosely
tied and slightly open at the neck. Marianna blinked at the
shock of dark, crisp-looking hair peeking over the top. Or-
dinarily, the improper sight would have elicited her staunch
disapproval, but not now. No cravat and no man to attend

to the viscount's coat or to cut his hair—these indicated Trowbridge could not afford a proper valet. She'd been led to believe the viscount was in some grave financial difficulty. She'd counted on it, in fact. Thus, his dishevelment served only to reassure her.

She dragged her eyes away from his exposed triangle of hairy chest, pulled her shoulders back, and waited for his acknowledgment, but the viscount only continued with his work, his fingers tracing a column of figures in his ledger. Marianna's eyes focused on his hands. He wore no signet ring or gloves. Though clean, his large hands were brown and rough-looking. She frowned again. Just what sort of man was the Viscount Trowbridge? Ophelia Robertson had led her to expect a gentleman, albeit a gentleman in strained financial circumstances. But those hands . . .

She coughed softly.

"Yes? Yes, what is it?" he said in a harried tone. He still did not look up. "I have much to do. State your business and be done with it."

Marianna swallowed her fear—along with a good deal of pride—and pulled from her reticule a tightly corked brown glass bottle containing a small fortune in loose gems. It was all she had.

"I am prepared to trade half of the contents of this bottle for a fortnight of your time and a lie."

She set the bottle on top of his ledger, right under his nose. Trowbridge didn't move, and Marianna held her breath, wondering what he'd do. She was desperate. Truth to tell, she would trade all of the bottle's contents if she had to, but promising only half left her room to bargain. She knew it was risky to present her entire cache of gems up front, but if she did not, he might assume she had more to offer, that she was holding out on him. The most reasonable course of action was to let him see right away her upper limit.

Trowbridge finally looked up from his ledger, and Marianna just managed to stop herself from gaping at him. *Saints and sinners!* At least one of the rumors about him was disconcertingly accurate. Truesdale Sinclair was so handsome, it felt like some sort of sin just looking at him. Except for the tiny scar neatly dividing his right eyebrow, he was shockingly perfect. Shockingly handsome.

Not that the slight imperfection did anything to mitigate his attractiveness. On the contrary, the feather scar gave the eyes something to rest on and the mind a mystery to ponder.

How had he acquired it? His countenance was one to inspire all sorts of wild imaginings. A violent encounter with a wolf or a bear, perhaps. Or, as the viscount looked more like a pirate than a gentleman, perhaps he'd earned the scar in a sword fight. Most anything was imaginable— except for Trowbridge ever coming away the loser. Even with him sitting down, it was easy to see he was quite tall and strongly built. Unwilling to look directly into his eyes, Marianna clung to his tiny scar, clung like a desperate, ship- wrecked woman to some piece of floating debris.

He was dangerous. Dangerously masculine. And he hadn't even so much as shaken her hand—yet. Marianna's heart beat a little faster in spite of her resolve to remain unaffected, for if Trowbridge accepted her offer, he would be doing more than shaking her hand.

He would have to kiss her. She would insist upon it.

He reached for the bottle and gave it a little shake, then examined the raised lettering on the front.

"Mrs. Beeton's Miracle Pills," he read. *"For the bust."* His flawed eyebrow rose into the disarray of dark curls that was his hair. "I am sorry, miss, but I find I have no need of miracles today, and you—" He allowed his gaze to slide downward over her ample charms. "You have had rather your share, I should think."

Marianna felt herself blush, the heat spreading from the neckline of her brown serge traveling costume to her burn- ing cheeks, and Trowbridge laughed.

Just then, a high-pitched, clearly feminine giggle ema- nated from the space under his desk, and Marianna's jaw, over which she'd thought she had control, finally did drop open. The bounder had a woman under there!

"Sir," Marianna said, narrowing her eyes to outraged slits, "I can see that you are indeed *busy.*"

Snatching her bottle up, she spun away and fled back through the cavernous hall to the front door, muttering. "I was announced. He *knew* I was about to enter, and still the bounder has a woman *under his desk!*" She'd conceded there might be some truth to the rumors about Truesdale Sinclair, but *this!* This was outside of enough. "He is a rake! No, he is worse. He is . . . he is . . ." Marianna couldn't think of an adequate descriptor.

She had just reached the front door, when a large, warm hand clamped over her arm.

"Leaving so soon?" True Sin drawled.

"Unhand me at once!"

"Not until you empty the bag about your business here. You said something about a lie."

"It no longer signifies. Good day!" She tugged at his arm, but she might just as well have been pulling against a pillar of marble, for all the good it did her. The man wasn't just big; he was enormous. She wasn't going anywhere. Marianna pulled herself up to her full height. She was tall, but the top of her head didn't even reach his chin.

"You, sir, are no gentleman. You are even worse than the rumors say."

He clicked the heels of his scuffed boots smartly together and gave a little bow. "I am pleased to know I do not disappoint. Now," he said, loosening his grip and offering her his arm in a show of fake gentility, "shall we return to the library and continue our most interesting discussion?"

Marianna was not fooled. She knew she had no choice in the matter. He would know the purpose of her visit one way or another. She glared pointedly at his arm and gripped her bottle tighter.

He grinned and let his arm drop. "I see you are an intelligent woman, Miss Grantham. I anticipate that whatever you have to tell me will be frightfully interesting, indeed. Shall we adjourn to the library?" he repeated.

"I would prefer another locale," she said tightly. "A parlor. Anywhere. Not the library."

"As you wish. This way."

The angry voices kept the little blonde cowering under the big mahogany desk at first, but then curiosity drove Eleanor to forget her fears. She crept to the great library doors and peeked around, just in time to see the blonde-haired lady disappear into the room with the blue sofa, the one Eleanor loved to jump up and down on when no one was around to catch her—which wasn't often enough for Eleanor's liking. She frowned, wondering if Uncle Sin were taking the Friday-faced lady there to jolly her up by showing *her* how to jump on the sofa. It certainly cheered Eleanor when *she* was cross. She darted through the front hall and scampered outside.

There was a sturdy bush beneath the parlor window just right for a five-year-old to stand in. She peeked into the tall window, but the view was disappointing. No jumping. The grown-ups weren't doing anything but talking. Boring. Grown-ups were like that, she supposed. She went in search of her sisters. They were older than Eleanor, too, but they were almost never boring. Especially not when Eleanor stirred them up a bit. She patted the salamander in her pocket and licked her lips in anticipation of mischief.

True motioned to a chair. Miss Grantham sat primly on the edge of it, her back ramrod straight. *Intelligent and proper,* he thought, making a mental list of the woman's attributes as he discovered them—a habit he had cultivated. It helped give him the upper hand. The trick was to discern his opponent's qualities before revealing his own. He looked at her expectantly, but she made no move to tell him why she had come. *Cautious,* he added to his list.

"You ran like a rabbit just now. Why?" True asked, deliberately blunt. Life had taught him to be an excellent judge of character, and he sensed this woman would prefer plain speaking to the indirect.

She only stared stubbornly up at him.

He'd seen that same look on too many other faces to misinterpret it now. It meant the same thing it always did: distaste and disapproval. In her mind, he'd already been tried and found guilty. He wondered briefly what he'd been convicted of this time. Not that it mattered. Not that it had *ever* truly mattered. He reviewed the last moments in his mind before coming to the only conclusion possible, as ridiculous as it was.

"You believe I have a lady stuffed under my desk," he said.

She scowled, set her chin a notch higher, and then arched one finely sculpted blonde brow. "No, my lord, I do not fancy she is a *lady* at all."

Sarcastic, he added, "A skillful riposte, Miss Grantham," he said, "but I am afraid you've gone wide of the mark." He sat opposite her. "You see, the young lady you heard under my desk—"

"So you admit it!"

"She is my niece, and she is—"

"Your niece!" Miss Grantham's skin went even paler than before, a feat he'd not have thought possible. "Saints and sinners!" she exclaimed and glared at him, leaving little doubt to which of the categories she thought True belonged.

He gave a bark of laughter before he could stop himself. The silly chit thought he'd just confessed to consorting with his own niece! She was determined to think the worst of him. He perversely decided not to help unknot the coil Miss Grantham had fashioned of her rash assumptions. In fact, he rather thought the lady deserved a little more rope.

"Aye," True continued slyly, "and a sweet little wisp of a thing she is. She was wiggling on my lap just before you arrived. Eleanor is her name."

She jumped to her feet and held up her palm. "I do not wish to know her name, my lord! I am leaving now, and if you attempt to detain me, I shall scream." She marched haughtily toward the door.

True smiled at her back, thoroughly enjoying the sport now. "Likely no one would pay you any mind if you did scream. Eleanor screams quite often."

The pronouncement had the desired affect. Miss Grantham made for the door in a mad rush.

"Of course," True said loudly, "most five-year-olds do."

Miss Grantham skidded to a rather undignified halt in the wide doorway and turned slowly around. She blinked her long, golden lashes once, twice, and then trained a piercing stare on him.

"Your niece is *five?*" she asked.

"Yes. Well, one of them is. I have three, you know." He was smiling openly now.

A ghost of a smile crossed her own lips. "No. I did not know."

True pasted on an expression of shock. "You don't say?" His sarcasm earned him a roll of her eyes, and he laughed. "They are my late brother's children—now my wards. Little Eleanor is quite terribly shy of strangers. She darted under my desk as soon as you were announced."

If he had expected her to offer him a cascade of apology, he'd have been disappointed, for she did not look in the least contrite. Instead, she moved slowly, thoughtfully, back toward the sofa and sat, frowning once more.

True crossed his arms over his chest. "Miss Grantham, you must dislike children very much."

She looked offended. "Dislike children? Rubbish! I am a schoolmistress, sir."

A schoolmistress? Perhaps he wasn't such a good judge of character after all. She carried herself more like a duke's daughter than a bluestocking.

She tapped her jaw thoughtfully. "Three girls, you say?"

"Yes," he confirmed.

"Ages?"

"Five, nine, and ten."

"I do not know if my parents will approve," she said.

"Of what?"

"Of the children."

He nodded. "I see."

"I think not, my lord."

True laughed. "You are correct. I do not understand at all. Perhaps I should ring for tea, and you should explain matters."

An hour later, True called for his coach, and Miss Marianna Grantham left Trowbridge Manor with his word as his bond. He shook his head. She actually trusted him to keep his word!

She was bound for London. She'd return the next morning with her belongings. She planned to reside with him at Trowbridge Manor for six weeks.

True walked to the window of the summer parlor and watched her mince primly down the steps. She was twenty-one years old, and already a high-stickler. She'd run like a striped ass when she'd thought he had a strumpet stashed under his desk. He couldn't help chuckling as he watched her now.

She moved sedately across the drive to the waiting coach. Even for that short distance, she had unfurled a parasol. Her pale, salt-colored skin matched the white-blonde of her hair, which she wore in a smooth, tight bun at her crown, and she walked like she had a poker shoved down the back of her corset.

He watched her board the coach and opened his palm. A large, deep green emerald, exquisitely cut, sparkled there in the bright August sunlight. The jewel was a sort of down payment, a guarantee of her sincerity, she'd said. The rest of the gems—sapphires, rubies, diamonds, pearls, and more emeralds—were still in her little brown bottle, which she'd tucked away in her plain, proper little reticule once more.

True watched the drive long enough to see four of his men start out with the coach. Outriders. The silly chit was traipsing about the countryside with a deuced fortune in treasure. She had intended to hire a post chaise back to London, but True had insisted she take his own coach. He didn't need any additional trouble.

That female was going to be trouble enough already.

She was heading back to London, where she would arrange her affairs and then start back for Trowbridge Manor on the morrow. It seemed she really was a schoolteacher—*practical, proper, and prudish.* But she was also an heiress. A wayward runaway heiress, a chit born and reared to be a lady. No wonder he'd not been able to size her up!

He strode back into his library and sat before the fire, pulling a decanter of brandy from a table as he passed. A gust of wind whistled down the flue. For a brief moment, the fire glowed brighter and then subsided, popping and hissing. That was about how long it had taken True to agree to Marianna Grantham's little plan, once she'd explained the purpose of her visit. He sighed.

She was an angel sent from on high.

Or perhaps she was a punishment sent to exact penance for all the many pleasures he'd taken from life.

He lifted the crystal decanter of amber liquid and poured a measure large enough to raise eyebrows in more proper drawing rooms, then tossed it down in a single burning gulp.

She didn't want much from him. True was to act the part of her betrothed for a month, at the end of which time she would cry off the engagement, give him three-quarters of her sparkling cache, and walk away. Simple.

True growled. Nothing was simple.

She'd come because she heard he was in dun territory and desperate for funds. He gave a derisive snort. Word always did travel quickly among the fashionable elite. He supposed discussion of the mull in which he'd recently found himself was standard fare in breakfast rooms across London. But the rumor mongers hadn't quite got it right this time.

They didn't know just how desperate True Sin really was.

He'd lost a ship. It had gone down in a storm with his

elder brother and sister-in-law aboard. The rest of True's small fleet had been impounded pending settlement of the lost cargo, and his wastrel brother's many creditors were demanding immediate payment. True was in danger of losing everything he'd worked so hard to achieve. Though he'd bargained for three-quarters of Miss Grantham's bottle of gems, he knew it wasn't enough to pluck his arse from the River Tick. Hell and blast, thrice her entire cache wouldn't be enough. No, True needed more, much more, and there was only one way to get it.

He'd have to marry the scheming chit.

True swore.

She had been astonishingly frank with him as she'd told him why she'd been sent to London. Her parents were wealthy. Simple English country folk by birth, the elder Granthams were nevertheless shrewd people, and they had made a vast fortune planting and trading in the West Indies. Miss Grantham was an only child, an heiress, and she had journeyed to England to marry a titled gentleman, a gentleman who needed her money badly enough to overlook her family's lack of connections.

True Sin qualified. Upon his brother's death, he'd become the new Viscount Trowbridge. Along with his brother's title, he'd inherited his brother's estate, his brother's three little girls, and his brother's mountain of debts. Franklin had been up to his cravat in angry creditors. There was scarce a person in London who didn't know True needed funds, and it was also well known he didn't give a fig about family connections—his own or anyone else's.

Of *course* Miss Grantham had come to him.

He was to play the part of her betrothed for a month, and then their engagement would be broken. Amicably, of course.

True wondered briefly why she needed a false suitor, why she hadn't been indulging in the boring crush of a London Season instead of masquerading as an impoverished schoolmistress. She hadn't offered any explanation, and he hadn't asked her. Whatever her reasons, he did not care.

True poured another brandy. He'd encountered young women of her ilk all too often. Invariably spoiled and grasping, they did not care whom they wed as long as their husbands could give them a title and a voucher for Almack's.

His lip curled as he imagined Marianna Grantham's course of action should she not manage to find a titled man who was anything but repugnant. Not all of the *ton*'s bachelors possessed titles. Would she abandon a titled but disagreeable man for a more amiable choice? Did she care one whit about love? If she could have only one or the other, it was not difficult to know what her choice would be. She certainly wouldn't abandon her quest for a place in Polite Society for anything as mundane as love. True tossed down the brandy. She would give up love for a title in a heartbeat. Not that he intended to let that happen.

Seduction came easily to True.

He knew he had a way of making even the most ugly of ladies feel beautiful, and when a man could do that, her affections were his for the taking. Marianna Grantham should present no challenge, for he had some raw material to work with; she was not altogether unattractive, though she was rather plain and terribly pale. Perhaps it was her agile mind more than her looks that made her seem within an ace of being pretty. He scowled into the fire and then slammed his brandy down onto a table.

She was pale and cold as a codfish, and True didn't know why he should find her any more fetching than a codfish. Neither should he care. The woman was an antidote. But he would make her fall in love with him, marry her, and then abandon Trowbridge for the coast and his ships—after he bedded her, of course.

But he'd bed her only once, and he'd take whatever precautions were necessary to avoid any . . . unpleasant consequences.

True told himself no guilt was necessary. Clever Miss Grantham would ultimately discover that she had not found love, yet True did not believe she would pine for it. On the contrary, she would soon revel in her situation. She would find herself the mistress of a large country estate and a fine house in London. She would have a title and her fortune, and thus the means to carry on in Polite Society. She would even have three children to satisfy any maternal longings she may possess. She would also have the freedom to carry on any sort of dalliance her heart commanded. What lady of the *ton* could ask for more?

And was that not what Marianna Grantham most wanted? To be a lady of the *ton*?

Thank God she hadn't met True's nieces. The three of them would have rubbed her fur in the wrong direction, starched-up hellcat that she was. If she'd spoken with them—or even seen them, wild as they were—Miss Grantham would have turned tail and run back to Town for certain. Back to the bloody drawing rooms of the *ton,* where the miserable chit belonged.

True sloshed some more brandy into his glass and sneered.

The *ton* was made up of men and women just like her. People who cared more for the loftiness of a man's title than the loftiness of his ideals. More for the size of a man's dwelling than the size of his heart. If anyone were in a position to know the ways of the *ton,* it was True Sin. Hadn't he been one of them? Hadn't he been as bad—no, worse!—than any of them? Aye, he'd been born to it, and he'd reveled in it, celebrating callous artifice along with the rest of Society.

The same sort of artifice he was about to employ against Marianna Grantham?

He shrugged the thought off. Miss Grantham aspired to be one of the *beau monde*. She was getting what she deserved. And the hell of it was, she wouldn't be unhappy about it.

For these past thirteen years, True had deliberately demonstrated he was not a part of the *ton*. He was a rogue. He kept his hair unfashionably long, dressed more like one of his sailors than a gentleman, and made it a practice to escort ladies no better than they ought to be—often one on each arm—to the most exclusive balls. He publicly sneered at Almack's. And, most outrageous of all in the eyes of the *ton,* he'd even dabbled in commerce, founding a shockingly successful shipping concern. And yet, in distancing himself from the *ton* so infamously, True had succeeded only in fixing its fascination.

He knew empirically that even the most prunes-and-prisms matrons secretly swooned for him, while their husbands emulated his mannerisms and boasted of his friendship. And yet, even as they vied to speak with him—or even to be seen standing next to him—at some ball or rout, among themselves, they professed to despise him. Such was the fickle nature of *le haut ton.*

Now he found himself on a path to marry a woman who would soon be one of them.

He didn't know whether to toast his good fortune or to drown his sorrows.

In the end, Truesdale Sinclair, the new Viscount Trowbridge, did a good bit of both, which was why, when Marianna Grantham returned in the middle of the night instead of in the morning, as she was supposed to, she found him singing in the fountain at the center of the grand circle in front of Trowbridge Manor, loudly accompanied by a couple of dear friends from the village, Whosits and What's-His-Name, and a duck, who was there to keep them all on key.

It was close on two in the morning, and ol' Mistress Mary didn't look happy.

Two

Marianna scowled at the three men up to their knees in the water of the enormous round fountain pond. The large structure dominated the center of the lawn, its dark gray stone well nigh fading into the inky depths of the night shadows. She wished the sounds emanating from it could be as unobtrusive. The three men were singing quite raucously.

She was tired and sore, having endured one jolting ride after another since close on dawn the previous day. There had been no accommodations for six extra men—the coachman, footman, and four outriders—at Baroness Marchman's School for Young Ladies, and she'd been obliged to start back for Trowbridge Manor as soon as her affairs were settled in London. She had thought to pass the night at an inn, but none of the four inns they encountered on the way back had any open rooms, and she'd been forced to press onward into the dark and weary hours.

She was so fatigued, she wouldn't have given the spectacle in the fountain a second glance if, from the window of the coach, one of the men had not looked suspiciously like her betrothed.

They appeared not to have noticed her approach. One of the viscount's companions had a half-empty bottle of brandy clutched in his fingers. Trowbridge brandy, no doubt, and Marianna was certain it was not the first of the evening.

"You are foxed," Marianna remarked to no one in particular.

"You're early," the viscount slurred.

"You look terrible."

"You, too." He grinned.

"At least I have a long day's journey for an excuse, my lord, rather than a large quantity of spirits."

"More's the pity," Trowbridge said, "for I'll wager that with a swallow or two o' brandy under your belt, you'd think I'm a right dasher, but here I've had half a bottle an' you're still plain as a post."

Marianna winced. She was well aware her looks were unspectacular. Skin and hair were colorless, her features nondescript. Once, she'd thought herself beautiful, but that time was past. She'd learned the truth here in England, and she wouldn't delude herself again.

The viscount swayed and clutched one of his friends for support. He was so foxed, Marianna doubted he'd remember his unkind remark in the morning. She'd have to remind him of it, if she desired an apology—assuming she would still be at Trowbridge Manor come morning, a circumstance under considerable doubt at the moment. One look at Trowbridge was enough to convince her she had chosen unwisely. He would never be able to masquerade successfully as her betrothed if he were often in his cups, with his tongue as loose as his stoppers.

And yet, if she did not stay, what was she to do? Her parents were to arrive in England from their home in the West Indies in little more than a fortnight, and they would expect her to present her betrothed without delay. She could not even lie to them and say the engagement was broken, for they would still want to know who the gentleman was. No, she had to have a besotted suitor come to scratch, and she had to have one soon. Too soon to take a chance on fleeing back to London now. What if she could not find another gentleman to agree to her madcap plot?

She looked at the viscount. It was quite dark, but even in the gloom she could see him grinning drunkenly at her and struggling to stand up straight. His two "friends" hadn't yet noticed Marianna—or perhaps they just did not care—and kept right on singing and hanging on to each other. One of them cuffed Trowbridge on the shoulder suddenly, and he joined them. They all sang loudly, and in different keys. The duck quacked right along.

Marianna pinched the bridge of her nose, closed her eyes, and shook her head. She had no choice. She had to stay. Some water splashed on her skirt and she swiped at it viciously.

Curse Ophelia Robertson!

The thought had no sooner surfaced than did Marianna give a guilty flinch. True, Ophelia was the one who'd steered Marianna toward True Sin in the first place, but she was certain the old woman had meant well.

She placed her hands on her hips and called to the footman, who hurried over. Marianna was not one to dwell on what she could not change. She was well used to giving orders, and there were definitely some orders that needed to be given here. Lud knew the viscount was in no shape to give them. The viscount was in no shape to do anything at all.

The four outriders had already disappeared, and the manor windows were all dark. Evidently, there were no servants on duty, for no one had stepped out to greet them.

It took both the coachman and the sleepy footman to pull the protesting revelers from the fountain and bundle the two villagers, one by one, into the coach. Marianna sent the servants on their way with orders to see Whosits and What's-His-Name home, which left her to attend to the viscount. He needed someone to assist him to his bedchamber.

She looked up at the large house, which stretched far to the left and right. No lights shone in any of the many windows.

She could wake up the household servants to see to his needs, but if she did that, there would be talk. After all, it was the middle of the night, and she was alone with a drunken viscount. It would be better if there were no witnesses. Certainly she could escort him to his bedchamber door and be back downstairs before the coach returned with her trunk.

The sound of the coach's wheels receded into the foggy darkness, and Marianna was left alone with the viscount. He looked down at her and hummed a little.

"You know 'Greensleeves'?" he asked.

"No."

"I will teach you, then." He grinned and filled his lungs with a huge breath.

"No! No, thank you. I cannot sing." She tugged him toward the front steps and got him moving in that direction, albeit slowly.

He exhaled. "Cannot? Or *do* not?"

"Where is your bedchamber—unless you would care to pass out in the library?"

"Changing the subject, Mary?"

"My name is Marianna, my lord, and I do not believe I have given you leave to use it."

"Ah, but we have an understanding. It is customary for a couple as affectionate as we are to call each other by our given names. And Mary is my pet name for you."

"Humph."

He laughed. "I ask again: do you sing? Up the stairs and to the right."

Marianna shoved him against the balustrade and braced herself half behind him and half beside him. "Up you go now." She gave him a hearty push.

As they climbed, Marianna became uneasily aware that the viscount was better able to negotiate the stairs than any man in his condition ought to be. In fact, by the time they reached the last step, she was sure he did not truly require her help at all. But, upon gaining the top, he stopped and hesitated, as though confused in direction. He swayed a little, and she put a steadying hand on his arm.

"You said your chamber was to the right."

"Oh . . . no. No, it is to the left. Quite so. Definitely to the left. This way."

She walked beside him down a long gallery filled with pictures that looked rather dark and eerie in the dim sconce light. She shivered.

He noticed. "Singing might help you feel better," he remarked.

"Singing would wake the whole household."

"What's the matter? Afraid to be seen with me tonight?"

"Yes."

He gave a shout of laughter and then held his fingers to his lips and shushed himself. "The next right," he said. They entered a long, windowless passage with doors at intervals on either side. " 'Tis a pity you don't sing, for your voice is quite lovely, and you'd be good at it, I wager. We're here." He stopped abruptly and turned to her. "In fact, I wager there are quite a few things you've never done that you would be good at." He waggled his flawed eyebrow at her suggestively.

She pointedly ignored his remark, stepping around him and working the door latch. The room was dark but for the weak sconce light shining into the room. She couldn't help it; her eyes were drawn to his bed, which was large and hung with sumptuous curtains. She was unsure of their color, but she thought they looked to be a deep blue. She wondered suddenly how many other ladies had looked upon his bed. A hundred, as one of the rumors said? One or two? Or none at all?

Disappointment stabbed her, and she realized in a lightning flash of understanding that a part of her did not want the rumors to be false. Even though she had no intention of . . . of cavorting with the viscount, it was still fun and exciting to think him a little dangerous. *Rubbish!* She shook off the illogical notion, grateful for the dimness of the light. She could feel the heat in her cheeks as she blushed. Quickly, she looked away and turned to bid him a hasty good night.

It was a mistake.

He was too close. Wedged as she was between the jamb of the open door and his massive, wet body, she found herself close enough to see the dark whiskers on his sculpted chin, the smooth whiteness of his teeth as his lips parted ever so slightly. His exposed skin glowed in the lamplight, and what was not exposed might as well have been, for his white linen shirt was wet and it clung to his muscular arms and torso, revealing every powerful contour. Her eyes fastened once more on the dark hair at his neck—only to follow it downward over his chest and his belly, where it tapered into a thin line before it disappeared altogether into his—She jerked her gaze back up to his face.

He laughed knowingly.

His breath was sweet with fine brandy. His eyes were like molten onyx, black as the deepest midnight, and as she stared into them, they changed suddenly. The laughter deserted them, and he became frighteningly intense. He leaned toward her, and for one horrifying moment she was sure he would kiss her. But he only reached behind her head and pulled out the comb that tightly secured her hair in place. The pale, limp mass fell down her back before she could stop it.

"Beautiful," he murmured, taking a handful and pulling it over her shoulder. "Shouldn't hide such a treasure up in a tight little coil."

Marianna danced away from his touch, and her hair slipped from his fingers. She knew, having grown up on an island frequented by sailors and plantation laborers, what drink did to a man. It made all women seem beautiful, desirable.

Drink and money. They both worked the same sort of black magic. She knew she was not beautiful—though once she had herself fooled into thinking she was. No, he was foxed, and she was an heiress. A plain heiress. She inhaled deeply. "Good night, my lord. I trust I can leave you now. You should be able to manage from here."

"I have done this a few times before," he agreed, his eyes sparkling.

"Yes . . . well. Good night, then." She turned and fled.

It took a little more than an hour for the coach to return

with the footman and her trunk. It was half past three in the morning when the footman, pulling a little cart with her green-painted trunk on it, finally led her through the dark passages of Trowbridge Manor to her own bedchamber. She was almost in tears from exhaustion. She'd endured two trips out from London and back, a flurry of packing at the school, a frenzied visit to Ophelia Robertson, and, of course, two encounters with the Viscount Trowbridge. She plodded behind the footman, barely able to keep to her feet and quite oblivious to her surroundings.

"Here we are, miss," he said. "Your chamber." He opened the door, and Marianna moved to walk inside, but he gave a sound of dismay. "Here now, miss, your room's not ready. We didn't expect you till tomorrow, so if you'll give me but a minute, I'll have a lamp lit and a fire—"

"No," Marianna said. "No, that is quite all right. I can see well enough to get into the bed. The room is quite warm already, and in the bed I shall be perfectly·comfortable." She thought she'd be perfectly comfortable in a cave with a covering of leaves as long as she could lie down and go to sleep.

"Yes, miss." The footman looked pitifully grateful and stifled a yawn as he deposited her trunk just inside the door. "I shall send for a maid to unpack it for you."

"No. Truly, I can manage. Thank you."

"Very well, miss." The man bowed and moved off down the hallway.

Marianna closed the door, latched it behind her, and sighed heavily. She didn't even attempt to extract her nightrail from her trunk. Instead, she pulled her tired brown serge over her head, untied her stays, and felt her way toward the bed wearing only her thin chemise. With the outer door closed, there wasn't even the dim glow from the hall sconces to light her way. It was darker than she had thought it would be, but she made it to the bed and burrowed gratefully under the thick, fluffy covers anyway.

The last conscious thought she had was that the sweet, heady odor of the viscount's brandy had somehow managed to cling to her clothes. The smell was oddly comforting. She fell into a dreamless sleep and did not wake until morning.

The viscount, for his part, lay in bed a long while before he slept, listening to the soft, even rhythm of Mistress Mary's breathing only a few inches from him. If she'd been perturbed to find him drunk and singing in the fountain, how much more dismayed would she be to awaken in bed with him? He smiled and fell into a deep sleep and dreamed of her.

She was splashing naked in the fountain and singing "Greensleeves."

Three

A bell rang somewhere in the distance, and Marianna cracked open her sleepy eyes. The room was swathed in dim light, though with the draperies closed it was impossible to guess how late was the hour. Her stomach rumbled, reminding her she had not eaten since her early luncheon the previous day, a meal hastily taken in the coach on the way from the school to Mrs. Ophelia Robertson's grand residence in Grosvenor Square. Still, she was in no hurry to rise and break her fast, for *he* was somewhere on the other side of that door.

How much would he remember of last night? Would he remember that she had accompanied him—alone—to his bedchamber? Would he remember saying that her voice was lovely, or loosening her hair, fingering it tenderly, and pronouncing it beautiful? Would he remember the provocative suggestion he'd made about her skill at things she'd not yet done?

And would he remember the whirlwind journey her wayward eyes had taken over his body?

One thing Marianna knew for a certainty: she did not wish to face him.

She could only hope he had no memory whatsoever of the night before, of the things he'd said to her, for he'd certainly not been sincere. Marianna knew that by the light of day and with a clear head the viscount would find her lacking.

But what did that matter?

It mattered not one brass farthing. She was not really his betrothed. After this month was over, they would probably only seldom meet. There would be an occasional glimpse of him across a crowded ballroom, little more. After a broken engagement, no one would expect them to interact. She tried to put him from her mind. She was still tired.

She closed her eyes and settled her head into the downy pillow once more. Perhaps she'd sleep another hour. Yes. She told herself she was not avoiding Trowbridge. She was just being certain she was getting adequate rest. The decision was wise. Prudent. Logical. Another hour would be—

Another hour would be another hour spent avoiding the viscount. She really did need to get hold of herself. After all, she could not stay holed up in her chamber for the next month, now, could she?

The smell of his brandy was still very strong. It wove its way into her troubled thoughts and evoked his image. The strong, angular features, the dark hair and eyes . . . the breadth of his shoulders and that intriguing thatch of chest hair that lured the eyes to follow to where it disappeared into his inexpressibles. She squeezed her eyes shut even tighter and sighed. It was no use. Trying to escape him by sleeping was an exercise in futility. He would follow her into her dreams. She had better get up and face him. It was best to get it over with.

Still, she hesitated. She did not want to get it over with. She wanted to hide there in her chamber all day. Coward, she berated herself, flopping onto her other side toward the center of the bed.

She froze in place.

She blinked. Her mouth worked, but no sound came out, which was a good thing, since all that would have emerged was a spate of babbling, anyway.

Truesdale Sinclair, the Viscount Trowbridge, was *in her bed!* He lay on the other side of the four-poster, asleep.

She held very still lest she wake him. Though her body was motionless, her mind was in a flurry, at sixes and sevens. Was he there by mistake or by design? Had there been some drunken misunderstanding, or was he a libertine? Not that it mattered, either way. She had made him a bargain, and honor demanded that she go through with it. Oh, who was she bamming? It wasn't honor but desperation that bound her to Trowbridge. It was simply too late for her to hie off to London now. There was no time to find another fake suitor.

Botheration!

She glanced at the door. Had she locked it last night? She was well nigh certain she had. She remembered the feel of the knob in her hand. But of course he would have a key. He must have let himself in after she had gone to sleep. She was a light sleeper, but she'd been so tired, she must not have heard him.

For what purpose had he come? If seduction had been on his mind, he'd certainly failed miserably—and somehow Marianna doubted that sort of failure was likely of True Sin. She knitted her brows together. The logic did not fit. It was unlikely the viscount had slipped into her room after she was asleep.

If he had not arrived after her, then he had to have come in beforehand.

When she'd escorted him to his bedchamber door, had he been so foxed, he'd led her to her bedchamber instead of his by mistake?

Another possibility occurred to her: perhaps this wasn't her chamber at all, but his . . . which might be the case had the footman led her to his master's chamber on the viscount's orders. Ah, but that would mean he'd had seduction on his mind from the time she'd left Trowbridge that morning. *Bells in Heaven!* Her heart hammered in her chest, and she grasped for a more reasonable—and more comforting—explanation. She was not fetching enough to incite such behavior. And the viscount needed her gems. He would not jeopardize their bargain in such a manner. No, logic told her he had to have come to her bed by mistake.

The only way to attack the problem was to assume that was the case. Which meant she had to get out of that bedchamber before someone discovered them together. She needed to get dressed.

Her eyes snapped to her trunk. There was no hope of opening its squeaky hasps without waking the viscount, and—*Lud!*—her poor traveling costume lay in a heap on the floor, dusty, wrinkled, and wet. But she could hardly appear downstairs in her chemise. Perhaps no one would notice if she wore the damp brown serge and went below to wait in the—She rolled her eyes, abandoning the thought. Even if no one raised an eyebrow at the gown, her hair was certainly a tangled mess, and her comb was in the trunk. There was no way she could appear downstairs. The servants would talk. Besides, if she left Trowbridge here and this *were* her bedchamber, a servant might discover him.

But what else could she do? Wake him? She'd sooner walk through fire with bare feet.

Next to her, he slept peacefully on, oblivious to her agitation. She shot him a black look and resisted an impulse to shove him roughly out of the bed and bounce his backside off the hard, cold floor. Asking him for answers was the only way she'd get them, but she had no intention of carrying on a polite conversation with a man wearing only his—

Saints and sinners, what *was* he wearing?

Her eyes widened as she realized for the first time that the narrow band of Trowbridge's exposed, muscular shoulders was quite bare. Her eyes darted to his lean, sun-touched face. He slept on. Marianna nibbled on her lower lip, her eyebrow climbing high on her forehead. He slept on. Heaven help her, she wanted to look at him. Not just a glance, either, but a long, satisfying examination. She told herself it was only natural that she be curious. She'd never seen a man's bare shoulders.

She stole another look at him. He slept on.

He was her betrothed, after all. Did she not have a right to look?

She did look, allowing her eyes a much more leisurely

journey than she had last night. He lay on his back with
the covers pulled over his arms and torso, warding off the
deep chill of the room. His face, though relaxed in sleep,
was still handsomely angular, his features sculpted. His
mouth had the look of an ancient Roman statue she had
seen in the British Museum. The wavy black mass that sur-
rounded his head seemed more a halo than a head of hair.
Even in its disarray, it did not look much different than it
had yesterday, when she'd first seen him. One errant wisp
curled over his ear and down his long sideburn. Her eyes
followed it downward, over a prominent cheekbone to the
line of his jaw, which, along with his slightly cleft chin,
was shadowed with unshaven whiskers. But her perusal did
not end there.

As her eyes ventured lower still, she gripped the blue
counterpane tighter. His bare shoulders were large and powerful. She stared at them, pressing her lips together and
raising her chin to get a better look. She could just see the
outlines of his collarbones, and her fingers went involun-
tarily to her own. His bronzed skin was smooth in spite of
its weathering. In fact, it looked almost silky, and she
couldn't help wondering if it felt silky, too. Her fingers
wanted to indulge in the same sort of wayward field trip
her eyes were enjoying. She shoved her hands under her
leg. But then logic took hold of her.

There was no use in denying Marianna was enjoying her
survey. And she need not feel any guilt. The viscount was
a magnificently formed man, and thus it was only logical
that she enjoy looking.

She could just see his pelt of chest hair peeking over the
white sheet and royal blue counterpane. She couldn't help
wondering just how far down that line of crisp, dark hair
marched. . . .

Saints and sinners!

Was he wearing anything at all under the bedclothes?

Phttt! She was out of the bed like a flushed pheasant,
looking wildly about. There! His clothes lay in a heap on
the floor beside the bed. She poked at them with her toe,

taking inventory. Boots, shirt, waistcoat, breeches, draw-ers—*oh, Lud!*—stockings . . . all of it. Every stitch he had on yesterday. Right there, on the floor of her bedchamber! Beside her bed.

And there he was, *in* her bed. Without his clothes.

Lud, she had to get out of there! No! Her unseeing eyes attached themselves to the hair on his chest once more as her mind occupied itself with other matters. No, she had to get *him* out of there! If anyone found out where he'd spent the night, she would be ruined.

If he did not offer to marry her, she amended.

And what would she do if he did offer for her? Would she marry him? Without love?

She stood stock-still in the center of the floor, her eyes fixed and glassy, her mind as firm as watered porridge and absently wandering the ether of future possibility.

"Enjoying the view?"

The masculine voice yanked Marianna out of her wool gathering, and she realized she'd been caught staring at him. Staring at his furry chest, to be more precise. His eyes spar-kled mischievously, knowingly.

"Did you enjoy sleeping with me last night?" he asked.

"Yes. No!" She jerked her eyes away from him. "That is to say, I did not know I was sleeping with you. No! That is not what I meant to say. I . . . I did not sleep with you. That is, I slept, but not with you. No, no, I mean . . . I mean . . ."

He was laughing, a deep, rich, and infuriating sound.

She rolled her eyes. "Oh! You know perfectly well what I mean."

"In truth," he drawled, folding his arms behind his head and causing the covers to slip lower, exposing what seemed to be a vast amount of muscled chest and belly, "I do not have the first notion what you mean, for I have absolutely no memory of what happened between us last night."

"I do," she blurted before she realized she'd put her foot in her mouth yet again. "Botheration! That is to say, my memory is unimpaired, and nothing happened between us. Nothing at all."

"How . . . interesting." He looked her up and down, and Marianna realized he was *not* speaking of the maddening mull in which they'd found themselves. She'd forgotten she was wearing only her thin white chemise. She snatched up a garment from the floor and covered herself with it.

"I do not know how you came to be here, my lord, but I believe we should discuss it later." She nodded toward the door. "Downstairs."

"I would be delighted to do so, but there is one problem."

"And that is?"

"You have my breeches clutched to your bosom."

Handing a naked man his inexpressibles was bad enough, but standing in the same room with him—albeit turned away—while he dressed was outside of enough! She could hear the fabric sliding against his skin, and she may as well have been sliding her own hands over his skin, for all the embarrassment the sounds caused her.

Marianna's cheeks burned as the clocks in the large house all struck one. She grimaced. She hadn't slept this late in over a year, and she was appalled. At Baroness Marchman's School for Young Ladies, she'd been required to be up with the rising sun, a habit she did not dislike. She supposed she had better get used to keeping later hours, however, as ladies of the *ton* rarely rose before noon.

It was no use.

No matter how hard she tried to concentrate on her vexation at having been a slugabed, she couldn't keep her mind from veering back to *him*.

Finally he left—without a word, thank goodness. She locked the door behind him and sagged against it. The room seemed infinitely larger now. Her eyes flicked to the bed. It had certainly seemed quite small when she'd found him lying there next to her. She shivered and pushed away from the door to see to her own needs.

Believing in the saying that first impressions were lasting, she dressed carefully and appeared downstairs an hour later in her finest gown, a soft ice-blue muslin sprigged with tiny sprays of embroidered delphiniums and, in her hair, a matching blue satin ribbon.

She'd come to London with a limited wardrobe, expecting to order new gowns without delay. She had been quite looking forward to it, in fact. But, of course, her circumstances had changed, and a closet of new gowns was not consistent with her assumed schoolmistress persona. Thus, she had nothing better than the ice-blue muslin to change into for dinner that evening.

Not that it signified, she thought with chagrin, for she anticipated retreating to her chamber with a megrim long before the evening meal.

To be sure, the Viscount Trowbridge had left her bedchamber quickly enough and with no further shenanigans, but that was not particularly reassuring. Marianna barely knew True Sin, but she didn't like what she'd seen so far.

She didn't like salamanders, either, but she did like little girls, which was a good thing, for she was no sooner downstairs than was she presented with three of them—three little girls, thank goodness, not three salamanders. There had been only the one salamander, but, as she'd found it squirming half submerged in the clotted cream on her tea tray that morning, one had been quite enough.

At the housekeeper's insistence, tea was taken with the three young ladies of the house. The stout woman introduced them as "the ABC's—Miss Alyse, Miss Beatrice, and Miss Eleanor." Apparently, there was no governess.

Not anymore.

The girls, Marianna discovered, had been motherless for a little over three months. Their mother and father—Trowbridge's elder brother—had died at sea while returning from a visit with relatives in Scotland. The girls did not seem vastly sullen for the event. They wore no black garments, and they seemed rather animated. Rather too animated, for Marianna was certain they all had their heads together on the salamander. She ignored it and wisely took her scones with brambleberry jam.

The three of them soon gobbled up their own scones and guzzled their tea, wiping their mouths on sleeves that couldn't be harmed too much by one more stain. Then they sat staring at her with wide eyes.

"Who are you?" the eldest finally blurted. Alyse had straight, dark hair, and she seemed much too grown up for her ten years.

"My name is Miss Marianna Grantham."

"What Alyse means," the middle girl said with a shake of her long, dark curls, "is what are you doing here?" Beatrice had dark hair past her shoulders like her sister, but it was curly rather than straight, and it hung in tangled ringlets down her back.

"I am . . . a visitor."

"Uncle Sin's lady friend?" Beatrice quizzed.

Uncle Sin? Marianna nearly spilled her tea, but she looked the middle child steadily in the eye when she said, "Yes. Yes, I suppose you might say that."

"Lady *friend,* or lady *bird?* "

"Beatrice Jessamine Sinclair!" the eldest cried in a parody of parental disapproval.

"What?" Beatrice shot back. "Don't you want to know which it is?"

"Of course I do," Alyse said. "It's just not polite to ask her, that's all. We'll ask Uncle Sin instead."

Beatrice plucked a heretofore unnoticed chunk of scone from the tea tray and crammed it into her mouth. "He will not tell us anything, silly. He didn't last time, did he?"

"Last time?" Marianna asked.

"The last time Uncle Sin had a lady visitor," Alyse supplied sagely. "We asked him if *she* was his lady friend, but he only sent us to the nursery for the rest of the afternoon."

Beatrice shook her head. "Aww . . . we don't need to

ask him, anyway," she said. "She stayed here last night, didn't she?"

"Yeth," the youngest lisped between the gap where her two front teeth had been. "Sheth a thoiled dove, all wight."

Marianna's eyes widened, and the two older girls dissolved into peals of giggles.

Little Eleanor, a darling thing with close-cropped blonde curls, scowled at her elder sisters and then turned haughtily away from them to tug on Marianna's gown. "How come you haven't asked 'bout my name?"

The other two girls fell silent. They watched Marianna, waiting for her answer. The question was clearly some sort of test, and Marianna very much wanted to give them a satisfactory answer. "Well," she said and took a sip of her tea. She had noticed, of course, that there was something odd about "the ABC's." Alyse, Beatrice . . . and Eleanor. C and D were clearly missing.

"I thought you would tell me about your names—all three of you—if and when you wished me to know." Marianna peered at them over the rim of her teacup. "One should never attempt to force a confidence, you know."

The elder sisters traded glances.

"Oh," Eleanor chirped. "Then I shan't tell you."

"I see you have met my nieces," her host's deep, rich voice boomed from the doorway, startling Marianna so that her tea did slosh over the rim of her cup. "I apologize for my absence," he said. "I had hoped to be here to defend you." He gave the girls a wry look. "I trust they have been perfect young ladies?" His voice was full of storm clouds. Marianna watched as three sets of eyes darted to the crock of clotted cream.

"They were no trouble," she said. Her assertion earned her a raised eyebrow, but the viscount said nothing to refute her claim. "Indeed," Marianna said, "They have agreed to do me a favor." She watched the ABC's' eyes widen.

"Which is?"

Ignoring the question, she leaned forward and gestured to the bellpull just behind him. "Would you be so kind as to ring for more tea, my lord? I find I am parched after yesterday's travels."

As Trowbridge turned his back to pull the cord, Marianna quickly replaced the lid on the crock and whisked it and the salamander into a lovely basket that stood empty on the side table. She thrust the basket into Alyse's arms and threw a meaningful look at all three girls, who clapped their mouths shut and glanced nervously in their uncle's direction.

Marianna said, "The girls have agreed to go outside and gather me a basket of ivy to brighten my bedchamber. Run along, girls," she prompted without waiting for Trowbridge's assent, and the three scurried out the door like mice.

"They are afraid of you," Marianna said when they were out of earshot. She did nothing to cleanse her voice of the disapproval she felt.

Trowbridge shook his head. "They are afraid of everything." He chuckled. "Except salamanders, it seems."

"You saw the salamander?"

"Aye." Deep, merry dimples appeared, and Marianna almost groaned. *Of course* True Sin's face would come equipped with dimples. They were the perfect boyish counterpoint to his manly scarred eyebrow. They were like laudanum for the face, and Marianna couldn't help returning his smile. "I rather thought the salamander was enjoying his swim in the clotted cream, didn't you?"

The dimples that had appeared left as quickly as they had come, and his face clouded over with concern. "I am afraid my nieces have had too little correction in their young lives, as you will no doubt agree."

"Then why, my lord, did you not scold them for the salamander?"

"For the same reason you did not betray their mischief to me, I expect. I am trying to win their loyalty"—his generous mouth tilted wryly—"or at least negotiate a guarded truce."

Marianna heaved a sigh of relief. At last, she'd found

something she liked about the viscount—besides his dimples and chest hair. She resisted the impulse to roll her eyes and fingered the delicately curved handle of her teacup instead.

"I was not aware that you had so recently inherited, my lord. I am sorry for your loss." As she said this, she noted the viscount's lack of mourning clothes. Something was terribly amiss here. "The wounds must still be fresh," she probed.

"Yes. Well. With an estate, three little girls, and an army of angry creditors thrust upon me, I have not had the time to grieve."

"And the girls . . . ?"

The new tea-tray arrived. He waited until the maid had withdrawn and then leaned forward. "Miss Grantham, I see no reason to stand on formality. On the contrary, considering our situation, you and I need to be rather . . . intimate. If we are to bam everyone successfully, we have a great deal to learn about each other and a devilishly short time in which to learn it, so you will forgive my speaking bluntly."

"I was not aware that either of us had thus far been anything but blunt. Do you ever express yourself in any other manner, my lord?"

He thought for a moment and then nodded. "When the situation calls for it, I can be quite . . . indirect, indeed." He sighed. "But this is not one of those times."

"Do go on."

He sipped his tea thoughtfully. "The truth is that my late brother and his wife saw little of me and even less of their own children. You must not pity my nieces or expect them to express any sorrow at their parents' passing, Miss Grantham, for they cannot mourn what they never knew."

"I see."

"And now . . . about us."

"Yes?" She swallowed reflexively.

"Where and when did we meet?"

"Why . . . yesterday, my lord. In the library."

He laughed. "No . . . where did we meet? In London? At a ball or musicale, perhaps?"

"Ah." She nodded her understanding. "I believe we met in Hyde Park," Marianna said, catching on. "I was strolling and lost my bonnet in the wind. You kindly retrieved it, galloping after it on your horse."

"And we met in the park every day after?"

She nodded. "I was staying at my good friend Mrs. Robertson's home, which is near the park. It was April, and the weather was fine. Then in May you escorted me to the Astley's."

He shook his head. "Do you not mean the opera? It is widely known I detest the Astley's."

She nodded. "I shall remember."

"When did we become engaged?"

"We have had an understanding since midsummer. Late June. Neither of us can recall the exact date. But there has been no official announcement. That will occur after my parents arrive."

He rubbed his chin. "Mmm . . . no. I think we should send a notice to *The Morning Post* right away."

"Why?" she asked.

His eyes flicked to the floor and he pursed his lips before he looked at her and smiled. But he did not speak, and Marianna couldn't help feeling his manner a little guilty. "My lord?" she prompted him.

He tipped his head rakishly to the side, and his flawed eyebrow rose suggestively as he said, "Well . . . the sooner our betrothal is announced, the sooner I shall have leave to kiss you. Unless, of course, sleeping in your bed again is an option."

Four

True watched her flush, thoroughly enjoying being an impertinent bounder.

She gathered herself quickly and said, "You jest, my lord." Her white brows came together to form a scornful valley.

True threw her his best smile and sipped his tea. "Are you certain?"

"I daresay," a voice chimed from the door, "she is quite certain, Trowbridge."

An old woman sailed into the room. Swathed in magenta-and-yellow spangled silk and with a matching turban engulfing her downy white hair, she reminded True of a Gypsy fortune-teller.

Marianna Grantham coughed. "Truesdale Sinclair, may I present Mrs. Ophelia Robertson?"

True stared at the woman incredulously. Ophelia Robertson was a celebrated London hostess, who was, in spite of her venerable age, considered a bit fast. How on earth had the starched-up Marianna become friend to the outrageous Ophelia Robertson?

"Do not get up," the old lady told True, though he had made no move to do so. "How are you, my dear?" she said with genuine warmth, plopping down beside Marianna on the sofa. "Are those poppy-seed cakes?"

The maid who'd shown Mrs. Robertson in stood uncertainly in the doorway. True excused her with a wave of his hand.

He glanced from Mrs. Robertson to Marianna Grantham. There could be no doubt the two were hand and glove with each other. "Why are you here?" he asked bluntly, earning a glowering expression from Marianna.

Ophelia chuckled. "Think to shock me with plain speaking, my boy? Won't work. I prefer it, in truth. I am here to serve as duenna to Miss Grantham."

"Duenna?" True asked incredulously. Ophelia Robertson's reputation was close on as questionable as his was.

"Of course," Marianna interjected. "A chaperone is essential. Mrs. Robertson will lend us propriety."

"Of course," True echoed.

Ophelia winked at him, stuffed a bite of seed cake into her mouth and motioned for Marianna to pour her a cup of tea. "You are to have the pleasure of Mr. Robertson's company as well," she said mischievously. Ophelia had shocked the entire *ton* this past spring by eloping to Gretna Green with a family servant.

"When will John arrive?" Marianna asked, referring to Mr. Robertson.

"Presently." Ophelia gestured vaguely toward the window. "He says your stables are a shambles, Trowbridge, and he is having a stern talk with your head groom."

True intercepted an apologetic look from Marianna. "I shall welcome any assistance your husband can render, Mrs. Robertson," he said, and he meant it. "My late brother's attention to such matters was often lacking."

"You mean it was nonexistent, don't you, my boy?"

True laughed. "I see you know the lay of the land better than most."

"You will find there is very little I do not know," she said, accepting a teacup. "When Marianna asked me which of the *ton*'s bachelors was furthest up the River Tick, I—"

"Ophelia!" Marianna gasped.

"Well? 'Tis true!" Mrs. Robertson defended herself. "You have had out with the truth, have you not? He does know why you have come?"

"Yes, ma'am. It just seems so . . . improper to speak of it!"

"I see no reason to waltz around the truth, my dear. It is all simple enough: he needs the money, and you need a bit of play-acting," the old lady said but then changed the subject anyway. "Did you enjoy the trip out, my dear? The fields and woods are so delightfully fragrant this time of year."

True sipped his tea thoughtfully as the ladies had a comfortable coze. He gathered theirs was a warm yet brief acquaintance. It seemed the two had met when Ophelia's great-niece had attended the boarding school where Marianna taught, and they'd struck up an immediate friendship. True could see why: independent and stubborn, Ophelia Robertson and Marianna Grantham were both bold as brass and twice as cold.

Casually, they informed him the Robertsons were to remain at Trowbridge Manor the entire month, whereupon a steady stream of heavy thumps and muffled curses commenced in echoes down the halls as their baggage was hauled upstairs. Marianna's speech faltered with each epithet. The language did not bother True. His sailors raised cursing to an art form, and he was able to ignore it, but he could see that Marianna was not immune. Perversely, he chose not to put a stop to it and simply pretended not to notice the servants' language.

A few minutes later, something fell with a sudden crash: a heavy trunk perhaps, for a particularly long and colorful string of words reached the parlor. Marianna flinched upon the yellow damask sofa and turned to True. "My lord, I simply must ask you to—"

"Oh, my!" Ophelia cried. "Marianna! Is that a mouse?" She pointed, and, as Marianna's head swiveled in that direction, the old lady executed a quick, furtive movement and then said, "No, I am mistaken." She clutched at Marianna's wrist and patted her own chest. "But I may still swoon. Do be a lamb and fetch my vinaigrette from my reticule upstairs."

"Which chamber is yours?" Marianna asked.

"Just follow the baggage and ask the servants. Hurry, my dear."

Marianna left in a rush.

True shook his head. "Your reticule is under your skirt, where you just tucked it," he said.

Ophelia turned to him. "With each of your servants' coarse epithets, that gel's spine grew straighter. I feared it might snap. Your servants' manners need correction, Trowbridge. Immediately."

True rubbed his neck tiredly. "Madam, there is jolly little at Trowbridge that does not need correction. If it is not my servants' manners, it is my stables." *Or my nieces,* he thought wryly. "Everything needs my attention."

"Oh . . . and now you've had to add a wayward heiress to the list. Poor boy," she added without a shred of true sympathy. "If you take my advice, Trowbridge, you'll move that gel to the top of your list. Marianna was reared carefully. She is used to a great plenty where attention is concerned."

"I gather she is used to a great plenty where *everything* is concerned," True remarked. "She was quite unabashed at telling me how wealthy her parents are."

"Indeed," Ophelia agreed.

"I gather all they lack is a bloodline."

"Of that"—Ophelia threw him a significant look—"I am not so very certain."

True regarded her obliquely. "What do you mean?"

"Only that you might ask yourself what else they might lack and if there is not some reason her parents did not accompany her to London."

True nodded. "Think you it has something to do with the fact that they sent their daughter equipped with color rather than drab?"

"You mean the rubies and emeralds?"

True nodded. "Instead of pearls—or diamonds at the outside. It is still considered improper for the newest misses to wear color, is it not?"

She nodded. "Quite beyond the pale."

"I thought so. Then there can be only one conclusion: the elder Granthams are not, shall I say, quite as polished, as our Marianna."

Ophelia shrugged. "Perhaps. They were both born and reared on English soil, but I gather they made all their vast fortune at trading in the West Indies, and they may be quite rough, for all I know. For all we know. And yet it does not signify. As you have seen, Marianna's manners are impeccable. Her entire life has been spent in preparation for taking her place among Good Society. Which reminds me, you really ought to speak to your servants, Trowbridge." She glanced down the hall from whence the occasional curse still emanated. "Marianna hasn't much tolerance for sailor talk. She possesses refined tastes and sensibilities."

"Would those be *ton*nish tastes and *ton*nish sensibilities?" True asked, allowing his well-known distaste to creep into his tone.

"Of course," Ophelia snapped. "And if you've any intention of winning her, you shall remember that. Marianna will be repelled by anything improper."

"Of a certainty. And of course that is why she came to me. 'True Sin' is known for his sense of propriety."

"Sarcasm becomes you." Ophelia paused with her teacup halfway to her lips and peered at him keenly over the rim. "Anyone but a fool would wish to wed her in your situation."

"I do not dispute that, madam. And I ask you again, why send Marianna to me?"

A smile ghosted across her lips. "I convinced Marianna to come to you because . . . because I happen to know you are not a fool."

True grunted and allowed one eyebrow to climb high on his forehead.

She waved her hand expansively. "You disbelieve me. You may not know very much about me, Trowbridge, but I know a great deal about you. I have watched you for a very long time. Knew your mother, rest her soul. So young . . ." Ophelia tasted her tea and made a face. "Too sweet." She rose, plucking her reticule from the sofa as she did so. "Ah. Here is my reticule. No doubt Marianna is still searching for it upstairs."

"No doubt."

Ophelia threw him a conspiratorial look, a pair of dimples appearing on her lined face, and True was suddenly struck by what a Diamond she must have been in her youth. "I am going upstairs," she informed him.

He nodded.

Ophelia swept toward the doorway and then paused halfway through. "Trowbridge . . ."

"Madam?"

"I meant what I said when I told you she was certain you were jesting."

True shook his head to indicate he had no idea what she was talking about.

"When I arrived! Do you not remember? Methuselah's kittens, you are forgetful, aren't you, Trowbridge? Forgetful and buffleheaded and—"

"You just said I was not a fool."

"—and impertinent as well."

"Guilty," he agreed.

Ophelia flashed her dimpled grin at him again and shook her head. "Marianna thought you were jesting about wishing to kiss her. She has no idea of the attraction she holds for a man—"

Neither did True.

"—and she has come to believe she is beyond plain and bordering on ugly. I trust you will do what you can to make her see herself as she really is."

True resisted raising a mocking eyebrow. Did Ophelia really believe Marianna was anything but colorless, rigid, and plain?

"Marianna is a fine gel, Trowbridge," the white-haired lady continued, "a good gel, and if you hurt her . . ." Her keen blue eyes pierced him, and her voice took on a hard edge. "If you hurt her, I will see you punished." She disappeared in a rustling swirl of magenta and yellow.

True frowned after her. Despite having attended some of her celebrated balls and routs, he'd never had occasion to speak at length with Ophelia Robertson. Unlike the rest of the *ton*, it seemed she had no interest in getting to know him. In fact, he'd fancied she actually avoided him, not that he had ever cared. She was a member of the *ton*, after all.

But after speaking with her now, he actually liked the flamboyantly garbed woman. He found her outrageously direct, ridiculously opinionated, and startlingly intelligent. Her frankness was refreshing, and he admired her loyalty to Marianna Grantham—though he certainly couldn't imagine what had inspired such feelings. Thus far, he thought sourly, he'd seen little in Miss Grantham to admire beyond a pair of large blue eyes and two other large features, which also came in a pair but lay a bit lower down.

Thought of the salamander slithered into his mind, and True was grudgingly forced to add *calm-headed, compassionate,* and *clever* to her list of qualities. Any other young woman of his acquaintance would have first screamed at the sight of the creature and then demanded the girls be punished. Not only hadn't Marianna Grantham screamed, she had also tried to hide the girls' transgression from him. And then, when she'd discovered that he'd known—and ignored—the prank, she had smiled at him.

He almost added *perfect teeth* to the list and scowled. It wasn't the sort of thing that belonged on his list. Such an addition was of no use. Come to think of it, of what use was the list at all? It did not matter what her qualities were. He was going to wed Marianna Grantham, and that was that.

No matter how much he loathed young women like her.

Presently, she rejoined him downstairs. He fixed his gaze on her and forced a smile. "Did Mrs. Robertson find you?" he asked as though it were a question of the greatest interest, as though *Miss Grantham* were of the greatest interest.

"Oh, yes," she answered. "Ophelia declared herself fatigued and said she would rest. She thought Mr. Robertson might need a rest, too, and she asked me to send for him. They were up late last night after having attended a ball in Town."

True well nigh chuckled, doubting the old couple would have any rest at all. They'd been married only that spring, and they'd been remarkably demonstrative in public since. Their marriage had been all the talk in Town, a match between a family servant of many years and a rich old spinster was enough to set tongues wagging even without their frequent public displays of affection. And then there was the manner of their marriage.

"It is rumored they eloped to Gretna Green," he said.

Marianna sighed, a smile playing at the corners of her mouth. "Yes. I know. It is exceedingly romantic, is it not? At their age, of course."

" 'At their age.' Do you disapprove of Gretna weddings for the younger set, then, Mary?"

"My name is Marianna—and, yes, a Gretna wedding is most improper."

"Ah. And are you always concerned with what is proper?"

"I am." She looked bemused. "Should I not be?"

"On the contrary," he said, "if you wish to secure a position among the *ton,* it is a necessity." He was unable to keep a note of scorn from creeping into his voice, and she detected it right away.

Her pale eyebrows rose. "You do not approve of the *ton,* my lord?" She looked appalled.

Blast. True knew he had to tread lightly. As practical, precise, and thorough as Miss Grantham was, she would certainly have learned of his more infamous behavior. She must know he didn't give a fig about what anyone thought of him. But he couldn't very well tell her exactly what he thought of her precious, bloody *ton* now, could he? Not if he wanted her to marry him. No, he'd let her believe his feelings were limited to a singular unconcern for propriety, for if she knew the actual depth and breadth of his contempt for the *ton,* she'd never marry him.

"You may call me True." He threw her a smile. "And no, I have never been excessively concerned with the opinion of Society," he said carefully.

"But surely you agree the opinion of Society—Good Society—is paramount, *my lord.*"

" 'Good' Society. I presume you mean the *ton.*"

"Of course. What else could I mean?" She looked genuinely perplexed with her pale eyebrows bunched together and her lips slightly pursed.

What else could she mean? Astonished, True realized Miss Grantham's bias ran deeper than he'd thought. It wasn't simply that she held the *ton* in greater esteem than she did other people, it was that the *ton* were the *only* people she held in esteem at all!

True thought of the men who sailed on his ships, hard-working, stalwart men it had been his privilege to know. He thought of the wives and sweethearts who waved to them from the docks, women who'd probably never owned a kerchief of silk, much less an entire gown of one. Those people worked hard, loved hard, lived honestly. They were, as far as True was concerned, the best sort of people, people from the finest society. Surely, in her guise as schoolteacher, Mistress Mary had met many such people. Had she not seen some of them for the good people they were?

"Mary, have you ever considered setting aside your goal of marrying into Society?"

"Of course I have. But why should I? The only good society—the only society worth being a part of—is the *ton.*"

Her response only confirmed his suspicions: to Miss Marianna Grantham, the *ton* was "good" and everyone else was . . . beneath her concern. He felt a stab of irritation but shook it off. After all, what else had he expected of her? The heiress had her cap set on securing a place among the *beau monde,* and nothing would steer her from that course. He supposed he ought to be grateful for her shallow bigotry. Was he not counting on it, in part, to secure her regard? That, and a few trinkets and fripperies and fancy words? He glanced at the mantel clock. "Eleven o' the clock," he said. "I've a surprise for you, and it should arrive any minute now."

She blinked at his abrupt change of subject. "What sort of surprise?"

"A dressmaker. You need a new wardrobe."

"Oh, but I cannot afford—"

"I shall give her the emerald you gave me."

"Oh, but I cannot let you make such a—"

"Indulge me, Mary. It is not a strictly altruistic gesture. Your appearance will have a direct impact on my own status," he lied. "You cannot have much in that one little trunk upstairs. Certainly not enough for a month's house party. I wish for my betrothed to be properly gowned. And, properly gowned," he said, turning a lethal and lazy smile upon her, "a young woman as lovely as you shall be the envy of all of my lady houseguests—and I shall be the envy of the gentlemen."

The compliment brought a soft pink to her cheeks, and she smiled at him shyly. True felt a corresponding glow of satisfaction. This was going to be very easy. He'd be wed within a fortnight.

"Well . . . I suppose I do need a few new things. A schoolteacher has little need for finery. I am afraid that this—" Her delicate fingers lit upon her pale blue muslin skirt and her blue sash before trailing along the lace that trimmed her neckline. "This is the best I have." Her nose wrinkled, reminding him of Eleanor when something vexed her. "It is not exactly *en vogue*, is it?"

True ignored the question and, leaning back on the sofa, asked, "Why have you been masquerading as a schoolteacher, Mary?"

"Why are you always so blunt?" she countered.

"Why are you so secretive?"

She hesitated, then fiddled with the ends of her blue sash. "I can see no reason not to confide in you, my lord. As you pointed out, we must get to know each other very well

and very quickly, and now is as good a time as any to start."
She poured herself more tea and seemed to be collecting
her thoughts. "As you know, I came to London alone a
little over a year ago. I was supposed to be fired off into
Society by a lady my parents hired for the task, the elderly
daughter of an earl, Lady Charlotte Cunningham."

"Cunningham. Did she not pass away?"

Marianna nodded. "Just before I arrived. And just after
I arrived, my maid deserted me. She was gone as soon as
the gangplank was lowered. She was a native of Shrop-
shire. . . ." She gave a small shrug of her shoulders. "I
knew no one in London, and I was utterly alone. I should
have sailed home forthwith. But I knew my failure to marry
well would surely have disappointed my poor parents."

True thought to point out that the failure would not have
been hers, but he decided to say nothing.

"I decided not to up and sail back home to the islands,"
she continued. "Instead, I decided to stay in London and
find a husband all on my own."

"A titled husband."

Mary nodded. "Of course."

"So you decided that living and working under an assumed name at a girls' boarding school was the best way
to snare a husband of the first consequence?"

She threw him a wry look. "Hardly. The school was my
only option. As I said, I knew no one in London, and living
by myself was out of the question. So I hid the jewels I
had brought with me—they were in ⁺he ship's safe, fortu-
nately, for my maid stole everything else I had, including
most of my clothes, and I took a position under an assumed
name—Mary Gant—at Baroness Marchman's School for
Young Ladies. At the time, I thought it an ideal solution,
for I did not wish to use my fortune to attract a husband.
I wanted to avoid fortune hunters, because I hoped to make
a"—a blush suffused her pale white skin a becoming shade
of pink—"a love match," she finished.

Nothing she could have said would have surprised him
more. "A love match?"

She nodded. "I know it is . . . unusual, my lord, for a woman in my situation to be so inclined, but I assure you that you have nothing to be concerned over. In all other matters, my behavior has been quite unremarkable."

"In all other matters? Such as in masquerading as a schoolteacher, for instance?"

She bit her lip, looking for all the world like a recalcitrant child, and True laughed. She corrected herself: "Most other matters, then."

"Go on with your story. What happened next?"

"There is little more to tell, really. I lived the life of a schoolteacher and wrote to my parents that I was living the life of a belle of the *ton.*"

"Why not tell them the truth?"

She shook her head. "They would have been sick with worry. No, no, fabricating a story was the only way." She pinched her nose. "You must think I lie as a matter of course. I do not. I wrote every one of those letters with a heavy heart. The only thing that kept me going was imagining my parents' pleasure as they opened and read each one. If only I had been having half as much success as I told them!"

"And then?" He looked at her intently. "What happened then?"

"And then . . ." Her voice trailed off and her eyes fixed on her teacup. "And then the summer wore on, and I did not find a husband," she said quietly, her blush deepening to an alarming shade of crimson. She looked down to finger the sinuous handle of her teacup and hesitated in spite of her spoken resolve to confide in him.

"Why not?"

She looked up suddenly. His question was impertinent and rude, and he expected for her to look him daggers, but her eyes held little more than . . . something True couldn't quite put his finger on. Embarrassment? Shame?

"I would rather not talk about it, my lord." She rose. "I believe I am fatigued, after all." Without another word, she quit the room for her bedchamber, leaving behind the faint aroma of starch.

He'd expected nothing less than a set-down, and he felt an odd pang of disappointment. He shook the feeling off. By the devil, what did he want from her? A stern protestation that her personal matters were her own? An indignant display? An argument? Certainly not! The last thing he needed was to quarrel with her.

Blast, True didn't truly give a deacon's arse about why she'd come to London or what she'd been doing since she came. The only details he needed were those to make his seduction easier: what were her favorite foods, colors, amusements, flowers, and gemstones. None of the rest of it mattered.

He wondered at whatever impulse had made him ask such personal questions in the first place. He supposed it was the old warrior's urge to "know thine enemy." Not that he really needed to know anything more. He was certain he knew exactly what sort of woman Miss Grantham was, exactly where her priorities lay.

If she were truly seeking a love match, she could have found one by then. Though she was no beauty, she was not entirely without positive qualities. She possessed sound, even teeth and a pleasing figure. She moved gracefully, if a bit stiffly. Her face and hands were expressive and nimble. With her quick mind, she might have found any number of shopkeepers or solicitors to satisfy her heart in spite of her lack of looks. But Marianna Grantham's heart was clearly not her first priority. She'd come to London to marry a title, and True knew in his heart just by looking at her that if given a choice between love and position, she would abandon her heart, as any young woman of the *ton* would do. She was no different from any of them.

She was already one of them.

Five

She was different.

True tried not to notice just how different as the next three days passed in a blur. While his body was busy bestowing flowers and devastating smiles upon Miss Grantham, he tried to keep his mind busy elsewhere. There should have been enough to keep himself distracted. He should have been able to dwell upon his lost cargo, his impounded ships, or the welfare of his sailors and dockhands and their families. But she kept stealing his attention.

He'd expected her to begin behaving like every other hopeful uncut, unpolished diamond. He'd been prepared for her to demand to be introduced to his more lofty-titled acquaintances—or to the upper gentry living within a few miles of Trowbridge. He'd been prepared for her to start ordering the servants about as though they existed solely to satisfy her personal whims. And he'd been prepared for her to question him concerning his infamous behavior within the *ton*. But she hadn't done any of those things. It was unsettling.

In the quest to know his enemy, True was failing miserably.

As he waited in the great front hall for everyone to assemble for a picnic on their fourth afternoon together, True took comfort in the predictable way she'd behaved toward her new feminine fripperies. It was one of the few areas where she hadn't managed to surprise him.

He'd expected her to order thrice as many gowns as

needed, and she had. She'd ordered twenty. True knew because he'd told the seamstress to send him the bill.

He'd expected Mary to be impatient to get her hands on the new gowns, and she had. She'd paid extra to have the first of them delivered in only three days' time. Not only that, but she'd paid even more on top of that to have the first several of the gowns delivered all at once. Three boxes had been delivered early that morning and taken upstairs. True sneered. Like all the other ladies of the *ton*, Marianna Grantham cultivated her own capricious, impatient nature. It wasn't enough to have one new gown. She had to have three. Otherwise, how could she keep everyone waiting as she decided which to wear first?

He took out his watch.

"Stop scowling," Ophelia told him. She was staring out the window in the direction of her husband, who was speaking with the coachman about the condition of the barouche that had been prepared for the seven of them—True, the Robertsons, Miss Grantham, and the ABC's.

True's nieces were still upstairs with Miss Grantham. Ever since she'd refused to betray them for the salamander, the ABC's had been her constant shadow. They adored her.

Ophelia grunted. "Marianna will believe you are cross with her for being late if she catches you with such a sour expression."

"I am not scowling."

"Humph!"

True wanted to ask Ophelia why she cared what Miss Grantham thought of him, but he knew better. Over the past three days, Ophelia had been exasperatingly close-lipped, making it clear that she would divulge information in her own time and not before.

True paced the marble floor a few more minutes and then glanced at his watch. "Miss Grantham has been an early riser until now. Do you think I should have a maid check on her? Perhaps she has gone back to sleep." Or perhaps the ABC's had lured her to the tower garret and tied her in order to have her to themselves the entire day.

They'd been quite put out with True for having to share her with him.

Ophelia shook her head. "New frocks demand extra time for dressing, Trowbridge. She shall be down presently—and you shall be properly appreciative of her efforts if you know what you are about."

A movement at the top of the stairs caught his eye, and True turned to see the ABC's floating downstairs in a cloud of pristine white muslin. They each wore a clean frock with lovely wide ribbon sashes of yellow, pink, and green.

Their shiny hair was dressed in matching ribbons. They were perfect, from their washed and glowing faces to the dainty black slippers they each wore on their usually unshod feet. They tried to act serenely dignified as they descended the stairs, but they spoiled their entrance by dissolving into excited giggles and running to crowd around True, where they posed and twirled for his benefit and all spoke at once.

"Are you surpwised, Uncle Sin?"

"Mary curled my hair to look just like hers!"

"Do you think we look all the crack?"

Ophelia spoke. "You should not say 'all the crack,' dear. It is not proper."

"Ophelia!" All three little girls squealed and ran to pose and twirl for her. The old woman admired their frocks, clucking over them appreciatively and, True took note, not reprimanding them for using her given name.

True smiled after them, and Miss Grantham appeared at his elbow. "I apologize that I kept you waiting, my lord. Beatrice's curls were dreadfully knotted."

"Miss Grantham," he said, marveling at the change in the girls' appearance. "Even God took six days to perform some miracles. You have managed to complete one in four."

She wrinkled her nose. "I wouldn't call this one complete. Eleanor still refuses to wear gloves, as you can see, and I had to bribe Alyse with the promise of an extra hour of reading to her tonight in order to get her to wash behind her ears. But I think I am making progress."

"Indeed," he said. "I would hardly recognize them. Do

you know, I have never seen them wearing their good clothes."

"Why, that is because they had none, my lord. I took the liberty of examining the children's wardrobes and then had these dresses made," she said. "Do they not look lovely?" She went to join Ophelia in praising and admiring the girls, and it was only then that True noticed what Miss Grantham was wearing. Or what she wasn't wearing, rather.

She had on the same plain brown traveling gown she'd had on the day she arrived. He touched her elbow to get her attention.

She turned to him. "My lord?"

"Pray, take your time in getting dressed. There is no need to rush. We shall be happy to wait."

She looked lost at sea. "But I am dressed."

"No, I meant that we will wait for you to don your new gown. Mrs. Robertson informed me that new gowns take extra time. Think nothing of it. Waiting will be a pleasure." He almost meant it. The change she'd wrought in his nieces was nothing short of miraculous, and it would truly be a pleasure to sit and watch them pirouette and preen for the time it would take Miss Grantham to change. "Take your time," he said again.

"Thank you, my lord, but my gowns have not been sent 'round yet. I asked Mrs. Bailey to complete my order for the girls first." She turned. "Out the door, young ladies. And remember, not one dot of dirt on those new frocks, or I shall not let you wear any of the others for two days." She herded the ABC's out the front door.

Ophelia chuckled. "Close your mouth, Trowbridge, or you shall have it full of flies." She glanced from Miss Grantham to True knowingly. "Not what you thought she was on first glance, hmm?" She gave a satisfied nod. "Good, because neither are you." She sailed out the door.

True frowned. Nothing was going according to plan.

* * *

Marianna smiled. Everything was going according to plan.

The weather was fine, and a gentle breeze blew over the sweet meadow grass where they picnicked, carrying the children's laughter to her on currents of clean summer air. She tilted her head back and looked up through the green leaves of the ancient elm tree, where she sat on a quilt, watching the girls play. Their uncle was with them, shepherding them back from a foray down to the brook to hunt for tadpoles.

Ophelia deserved a medal for directing her to Truesdale Sinclair.

Though the beginning of their acquaintance had not been promising, the viscount's behavior ever since had been nothing short of perfect. *Everyone has a lapse in good judgment now and then,* she thought, giving a silent nod to her own transgressions.

Trowbridge was not perfect, but—except for a few lapses she suspected had more to do with a somewhat *fast* sense of humor—he was a perfect gentleman.

Though the rumors concerning his stunning good looks were not exaggerated, a steadfast application of logic coupled with well nigh a week's observation told her that the balance of the rumors were false. The very idea of Trowbridge having had hundreds or even dozens of romantic liaisons was ridiculous. He was a gentleman, and gentlemen did not behave in such a manner.

No, the viscount was everything that was amiable. Polite and attentive, he seemed genuinely glad to be of help to her, and he was eager to learn everything he could about her. Of course, that was only because that was what was required of him according to the terms of their bargain and not because he desired to seduce her. As he had pointed out that first day, they had to learn all they could of each other in order to carry out their ruse successfully.

Still, there had been moments these past two days when she thought his interest ranged beyond that which was strictly necessary. Take, for instance, the flowers he had brought her yesterday morning and this. He'd presented them, saying he was acting his part as thoroughly as he could now, so that he might be more convincing when their guests arrived. The lovely single pink roses were no more than a besotted suitor might bestow upon his beloved, to be sure. And yet the way he had placed them into her hand, his fingers lingering over hers as he had looked into her eyes . . . She shook her head. She was telling herself tales. Truesdale's interest in her lay no deeper than the bottom of her gem bottle.

She wondered if he would have agreed to help her at all if she hadn't had any gems to offer him. Three days ago, she would have rejected the idea, but now . . .

He had surprised her.

He was not the gruff, unbending man she'd thought he was at first. Especially toward the ABC's. Nothing in her education—or her upbringing—had led her to expect a gentleman to take such an active interest in children. Why, even her own papa, who loved her excessively and who had told her a thousand times he wanted only what was best for her, hadn't had much contact with her. But, as Marianna sat weaving daisy wreaths for the ABC's, she watched Truesdale Sinclair playing blind man's buff with the girls, and she was forced to reexamine her views. Either Truesdale Sinclair was an unconventional man, or ideas of child rearing had changed since her parents had left England some twenty-five years before.

Each day, the neglected condition of his late brother's estate demanded more time than the viscount had to devote to it. Yet, as busy as he was, Trowbridge still took time out to speak with the girls whenever they asked, and he made it a point to breakfast with them each day. He loved them. Of that Marianna was certain. He even tucked them into bed at night, kissing their brows and smoothing their hair, and telling them silly stories of sea monsters with sore tentacles or mermaids who forgot how to swim.

She sighed, missing her own papa and wondering what sorts of bedtime stories he would have told her if he'd had the time. Poor Papa, he worked too hard when she was small. She gave a guilty flinch, for she knew all his hard work had been for her, and here she was, perpetrating a ruse to fool him into thinking she was going to marry the Viscount Trowbridge. She finished one daisy wreath and began the next, dwelling upon her reasons for the ruse. She did so want to marry for love!

But it was no matter.

One way or another, she would marry before the first snowfall. She knew her duty, and she would not disappoint her mama and papa. They had sacrificed too much for her. She would marry whether she found love or not.

Ophelia appeared next to her, a welcome diversion from such unpleasant thoughts. She motioned to the three daisy wreaths Marianna had fashioned. "You'll have to make one larger than that to fit over my turban."

Marianna's morose thoughts scattered, but her mood was not so easily dispelled. She tried to smile, but she was not terribly successful, and Ophelia said, "Come now, dispel those blue devils. Tell me what troubles you."

Marianna didn't even try to offer a denial. Ophelia was astute enough to know when Marianna skirted a direct question. Besides, she was Marianna's friend, and as such she was owed a confidence.

The old woman settled herself upon one of the chairs the footmen had set up for them. "Well?" she prompted.

Marianna shook her head and stared at her hands. "It just seems incomprehensible that somewhere there is a man to whom I shall soon be wed. A man I do not know. A man I have never even glimpsed."

Ophelia shook her head. "That is not what troubles you."

Marianna threw her a questioning look. "Oh?"

"No. You, Marianna, in spite of your otherwise sensible mind, believe in foolish fairy-stories. You were brought up knowing what is most important in a husband: wealth and title. But you have always harbored a secret belief in all that *one-true-love* rubbish, and now you fear not finding your own true love. Even worse, you are beginning to doubt any such man exists."

Marianna lowered her gaze to her lap.

Ophelia reached out to tip Marianna's chin back up. "You are wrong, Marianna." Her blue eyes were soft and kind. "He does exist, and you will discover him right here at Trowbridge. Very soon."

Marianna knew she referred to the army of bachelors who would soon be descending upon Trowbridge Manor along with the rest of the house party guests. They were hand-chosen by Ophelia, an exemplary group of men to be sure. Yet Marianna held no confidence that she would fall in love with one of them. She wanted to ask what made Ophelia so certain it would happen with one of the gentlemen coming to Trowbridge, but she did not wish to spoil her old friend's pleasant fantasy. A wistful smile had claimed the lady's lined face. If Ophelia could find a few days' pleasure believing that she could bring Marianna together with her own true love, why spoil it for her?

Marianna said nothing and began weaving a much larger, turban-sized wreath.

True set the girls upon a hunt for a four-leafed clover, and wandered back over toward the picnic quilt. As he approached, Ophelia rose and went in search of her husband, who was with the coachman and footmen, talking horses, no doubt. The man loved horses, and he was spanking good with them. After only three days with him present, True's stables were already in much better shape. He had expected to wait an hour or more for the barouche to be brought 'round this morning, but it had taken less than a quarter hour. He was certain Mr. Robertson—John, as the man insisted True call him—was responsible for that.

Ophelia threw Truesdale an amused look as she quit the shade of the elm tree, and True sat down on the blanket next to Miss Grantham.

"They are quite taken with you," he said, nodding toward

the ABC's. "When I suggested they look for a lucky sham-rock, the three of them cast about with a decided lack of enthusiasm—until Alyse said that when she found a four leaf she would present it to you. Then the other two threw themselves into the hunt with alacrity, and now all three of them are racing to see who will be the first to find one. They all want to please you."

Mary smiled. "The feeling is mutual. They are darlings, if one takes the time to get to know them. Do you think they are hungry?" She changed the subject. It was indicative of another of her traits—another surprise for True—for, un-like most other people, Mary did not trumpet her own ac-complishments.

True tapped the picnic hamper. "I am not at all certain anything in here is edible."

He had ordered a hamper to be laden with whatever largesse the cook could produce, though True did not expect much in that regard. Thus far, he'd seen Cook spend as little effort as possible in pleasing anyone—though he was un-certain the result would be noticeable even if she did put in special effort, for Cook was as incompetent as the rest of the Trowbridge servants. Incompetent and ill-mannered. Her expression was invariably as sour as her quince pies.

True had learned Mary Grantham's favorite foods early on—bacon, shortbread, roasted chicken, and anything made of apples—but requests to Cook to prepare them went largely unheeded. He intended to dismiss the woman as soon as he had time to procure a suitable replacement.

Not that it really mattered that much. After all, he would be leaving Trowbridge Manor before too long, and he did not need the food to entice Mary to stay. Not when he had his smile, his attention, and fields of bluebells to bestow upon her. Not when he had his mother's engagement ring to spring upon her when the time was right.

No, he did not need special food.

He opened the hamper to begin taking out its contents and blinked in surprise. Cold milk lay in ice, along with a jar of summer pickles and a small crock of fresh butter.

Beneath that lay a box of tall, light, fluffy-looking biscuits. Farther down, he discovered a pot of plump apple dumplings, a tin of delicate shortbread still warm from the oven, and two roasted chickens.

John and Ophelia joined them, and True motioned to the footmen, who were standing nearby. "Is Cook ill this morning?" he asked them, certain he knew the answer. Whoever had filled in for her might make a suitable replacement.

The footmen traded looks, and one man shrugged. "No, my lord. Cook was right as rain and singing loud enough to wake up the King before dawn this morning."

True frowned. "Well, then, who prepared the food?"

The footman shrugged. "I reckon it was Cook, my lord."

"Impossible."

"Oh, no, Mr. Fitts is correct," Marianna said. "Cook asked me this morning at breakfast if I preferred apple dumplings or apple pie for our picnic."

"At breakfast? You slept through breakfast."

She laughed. "No, I was up quite early working on . . . on my embroidery. I was peckish, so I wandered down to the kitchen to beg a crust or two and ended up having the loveliest breakfast with Cook. She's such a dear woman."

"Cook? My cook?" he asked, genuinely all at sea, but Mary's attention was focused on the ABC's, who had given up their search for a four-leafed clover and now produced ratty bouquets of wildflowers for Mary instead.

Ophelia approached. "Humph!" she grumped with mock sincerity. "I suppose I shall have to pick my own flowers." She marched dramatically out into the meadow. The ABC's traded guilty looks with Mary, and soon all five of the females were far afield, scouring the meadow for more wildflowers.

John shrugged. "No tellin' when they'll be back, an' my belly's too empty for waitin'." He reached for a leg of chicken and a pickle. Tucking in, he smacked his lips. "Delicious!"

"It is?"

John nodded, taking another bite. "Mmm . . ."

Experimentally, True tasted the chicken. It *was* good. He tried the biscuits next, then the shortbread, and finally the apple dumplings. All were exquisite. "I do not understand," he said absently.

"Mmm?"

"I thought my cook incompetent. I had intended to dismiss her. I had intended to dismiss quite a few of the incompetent servants my brother hired. But now I find she can cook like this."

"I been in your stables a lot these past days, my lord—"

"For which I've been meaning to thank you."

" 'Tis nothin'. I'm right glad to help. Anyways . . . I come to know the lads in the stables fair enough already, and I'm guessin' your brother didn't hire no bad servants. It's just that they ain't willin' to work their hardest for a man who ain't likely to appreciate it, if you take my meanin'."

"Meaning my late brother was an ungrateful knave who thought himself above everyone and made sure they all knew it?"

"That's it. And of course you're guilty by association."

And by reputation, True added to himself. There was a time when his own behavior had been no better than his brother's.

"But now," John continued, "your servants all think Miss Marianna's goin' to be their new mistress, see?" He plucked a biscuit from the box and motioned toward the footmen, who were following behind Mary, baskets in hand, to help carry the wildflowers she gathered. "She's got them charmed, my lord, and they're doin' their best to please her."

Just like the ABC's, True thought. The girls had actually refused to take their shoes off and tramp into the water after the elusive tadpoles. They hadn't wanted to take a chance on getting their new frocks spotted.

Trowbridge had been neglected. Usually, True's brother and sister-in-law had stayed at their town house and chose to travel to friends' homes during the fashionable months to flee London for the country. They left their daughters at Trowbridge, rarely seeing them above two or three times a year, and then never for more than a week at a time. The girls had never truly known their parents. They'd seen True more than they had their own father, and True had always regretted not being able to spend more time with them. He was always there at Christmas and as often as he could get away from his shipping business, still in its struggling infancy, but he was painfully aware that it had not been enough.

The ABC's had needed a firm attachment to an adult. They had grown wild, and keeping a governess had become more and more difficult. Intervals between governesses had lengthened, until Franklin and Sylvia had just given up. True remembered having spoken to Sylvia about it during one of his rare visits to his brother's town house. Lounging on a sofa in her lavishly decorated parlor, she'd declared interviewing "stodgy old spinsters" a tedious bore, and she was much too busy, she said, to be bothered every week with it. If her brats back at Trowbridge Manor insisted on chasing off their governesses, then they would just have to do without them. She and Franklin had washed their hands of the entire matter. True had looked to Franklin, but the elder Sin had simply shrugged his abstention and unconcern. True had given a tight nod and left, seething. It was the last time he saw either of them alive.

Overseeing the girls' day-to-day existence had fallen to the Trowbridge staff—but they already had more than enough to do. Franklin refused to spend a farthing on the estate. The idiot bled off the profits and never put anything back into the land. As servants and tenants moved on or died, Franklin made no effort to replace them. The workload increased, and the only contact the people of Trowbridge had with Franklin was the occasional angry letter demanding to know why the revenues were down. The steward had quit in disgust three years before. With no improvements to the estate and a shrinking staff, Trowbridge had been slowly dying.

Since his brother's death and until Mary's arrival, True had been working day and night to turn the estate around. At first, he had thought that if he could bring Trowbridge back to its former profitability, he could stave off his brother's creditors long enough to settle the debts one by one. He had given it an honest go, visiting each creditor personally. To a man, they were unmoved. Franklin had taken out enormous loans, and every one of his creditors demanded immediate payment from the new Viscount Truesdale. It was blunt True just didn't have.

Next, True had tried to secure a loan. He had thought his own successes in founding a shipping business, coupled with the recent improvements to Trowbridge and his diligence in attempting to bring the estate back from the brink, would be enough to convince them. But each man he spoke with had laughed in his face. He was at point-nonplus.

It seemed no one believed True Sin would keep his word. They all expected him to use the money to have his ships released and then to simply disappear onto the high seas. The hell of it was, the thought had occurred to True. Deep inside, he knew he was no better than his brother. He was one of the Sins, after all. Deceit and treachery were in his blood.

There was still a long way to go before he could depart Trowbridge and leave it in the hands of his current steward. When it came to managing the land and the accounts, the young man he had hired the previous month was capable, but, fresh from University, the lad was lacking in the skills necessary to handle the staff. Even a trained and disciplined staff. True spent most of his time repairing the damage that years of neglect had done to the servants and tenants. He had to teach them to work together once more, and it took every ounce of leadership skill True possessed to affect any change at all. The staff's return to cooperative efficiency was painfully slow. At the same time, he had to teach his steward to manage people—a task that would have been delicate enough even if the staff and tenants had already been working smoothly together.

In spite of the challenges, Mr. Montescue was doing quite well indeed. He had been a good choice. Eager and intelligent, he was young to hold such an important position as steward. But it had been impossible to find another, more experienced man to take Trowbridge in hand. Trowbridge was a large estate, and its problems were well known. True had advertised in the papers, and several candidates had shown, but all were far from worthy. Most either smelled of gin or had no references. Montescue was glad to have the job and was willing to work hard for a small percentage of future profits. True was satisfied that Montescue would be earning a tidy sum in less than a year, and Trowbridge would have a loyal steward for years to come. Montescue needed him less and less now, and True believed that as soon as he was wed to Mary Grantham, he could leave Trowbridge for the sea, and the estate would prosper in his absence. Assuming he had any ships left to return to. Even now, forces in London and Portsmouth were gathering to take his ships from him.

As it turned out, even with Mary there, he could still give some attention to the estate. Mary took a surprising interest in how the estate, so different from her parents' holdings in the islands, were run. At first, when Mary requested to accompany him on his rounds, he had balked. He had thought she would become bored quickly and demand to return home, but she never did. She listened attentively and asked questions that showed an innate shrewdness about money. In his more cynical moments, her behavior reminded him of her avaricious and overly ambitious nature, but in less guarded moments he found himself almost enjoying her company.

She was an excellent rider, and she seemed to have an innate understanding not only of her own mount, but of True's as well. When True's normally steady horse shied violently as they veered off a path, she correctly guessed the beast was uneasy with the brook, which could be heard splashing over stones a short distance away.

"Has he ever been in an accident involving water?" she asked.

"Indeed. Journey caught his hoof between two stones in a brook as a youngster. He always balks at crossing water now. I take him over bridges, rather than fords, even when doing so will take me some distance out of the way." He glanced over at her. "You surprise me," he said.

"Oh?"

He shook his head. "You ride that mare as though you've known her all her life, and your guess about the origin of Journey's fault was uncanny."

"Not really," she answered. "Horses are a great deal like children, and I already know a great deal about them."

The remainder of the week passed pleasantly enough. In the evenings, after the ABC's went to bed, True and Mary passed the time with chess or backgammon. She was terrible at both of them, having never played them as a child, but she was a fast learner. They formed an easy camaraderie, which was understandable because they knew more details of each other's lives than most couples married for years, True fancied.

He began to think that marriage to Marianna Grantham would not be the odious undertaking he'd first imagined. They would never be true lovers or true friends, but perhaps they could share a guarded truce.

Ophelia was correct; there was more to Mary than met the eye.

Take for instance her mischievous streak, which was coupled with a wicked sense of humor. He had discovered them both when, two days before their guests were due to arrive, he walked into the morning parlor unannounced to find her embroidering furiously on a pair of ladies' stockings.

The things were finely knit of white silk and bright blue brocade shot with silver. She'd embroidered blue and silver flowers down the sides and added three tiers of white lace. As though that were not enough decoration, she had attached blue and silver satin garter ribbons with silver tassels and tiny silver bells hanging from the ends. The whole effect was nothing less than hideously gaudy.

As soon as she saw movement in the doorway, she shoved the outrageous stockings behind her back, but it was too late. He'd already seen them, and she must have known it by his expression.

"They're not mine," she said.

"Naturally," True drawled. "They have to be for Ophelia—"

"Hardly!"

"—or for your mother."

"Oh, my lord, you jest."

"I do." He smiled. "So, who are they for?"

"My friend Agnes." She took the stockings from behind her back and stroked them lovingly. "I miss her."

"Agnes Marchman, the baroness?"

"Yes, the same. Founder and headmistress of Baroness Marchman's School for Young Ladies."

He motioned to the stocking. "Somehow, Lady Marchman does not strike me as the sort to wear—oh, I see. Blue stockings for a bluestocking!"

Her cheeks blushed pink. "Yes."

True chuckled. "Mary, you are not the proper miss you would have everyone believe you to be."

"My lord, I see no reason for insults!"

"It was not intended as such, for I much prefer you the way you truly are."

She rolled her blue eyes at him before smiling shyly.

"Care to ride with me? My presence is required at the mill and then in the high fields to the east. Mr. Montescue wishes to discuss irrigation and how it will affect the tenants who live in that area."

"I would like to, my lord. But I shall have little time to work on these stockings after our guests arrive. I will finish today and join you this afternoon perhaps?"

He bowed quickly and left her to her work, chuckling as he went to meet his steward at the mill. When she smiled, she was almost pretty. Almost. If a man liked pale, colorless women. Which True did not. Blonde curls and blue eyes were all the crack among the *ton*. He'd always preferred dark hair and eyes, as everyone knew. He'd taken two Romany maids to Lady Elgin's ball once.

Half the day passed and True's hands were sore before he realized he'd forgotten to retrieve his riding gloves from the morning parlor, which was why he'd gone there in the first place.

She beat him at backgammon that night, six games to four.

Six

Rain pattered softly on the roof and the wet ground outside, filling the darkness with a lulling music. It felt as though the entire house had been put under a spell. The world had a sleepy feel, and the ABC's and the Robertsons, who had all been yawning by midafternoon, were already abed.

It was True's last night alone with Mary, and it was time to deliver his *coup de grâce*.

If all went well that evening, he would make a hasty trip to London on the morrow, leaving before dawn and returning just before the Trowbridge houseguests began to arrive that afternoon. He was well nigh certain his seduction had been successful. He'd been the recipient of several more shy smiles, and he'd thought he'd seen Miss Grantham surreptitiously pinching her cheeks to bring up their color earlier in the day.

Mary sat on a sofa reading *The Faerie Queene* to him in the glow of the lamplight. So absorbed in the poem was she that she had tucked her feet up underneath her, abandoning her pink kid slippers on the floor beside her.

She was wearing one of her new gowns, a delicate muslin in a becoming shade of salmon. It seemed to emphasize what little color she possessed. The damp weather had given her hair a little curl, and wisps escaped to frame her face. Her blue eyes shone with excitement as she read the ending of the work.

He feigned rapt attention until the last word faded from her lips and she had finally closed the book.

"Beautiful," he murmured.

"Quite so," she said on a sigh, "the poem is deeply allegorical, of course, but I always get lost in the story, especially the last section where Calidore rescues Pastorella."

"He does?"

"Were you not listening?" she exclaimed.

"On the contrary, I was listening. To you. To your voice. That is what I meant. You have a beautiful voice, Mary."

She stood up. "Rubbish."

"Not at all. I told you what a fine voice I thought you had that very first evening you came to me. Remember?"

"How could I forget?" She smiled. "You wanted me to use it to sing 'Greensleeves' in the middle of the night. And if I didn't know the song, you were going to teach it to me."

He threw her his best mischievous grin. "The offer still stands."

"My lord," she said, her stern tone ruined by an ill-concealed chuckle, "I do not sing."

"You should have a go. You would excel at it. You excel at a great many things, Mary."

"More rubbish. Name one thing."

"You are good with the children."

"Humph! That does not signify. I was a schoolteacher, after all. I am supposed to be good with children. What else?"

He sensed the challenge in her voice. She didn't think he could come up with anything else. "You are wonderful at managing the servants. You are good to them. You treat them like the individuals they are."

"I was a servant when I was a teacher, my lord, and—"

"True. You should get used to calling me True. It will help our ruse if you let the name slip in front of our guests once in a while."

She nodded. "Truesdale," she conceded.

"Ever the proper miss, aren't you?" he asked. She raised

her eyebrows and nodded, and he said, "I interrupted you. Go on."

"Oh, yes. I was going to say that being a servant brought me an appreciation of what their lives are like. I fancy I am much more sympathetic to them than I was before I came to London. But that hardly qualifies as something I am skilled at. What else am I good at?"

Now she was enjoying the sport. "Embroidery," he answered.

She blushed crimson. "Pray do not mention the things again. As soon as I have them finished, I will give them to Agnes—and you will pretend you never saw them." She threw him a look of mock severity. "They are meant to be a humorous hum. I doubt she will truly wear them—though she might. Agnes has a rebellious streak much like Ophelia—they are old friends, you know. That is how I met Ophelia—and no one would know Agnes was wearing them."

"Except for the bells jingling."

She covered her mouth and laughed. "Do you think I went too far with the bells?"

"No . . ." he said with mock sincerity. "In fact, I believe you should add a few more. Or a pair of tiny cymbals or castanets, perhaps? She could *crash*-clickety-click-*crash*-clickety-click as she jingles on past." They laughed together. "Really," he said, "if Lady Marchman has half the sense of humor you do, she will love the stockings."

She nodded her thanks.

"Speaking of giving . . . I have something to give to you."

"Oh?"

"Yes." He walked to the mantel and opened a small porcelain box there. "When our guests arrive, we must in every way appear as a betrothed couple. If anyone discovers our ruse, we shall both find it devilishly uncomfortable. Any potential investors I have would dry up, my shipping business would be lost, and you—you would be utterly ruined."

Marianna swallowed hard. She knew what he said was true.

"We must do everything our guests expect of us, everything they would expect of a betrothed couple. We have done well this past week. We have constructed a believable story, all the stronger for its simplicity, and we have learned each other's habits. I think we are ready but for a few small details."

"Which are?"

"This is one," he said, and lifted from the porcelain box an object that sparkled in the lamplight. "A ring. It was my mother's."

Marianna blinked and felt her heart constrict. His mother's ring. She wondered about the woman who had last worn it. Ophelia had said Truesdale's mother was not a happy person, though she would say no more, and Truesdale never spoke of his family. The ring was a very large ruby ringed with diamonds in a setting that looked like a rose just opening and sprinkled with dew. She stared at it.

He sat beside her and took her hand in his. His fingers were warm against hers. She expected him to slide the ring onto her finger and let go, but he lingered, stroking the back of her hand with soft, slow circles of his thumb.

"It . . . it is lovely, my lord. Shall I put it on?" she asked, unable to keep a nervous flutter from her voice. Was he aware of what he was doing to her hand?

"My mother never took this ring off ," he answered without letting go. "Roses were her favorite. She always said that if she'd ever had a daughter, she would have given her the name Rose." He reached for her other hand and then rubbed both her palms with his fingertips. How could he *not* know what he was doing?

Gently, Marianna tried to pull her hand free. "I . . . it . . . under the circumstances, it seems improper to wear your mother's ring."

He shook his head. "You must. It is a family heirloom. Our guests will expect it, and they will think it odd if you are not wearing it, just as they will think it odd if—"

"If, my lord?"

"If you try to pull your hands away when I touch them, as you are now."

"Oh!" So he was not caressing her hand to express affection, he was simply making a point. Her cheeks flamed. She felt foolish for having thought, even for a second, that he had formed some sort of *tendre* for her.

"Our guests will also think it odd if you balk," he said, leaning toward her, "when I do"—he took her into his arms—"this." He kissed her.

Instantly, she stilled, but her mind was awhirl. His reasoning was sound. She'd known from the beginning that nothing would be more convincing than to be "caught" kissing once or twice as all betrothed couples usually were. She had even planned on insisting they be seen kissing— though that part of her plan had become more and more uncomfortable for her to contemplate as time went on and she'd got to know the viscount.

Using her logical mind, she analyzed his movements, noting how he curled his arms behind her and drew her against him, how he slanted his mouth over hers and pressed gently. How he skimmed his hands over the flesh at the back of her neck and cradled her head. How his fingers dug into her hair, and how he began guiding her movements. She wondered how such a kiss would feel if she were not so unattractive, if the man kissing her really wanted to kiss her. She noticed his eyes were closed. Hers were not. Should they be? Yes. Elsewise, someone might notice. She shut her eyes, and then, realizing she was very tense, realizing an observer might notice that, too, she relaxed against him and did her best to kiss him back.

His breath was sweet, his lips surprisingly soft and warm. The thought occurred to her that if she stopped analyzing the kiss for a moment, it might be quite enjoyable.

She tried it.

Focusing on his warm, soft lips, his sweet breath, and the way his mouth seemed to be coaxing hers, she sighed against him and allowed him to show her what to do.

He moaned.

Instantly, she set her hands against his chest and pushed away from him. He opened his eyes, and she was stunned by what she saw there. Desire! She didn't know how she knew, but every part of her—not the logical parts, but the feminine—confirmed it. True Sin wanted her! Wanted her in a physical, masculine way.

She stood and murmured something unintelligible, even to her, and fled.

She found herself in her chamber a few minutes later, not remembering the journey, the path she'd traveled, or even how long it had taken her to get there. Her mind worked furiously, sifting the logic from the frenzied feelings his kiss had conjured. Marianna had never been kissed before and did not have much experience with which to judge, but she was nevertheless certain that *that* kiss had been more than was strictly necessary to acclimate her to his touch.

But that could not be, could it? What had just happened? She had to think! She fought for control of her frenzied feelings, pacing the floor of her bedchamber like a caged tigress. He had complimented her, smiled at her, touched her hand, given her his mother's ring . . . and kissed her.

Gently, insistently, hungrily.

She thought about the past week, about the flowers he'd given her, the smiles, the dozens of small kindnesses he'd shown her. They'd increased in number as the week had worn on.

Could it be that he'd come to care for her? She didn't know. Logic told her there was no way to be certain of his feelings.

But she ought to be certain of hers.

Did she care for him? There was much to admire about the Viscount Trowbridge. He was a loving guardian to his nieces, a fair and respectful master to the servants, and a tolerant host to Ophelia, who would try anyone's hospitality. He had an engaging way about him and a delightful sense of humor. He'd been attentive and amiable all week. And surely he hadn't felt obligated to listen to her read the entire text of *The Faerie Queene* in one afternoon. He'd wanted to spend time with her. Hadn't he?

Oh . . . saints and sinners! She did care for him! Was he the one? Was he the man she was destined to marry?

That kiss hadn't been a lesson, a taming, a strategy, or anything like that. It had been a conquest. No, she amended. Truesdale was a gentleman, and gentlemen were not conquerors. His kiss had not been a conquest, but a . . . an exploration.

But why explore her? Was she such a mystery? Such a treasure to search for and covet?

No. She was not.

Her racing mind came to a sudden halt. She was far from a treasure. She was no Diamond. She was a colorless spinster who still smelled of starch, while he was a much-admired and dashingly handsome viscount. Ophelia had warned her the ladies among their houseguests, married or not, would be vying for his attention. Apparently, he was a sought-after *parti* among the untitled ladies of the *ton*. Surely, the viscount could no doubt have his choice of any of them? Marianna was plain as toast, and she knew it. Why should Truesdale choose her?

The answer lay in simple logic: he wouldn't.

She had to have been mistaken. He didn't desire her. He had been acting a part during that kiss, or perhaps she'd just made up the whole idea. Yes, that was probably it. Ophelia was right, Marianna did believe in silly fairy stories. She did believe in one-true-love, and just for a moment—for one *insane* moment—she'd believed that perhaps Truesdale Sinclair was The One.

She went through the ritual of getting ready for bed, and then she lay down but slept hardly at all. All night long, in spite of all her careful, controlled logic, in spite of her resolve to abandon her impractical, fantastical fairy stories, the moment she'd thought she'd glimpsed genuine desire in his eyes kept coming back to her, and she wondered: was there any chance he really cared for her? Was there any chance at all that he really was the one? The one man she was destined to love?

Morning came. She dressed in one of her new gowns—the aqua. It was his favorite, he'd said when the gowns had all arrived. She'd thought to save it for when her parents came, not because it was his favorite but because it matched her eyes, and she thought it would look the prettiest of all the gowns she had. She dressed her hair in a rather careless twist with a matching aqua ribbon. She allowed some of her curls to frame her face. He had remarked that he preferred she give her hair some freedom.

She went downstairs at first light, where she knew she would find him at breakfast with the ABC's. Her heart pounded. She had made a decision. She would ask him. She would ask how he felt about her. There was no other way to be certain. She preferred plain speaking, and so did he. She wasn't sure how she felt about him, but it was best to get their feelings—or lack of them—out in the open.

She swept into the morning room, where the ABC's sat looking morose. Three places were set upon the table. Three places, not four.

"Where is your uncle?"

"Gone," Alyse said in a sulky voice.

"Gone where?" Marianna asked.

Eleanor shrugged. "He left while we were asleep."

"Yes," Beatrice said. "The coach is gone, and they will not tell us where he went or when he's coming back."

Seven

London was wretched. The streets were muddy from the recent rain, fog had shrouded the church spires deep into the afternoon, and the fetid odors drifting in from the Thames seemed to cling to everything. The air was too still. True wished a breeze would blow in from the North Sea. By Jove, how he missed the ocean!

True hadn't even seen the sea in two months.

It wouldn't be long before he returned to that life, he thought as his coachman maneuvered the vehicle into fashionable St. James's Street. He patted the pocket of his waistcoat and, withdrawing an envelope, threw it onto the seat opposite him. It was a special license. With it, he could wed Marianna Grantham wherever and whenever it was convenient.

Not that True cared where or when—only that the deed were done.

He rapped on the ceiling of the coach, signaling he wished to debark. Out on the street, he made his way to a nondescript shop with a small sign at the top. "Chancellor and Gale," the sign read. "Jewelers." Their wares were overpriced, but True didn't mind. The shop traded in discretion as much as it did in jewels. Not many of the baubles purchased there ever made it onto the hands or neck or ears of a wife.

Leaving the shop a half hour later, True ordered his coach to his town house in Silver Street. The afternoon sun slanted low across the rooftops, wives scurried forth to bring a meal to their tables. He'd hoped to make it back to Trowbridge before now, for his houseguests would already have begun arriving, but the delay could not have been helped. His order from Chancellor and Gale could not be made ready before then, and, with the roads as sodden and rutted as they were, it would take him a good four hours of neck-or-nothing riding to make the journey back to Trowbridge Manor. He would not start until morning.

It was no matter.

Truesdale suspected that his betrothed would take his absence gracefully, as she did most everything. She would give some excuse or other and carry on with her activities as though nothing were amiss. He honestly didn't think she'd mind much. Like a cat, clever and quick, Marianna Grantham would always land on her feet.

He stared out the window as the carriage wove through the crowded, rain-soaked streets. He knew with an experienced certainty that his seduction had been successful. She'd blushed in his arms last night, and she'd run from the room as though the soles of her feet were on fire.

A growl of frustration cleared his lips. Thank God she'd run.

The truth was, when she had finally relaxed against him and begun to kiss him back, True nearly abandoned his wits. Though it was obvious she'd never been kissed, Marianna Grantham had proved to be as apt a pupil at kissing as she was at everything else. Too apt! He snorted. He could still feel the silken strands of her golden hair entwined in his fingers, could taste her sweet mouth on his own hungry lips. He'd wanted to go on kissing her.

Bloody hell, what he'd wanted to do was to carry her up to his bed!

True shook his head. What had come over him? He'd been rusticating in the country for three months, that's what. It had been too long since he'd enjoyed feminine company, that was all. It was not as though Mary were the least bit attractive. Quite the contrary. Her pale looks held no power of fascination. By candlelight, a man couldn't even see she had eyebrows.

Ah . . . but with no candles at all . . .

True's mind went a-begging as he imagined how her body might feel beneath his in the darkness, how her voice would sound when drugged with passion. She would smell like a field of dewy flowers from walking with him in the rain . . . hand in hand . . . singing "Greensleeves" . . . swimming in the brook . . . together . . . naked in the brook. . . .

Out the window, someone whistled a greeting to the coachman, and True shook the images of Mary from his mind with annoyance. Indulging in such fantasies would get him nowhere. Marianna Grantham was not the sort of woman to sing or swim naked in the brook, and she was not the sort of woman to inspire such heated thoughts. She was drab, colorless. And she did not smell of wildflowers and rain, but of starch.

The trouble was, her personality wasn't as colorless as her countenance. The trouble was, he'd been forced to get to know her. She'd become a person to him this past week, a person with dreams and ambitions. Ambitions, he'd come to realize, which were equal in intensity to his own.

Too bad they were all centered on her future position among the *ton*. They could have been friends but for that.

If he were not careful, he would begin to believe that he truly liked the chit, by Jove! He had to remind himself that her shallow focus on gaining a position in Society far outweighed the list of good qualities he had assigned to her. Kindness, cleverness, compassion, none of it mattered. Not when she believed that the upper ten thousand were the only people who really mattered.

He had to concede that she was not what he had at first believed her to be. Where Mary was concerned, True's uncanny ability to instantly assess a person's character had abandoned him. She was not the empty-headed and selfish chit he'd first thought she was, and she was not as high in the instep as her rigid bearing and aroma of starch had led

him to believe. Those blue stockings of hers were evidence
enough of that. He recalled the painfully ornate things she'd
made for her friend Lady Marchman. The stockings were
a slyly playful gift and evidence of a delightful wit Mary
usually kept hidden away.

He wondered why. Why was she so serious? Why did
she feel she had to keep her naturally buoyant personality
in check? What had her upbringing been like? What sort
of people were her parents?

As the coach made its ponderous turn into a less crowded
street, he wondered what she'd think of his brother's town
house there in London. Would she find it as vulgarly lavish
as he did? When she finally breached the sanctum of Almack's, would she find it as much of a tedious bore as True
did? Perhaps she would eventually grow tired of London
and retreat to the country. She seemed quite content at
Trowbridge Manor, but what if she grew tired of it, too?
She might travel. She hadn't complained about her long
journey from the islands. He wondered if she had merely
endured the trip, or if she actually liked traveling by ship.
The *Lady Jane*, True's largest ship, had fine quarters. He
would be proud to show them to her. She would enjoy seeing—

He stopped mid-thought. That would never do. As soon
as they were wooed and wed, she'd be happy, and he'd be . . .
gone. For now, he'd set her firmly from his mind. True
spent the rest of the drive to the town house scowling out
the window.

Marianna wished True Sin to perdition.

She had occupied the parlor all day, forced to greet the
Trowbridge houseguests alone, when she should have been
standing beside the Viscount Truesdale. The servants had
naturally been deferring to her, as they had been doing all
week, and none of the guests knew exactly what to make
of that. It was certainly enough to arouse their curiosity,
however. They all had to be wondering about Marianna's

status with the viscount, but Marianna could hardly announce their engagement without him, especially since she didn't know when—or if—he would be coming back, the bounder!

It was late afternoon, the last of their guests had arrived an hour before, and Marianna hadn't the first idea what to do next. She smiled wanly and looked about the parlor, where most of the guests had now assembled. They sat in groups, talking amongst themselves, and it was clear they were all waiting for Trowbridge to arrive. Marianna sat with Ophelia next to the window.

"I shall strangle him," she whispered through her carefully benign smile.

Ophelia looked up from the letter she was reading and patted her hand. "Do not be too harsh on the boy," she whispered. "He would not have been late on purpose. Probably a broken axle or some such."

"A broken axle, or a broken promise?"

Ophelia lowered the missive to her knee. "He would not. He needs—" She glanced about her furtively and lowered her voice even more. "He needs you too much to cast you to the wolves."

Marianna felt as though that is exactly what he had done. She didn't know any of the guests, and they were all clearly curious about her. They were all *Good Ton,* but—honestly!— she still felt as though they were wolves, circling before the kill. She smiled at a dowager duchess whose raised eyebrows did nothing to calm her nerves.

"This was not what I fancied my introduction to Society would be like."

Ophelia tapped the letter. "It is a pity my grand-niece and nephew could not attend. Having someone here you are acquainted with—besides your duenna, of course," she said, meaning herself, "would have made the time pass more smoothly." Lord and Lady Blackshire had been on the guest list but they had sent word that Lady Blackshire was increasing and could not travel. Ophelia was delighted with the news. She had taken out their letter to reread it every five minutes or so, and she had been quite blissfully distracted since it had arrived that morning.

Marianna shifted uncomfortably. "They are all staring at me."

"A little mystery concerning your connection to the viscount will not hurt."

"As long as he comes back," Marianna muttered.

"He will return. Soon," she added. "Do not worry so. You will give yourself gray hair."

Marianna tried not to worry, but she found that impossible. She had the Trowbridge ruby on her finger, but so far it had gone unseen, camouflaged as it was beneath her gloves. The gloves itched her fingers, and she longed to take them off. She had never enjoyed wearing them, and since she had come to England, she had grown too accustomed to being free of them. Schoolteachers had little call for gloves, and, given the viscount's lack of formality, she had forgone them here at Trowbridge Manor almost as much as at the school.

She tried not to fidget, tried not to notice the furtive glances cast her way. She knew the guests were all attempting to guess her connection to True Sin. Of course, as members of the *ton,* they were too well mannered to say so. It would have been intolerably forward to come right out and ask. And, by the same code of behavior, she could not volunteer the information, no matter how much she longed to.

Did they imagine she was an impoverished relation? A governess? A housekeeper? Whatever they thought, they all seemed to be awaiting True's arrival to confirm their surmises. They talked of little else but the viscount, though their conversation somehow felt . . . restrained, Marianna thought, as though they all had more to say but didn't for some reason. They must all be wondering where Trowbridge was. Marianna was wondering the same thing. Blast the man!

One young man, a tulip wearing a pink striped waistcoat, finally addressed the company, though he looked straight at Marianna. "I say, this is deuced odd. Does anyone know when we shall have the pleasure of the Viscount Trowbridge's company?"

Marianna caught Ophelia's eye and silently beseeched her for help.

Ophelia rose suddenly and with the kind of flourish only she could produce. "It is deadly dull inside, and the weather is fine. I am venturing outside to stroll the gardens." She looked at Marianna. "Did you not say tea would be served on the lawn today, since the weather is so fine?"

"I did? Oh! Yes . . . yes, I did."

The guests exchanged looks and rose *en masse*. Ophelia led the exodus. Everyone seemed genuinely glad to stretch their limbs after their long journeys, and Marianna was simply glad to get away from them for a few moments—though she couldn't help wandering into the library, which provided not only fine vistas of the gardens through its tall windows but also voluminous curtains to hide behind as one spied on those who strolled there.

She perched on the edge of a chair covered in green damask and peered around one of the matching curtains. Her eyes fixed upon one handsome gentleman after the other as their deep voices floated to her through the opened windows.

Ophelia had helped her assemble the guest list. It included well nigh twenty young bachelors, men Ophelia considered the most eligible *partis* among the *ton*. They were all titled, wealthy, or both, and most of them were quite good-looking.

One of them would be her husband. Her heart beat hard and fast in her chest, and she felt herself begin to perspire. Her parents' fortune was so vast that she was certain to attract the attention of several of the young lords. She would soon have a choice to make. She would have to decide which of them she wanted to wed. And her fake betrothal to the Viscount Trowbridge was designed to allow her to choose wisely, logically.

It was all planned.

As soon as the viscount arrived home, they would announce their betrothal. As Trowbridge's betrothed, Marianna would be off the marriage block. The bachelors on the guest list would know it could do them no good to try to impress her. They would not be displaying false manners or sweetening their words for her benefit. They would be at their ease, behaving naturally—and Marianna would have an entire sennight to observe them. She would see their true colors, and she could decide which one she should marry. Meanwhile, everyone would have time to discover—with a little help from Ophelia—just how large a fortune Marianna was heir to.

Finally, Truesdale and she would end their betrothal amicably and publicly, and then the object of her affections would have a clear way to courting her.

It was simple. Foolproof. Logical.

She sighed and rolled her eyes. The plan may have been logical, but Trowbridge's continued absence proved it was neither foolproof nor simple. She looked at the sky. In a couple of hours, the slanting shadows would begin to disappear into the darkness. Already, the sun was beginning to turn the sky to the east a luminous pink.

Where was he? Had she been so disagreeable that he had abandoned her bottle of gems and hied off to escape her? Was she so ugly that he could not bear to be seen standing as her betrothed? Or had he gone away on some errand, and had his carriage overturned? She imagined him pinned under the wheels, broken and bleeding. Should she send the servants out looking for him?

She rose and turned from the windows. No one even knew what direction he'd gone. If she did send the servants out after him, how were they to find him?

She crossed her arms in front of her and shook her head. One thing was certain: if he were not bleeding when he returned, Marianna would do him an injury herself.

A movement at the window caught her eye. A couple had strolled quite near the library, speaking in hushed voices. Marianna did not wish to eavesdrop, and she began to hurry from the room, but a snippet of their conversation stopped her in her tracks.

"Care to venture a guess who she is?" the lady asked.

"His latest light-skirt, I daresay."

Marianna stepped back to her curtained alcove and, peeking outside, caught a glance of emerald satin and a cream waistcoat embroidered with *fleurs-de-lis*. Lord and Lady Somebody-or-Other. An earl and his wife. Marianna did not remember their names.

"How like True Sin," Lady Somebody said. "To leave a trollop to play the part of hostess. If he is not going to be here, perhaps we should leave."

"And chance displeasing him? My dear, one does not rebuff the invitation of True Sin. When would we ever get another?"

"Why were we invited, do you think? To meet this new trollop?"

They both laughed, then the man said, "I doubt it. Why would he go to all this trouble? He'd just drag her into one of Lady Jersey's routs as he always does."

"Or to the opera!"

"O-ho, quite so! Yes, the opera, True Sin's market fair, where he peruses the wares and pinches to test freshness before taking a sweet home. God knows he never watches the stage."

The lady laughed. "How can he, when his glass is always trained on the bosoms of the two-shilling patrons?"

"I doubt True Sin will be attending the opera as long as he holds on to this one. She looks too practical to allow him anywhere near a stage."

"You are right, dearest. Why, she looks almost respectable. She is certainly not True Sin's usual fare, is she?"

"No. Unless you count the chit's figure. True Sin always has been partial to ample bosoms."

"Indeed. She does have that in ample proportion. How *could* he resist?"

The two laughed gaily and strolled on out of earshot, and Marianna stood quivering with shame and confusion.

They thought Truesdale had her there because of her bosom? They thought she was a . . . a kept woman? And why? Because Truesdale had kept many such women?

If she believed what she had just heard, she would be forced to think Truesdale Sinclair was a libertine, a rake.

No . . . She shook her head. It must not be true. It couldn't be true. Truesdale had proved himself to be a gentleman. And Ophelia Robertson—her dear old friend—would never have suggested she ally herself with him if he were not completely worthy. Would she?

Marianna knew it was wicked, but she suddenly had her doubts.

She retreated to the comfort of logic. There was only one thing to do under the circumstances: speak with Ophelia. She sailed out the door to find the old lady. She would relate the conversation she had overheard and ask what it could mean. Surely Ophelia would have a logical explanation. A reasonable excuse for such odious accusations. Yes, it was all a misunderstanding, and Ophelia would confirm that.

Marianna headed for a particular spot in the garden. She knew that, in spite of Ophelia's assertion that she was going to stroll the grounds, the old lady did not enjoy walking, and the shady bench in the rose garden was her favorite spot to pass the time at Trowbridge Manor. The rose garden was ringed with trees, and a little pond with goldfish was nestled in the center. Ophelia had spent many happy hours there since she came to Trowbridge. Marianna fully expected to find her there now, but the stone bench was empty. She searched the house, but no one had seen her. Ophelia was not in her bedchamber, and she was not with John in the stables. Ophelia simply could not be found. And yet, in the end, it did not signify, for as Marianna roamed the rest of the grounds, looking for her friend, she found the other guests—now that they could speak with her in greater privacy than the parlor had afforded—quite willing to regale her with all sorts of information about True Sin. And the more she heard, the angrier she became, for, as it turned out, the Trowbridge houseguests had good reason to believe Marianna was no better than a common trollop. Truesdale Sinclair, the Viscount Trowbridge, was no gentleman.

The stories she heard about him were shocking. Saints and sinners, she had almost convinced herself she was in love with him! Now she didn't know which was worse—to be masquerading as his betrothed or mistaken for his bird of paradise. She fled to her bedchamber, heartsick. She tried not to cry. Tears would serve no logical purpose, but they came anyway. Dear God, her parents were due to arrive any day, and they would certainly discover the viscount's scandalous past the same way she had, soon after they arrived.

The poor darlings would be so worried about her. And disappointed. In fact, she wouldn't blame them if they were quite angry.

Marianna, for her part, was livid.

True sighed as he arrived home. He was weary.

He had decided not to wait until morning to start back to Trowbridge. He'd known when he set out from London that he would arrive at Trowbridge jolly late indeed, but if all the visiting *beau monde* kept Town hours, most would still be awake when he arrived, he'd thought. He had hoped he and Mary could still announce their engagement.

He'd started from London after dark with instructions to his coachman to make the journey as quick as possible, and although he had been willing to endure the jarring, jolting, and bouncing, his coach, apparently, was not. A wheel had broken halfway to Trowbridge. Rather than wait for it to be fixed, he'd walked the three miles to the next village to borrow a horse, slogging through the mud from one farmhouse to the next until he found a family with a horse they were willing to "lend" him for a price. He had paid thrice as much as the miserable animal was worth. And still it had taken him several more hours to get home.

The roads were wet and slippery, and he was caked with mud and chilled to the bone.

It was well nigh three o' the clock when he climbed the front steps. He awakened the footman on duty, who had fallen asleep, and directed the man to take care of the poor horse, who, by the look, would be even more grateful to be warm and dry than True. He took off his filthy boots and coat before coming inside. No need to muddy the floors and create work for the servants. He stopped in the entry hall to listen. Everything was dark and quiet. Three in the morning was late, even for Town hours.

He started toward his parlor to pour himself a brandy, but a glow appeared down the hall as someone approached, carrying a lamp. He tugged off his gloves and waited to see who would appear.

Mary!

She appeared like a wraith out of the gloom, and he knew something was wrong the moment he saw her. As she approached, he noted the high color in her normally pale face. Her features were tight, and her bearing was even more erect and stiff than usual.

"You are angry," he said.

"Bloody right, I am." The words came out as little more than a hiss, and she blew right on past him and into the library.

True followed, and shut the doors behind him. "Bloody?"

"Yes, bloody!" she sputtered, losing her composure. "Bloody, bloody, bloody! There! I said it. And do not even have a go at pretending you are shocked, for I am certain it is not the first time you have heard a—a *lady* curse."

True held out his hands, palms up, in supplication. "I apologize, my dear, and beg your humble forgiveness for returning too late to greet our guests. I tried—"

"Do not 'my dear' me, Trowbridge. Or, should I say, 'True Sin?' "

"True Sin." He lowered his hands. "You have never called me that before."

"I never had reason to before now. But now I know the truth."

"The truth? What are you talking about?"

She did not answer him but spun on her heel and began to pace in front of him. "Oh, what a fool I have been! I did not listen to the rumors. I did not believe a man could have so many paramours. It was not reasonable. It was not logical. But I should have suspected it was true the moment I looked at you, the moment I saw how—how bloody handsome you are! I should have believed the rumors were true the moment we met!"

"Which rumors?"

"Which rumors? Take your choice? Let me see . . . you might consider the one about you and a certain woman you took to the opera half naked. Or the sisters you escorted to Lady Jersey's ball last spring. Surely you remember the ones? They're the pair the gentlemen refer to as the Moon Goddesses. Or how about the time you became foxed and shot the hat from the top of a gentleman's head?"

"It was a duel."

"In Carleton House?"

True nodded, confused. "Do you mean to tell me you did not know of these things before you came to Trowbridge?"

She rounded on him. "Of course I did not know about them! Why on earth would I have come to you if I had? Why would a young lady in my situation connect herself to a man who had so thoroughly disgraced himself? Your dishonor is legendary. No, I knew nothing about it until our guests arrived, but it was not long before they hastened to my side to ply me with stories about the infamous True Sin."

He raked his fingers through his hair. "I assumed you knew all the *on-dits* before you came to me."

She shook her head violently. "I was working as a schoolteacher, not attending the . . . the opera!" She threw him a venomous look.

"But did not Ophelia Robertson tell you—"

"Apparently, my duenna neglected to mention a few

things, and I want to know why." She plunked one hand on her hip, clearly waiting for True to supply the answer.

"I do not know why. Why did you not ask her?"

She threw her hand into the air and began to pace the floor in front of him. The lamp she carried marshaled the shadows, and they marched with her. "I have been wanting to speak with her since this afternoon. But she slipped away from me and disappeared for above two hours, and then the next thing I knew she was shut up in her room with the complaint of a severe megrim."

"She escaped you."

"So it seems."

"Cannot say I blame her. I wish I could escape your ire, too."

She shot him another black look. "What do you expect? You left me entirely alone with a house full of guests, a ruby the size of the Tower of London on my hand, and no dearly betrothed in sight. I did not know where you were or when you were returning or even *if* you were planning to return. I sat through two meals knowing that most of my guests believe I am your mistress, and, as though that were not enough, I had to protect the guests from the ABC's, who thought it flaming keen to have so many new places to deposit salamanders! I think I am entitled to a little anger." Her feet stilled with her back to him, and she gave a sniffle.

"I am sorry," he said, and he actually meant it, "but all will be set to rights when we announce our betrothal on the morrow."

"Set to rights?" She whirled back toward him, even more at dagger drawn. "Surely you jest! Nothing can be put right. You, my lord, are not a suitable suitor," she said, "even if you are merely a temporary one. My parents will be most displeased." She rolled her eyes and shook her head. "No, that is calling it too brown. They will be furious, and for good reason, not that you care, I am certain. You obviously care not one whit about anyone but yourself."

He wasn't prepared for her brittle, caustic manner or for

the sheer distaste in her expression and voice. He had just spent seven hours racing home to please her, and she hadn't even seemed to notice that his clothing was wet and caked with mud. He was dangerously weary.

"If you cared about anything but my bottle of gems, you would not have entered into our bargain to begin with. You are not *Good Ton*. You knew perfectly well that no one of good breeding—and certainly not my parents—would find you an acceptable husband."

Something inside True twisted and snapped.

He leaned insolently against the library door frame. "Ah, Mary . . . we are well matched, then, for no one of good breeding would attempt to buy a title or lie about being betrothed."

His barb found its mark. She plunked the lamp onto his desk, sloshing the oil about the chamber and sending amber shadows dancing over the book-lined walls. "How dare you stand there and compare your own behavior to mine or my parents'? You know perfectly well there is nothing like your behavior in ours." She put her fists to her temples. *"We* have not driven breakneck through Hyde Park at four in the afternoon. *W*e have not attended a ball *sans* cravat or coat. *W*e have not placed public wagers on which royal prince a countess's newborn babe will resemble." She thumped the wall with her hand. *"And we have not washed our hands in the lemonade at Almack's!"*

True affected a bored stance. "The refreshments at Almack's are frightful. Their cakes are stale, and their lemonade is too watered. Someone needed to point that out to them."

"Ohh . . . !" She seethed. "So you will not even make an attempt to deny these claims?"

"Deny them?" He laughed. "Not only do I not deny them, I claim them as my own and celebrate them. In fact, you seem to have missed a few." He allowed his mouth to curl into a wicked smile and then sauntered over to pour himself a brandy. "I played the prince at piquet-loo."

She narrowed her eyes and crossed her arms. "And?"

"The cards fell perfectly, and I won."

She rolled her eyes. "That is nothing. I have heard he is not the cleverest—"

"You did not ask what were the stakes."

"I do not care."

"Liar. I won his dessert. Carried her right away from his supper table."

"So? What does the prince care? He can have his cooks make any number of—Did you say 'her'?"

True nodded. "Quite so. Took the sweet away during the third course." He grinned. "Carried her out over my shoulder."

"Saints and sinners," she murmured.

"And then there was the time I went to a masquerade dressed as a shepherd—"

She shrugged.

"—ess," he finished.

"Enough!" she cried, and covered her ears. "Your behavior puts me to the blush. It is an embarrassment. It sets my reputation in jeopardy."

True nodded, bending his mouth into a snide shape. "What reputation?"

She ignored him. "I order you to amend your ways for the duration of the house party," she said. "I demand that you attempt to convince everyone you have changed your character. If you do, perhaps everyone can still be convinced that I have managed to reform you."

"They might just believe it—"

"Good."

"—with a stiff-rumped, starched-up, stick-in-the-mud spinster like you to pull it off."

"Starched-up? Stiff-rumped! Why, you . . . you capricious . . . careless . . . skirt-minded scoundrel! You are deviant. And despicable. Just like the rest of the Sins!"

True drew back sharply, as though he'd been slapped. There was nothing she could have said that would have cut him any deeper than that. Feeling angry—and not a little hurt—True laughed mirthlessly. "A scoundrel? You flatter me. I am going to bed." He opened the doors and started for the staircase. "Care to join me, Mary?" he tossed over his shoulder.

"My name is Marianna, and I would rather kiss a sheep."

"And *you* call *me* deviant!"

A shoe flew through the air, missing his head by an inch.

True let his laughter echo down the stairway. It was genuine, he realized with surprise. Thunder and blazes, he felt alive, exhilarated. He hadn't had a good argument like that one in months, and never one with a woman. She'd given as much as she'd gotten, by Jove!

By the time he reached his chamber, washed, and got ready for bed, though, he was a little more circumspect. He should have avoided an argument at all costs. He should have done whatever he had to do to smooth the hellcat's fur. He certainly shouldn't have agreed with her.

But the hell of it was, he did agree with her. Every word she'd said about him was true.

True Sin was no better than the rest of the Sins. No matter how hard he tried to rid himself of their influence, he still felt their wildness, their impulsiveness. In spite of his renowned disregard for the Society they had prized, he was, deep down, no different from any of the rest of the Sins. Did he not take an almost sadistic pleasure in shocking the *ton?*

Aye, his behavior went beyond merely distancing himself from Society. He was not seeking separation, but revenge.

Revenge, an art he had learned at his father's knee along with the other blac' arts that dovetailed so perfectly with the wildness coursing in his blood.

He turned over and punched his pillow.

No matter how far he distanced himself from the rest of the Sins, he would still share their blood. Their wickedness was his own. He was born with it, and he would die with it. The best he could do is attempt to tame it. To hide it. To be certain he did not perpetuate it.

Which was why the Viscount Trowbridge would never father any children.

True Sin would be the last Sin. It was something he had promised himself long ago.

He lay in his bed, unable to sleep in spite of his weariness. Things with Mary were all in disarray, and he didn't know how to repair them. Ophelia had deliberately kept her ignorant of his behavior amongst the *ton*. Why? Why was she so interested in helping him? It was no use asking her. The stubborn old harridan had made it clear she would tell him nothing.

God, he'd made a muck of things with Mary! She was angry with him, and he had to admit that, even had she not discovered his infamous reputation, she had reason to be angry.

When he'd left for London, he hadn't told anyone where he was going. He'd thought about it, but he wasn't used to reporting his movements to anyone, and the idea had chafed him. Besides, he would have had to lie about his purpose anyway. He could hardly have told her he was going to procure a special license to marry.

Not that it mattered now, anyway. The paper gleamed in the moonlight on his dressing table. He was grimly aware that losing his temper with Mary may have rendered the special license useless. Unless he could affect a major change in Mary's opinion of him, there was no way he was going to get her to agree to marry him.

And yet it would take a miracle for Mary to wed him now. His character was as carved in stone as his past deeds. He could change neither of them. How was he going to turn her up sweet once more?

He lay in bed thinking, the moon sinking low in the west before an idea came to him. If he could not change his own character, perhaps he could change Mary's instead. Perhaps if she were involved in some small scandal, she might be more forgiving of his own disgraces. . . .

Eight

Marianna avoided Truesdale the next day, fleeing from their argument into the company of one of their guests, Orion Chase, the Earl of Lindenshire, a handsome young man.

All of the Trowbridge bachelors were impeccably dressed, but Lindenshire was *perfectly* attired. His attention to detail bespoke a heightened sensibility where others' opinions were concerned. He knew the importance of appearances—though *his* good manners, she was sure, were not made up, but natural.

Attentive and soft-spoken, Lindenshire squired her about the estate all day quite amiably. They were both surprised and delighted to discover they shared a scholarly interest in insects. He seemed quite interested to hear of the insects she had encountered in the West Indies, and they strolled about the grounds most of the afternoon, collecting interesting specimens to take with them into the library to look at under the spying glass, which was kept there for peering at the atlas. Lord Lindenshire seemed a good man, a kind man, and if Marianna's thoughts had not been preoccupied with her argument with Truesdale and upon how her parents would react when they found out she was betrothed to a rake, she would have been quite content to pass the time in his pleasant company.

He did not seem to think she was starched-up or stiff-rumped.

"Do you think I am odd for my interest in such things?"

she said suddenly as they sifted through a trellis of wisteria, searching for beetles.

"Yes," he said, smiling, "I do. And I am most grateful. I expected the viscount's house party to be deadly dull." He brushed his wispy, straight brown hair from his startlingly clear and intelligent brown eyes and smiled at Marianna. "I was wrong. I have found lovely company."

He gazed at her so earnestly, Marianna looked down at her hands. "Why did you agree to attend?" she asked uneasily.

"Curiosity, I suppose." He shrugged. "And you?"

Marianna flushed guiltily. She was certain the studious earl had formed a quick and fragile *tendre* for her, but she would be announcing her engagement to Trowbridge that evening at supper. She hoped. It seemed wrong not to confess that to Lindenshire right then. And yet it seemed wrong to confess any such thing, for Marianna was not engaged at all! In spite of her misadventures, Marianna was possessed of an honest nature, and she especially hated to lie to someone like Lindenshire. There was a kindness about him, a gentle nature that made her trust him.

She gave a guilty flinch, knowing that he could not trust her in return.

"What is wrong?" he asked suddenly, genuine concern in his eyes. "Is there some way I can help you? Something involving Trowbridge, perhaps?"

"Your intuitiveness is admirable," she said evasively.

He shook his head. "You flatter me."

You flatter me. The same words she'd heard Trowbridge say not twelve hours before. How different they sounded when uttered with kindness and sincerity!

Suddenly, the thought occurred to Marianna that Lord Lindenshire might make a good husband. Love grew from seeds of friendship and trust, did it not?

How different he was from True Sin! He cared about the *ton,* he would never be seen without a cravat. Walking beside him brought her a sense of comfort rather than unease. When she was close to True Sin, she was aware of every movement of his body. With Lord Lindenshire, she was completely relaxed. She had known him for less than a day, and already she felt as though she had known him a lifetime, while even a fortnight of True Sin's constant acquaintance could not uncover his secrets.

She was at sixes and sevens. She knew she had to go through with her engagement. It was the only way to convince the *ton* she wasn't True Sin's mistress.

Saints and sinners! Did Lord Lindenshire think she was a bird of paradise, too?

She felt sick at the thought. Without thinking, she turned to him and opened her mouth to offer a denial, then thought better of it and bit her lips. What would he think of her if she confided her engagement to Trowbridge? A lady just did not do such a thing. Did she?

She wished she could ask Ophelia's advice, but the old lady was still missing, and Marianna wasn't entirely certain she could trust Ophelia anyway, not after she'd misled Marianna so disastrously about True Sin's suitability for her plot. Talking to John would not help. He had been a family servant until Ophelia married him. The man was sweet, but he knew little of the *ton* and cared even less.

Wasn't there *anyone* she could confide in?

Even if her parents, who were to arrive any day now, came immediately, she couldn't speak to them of her troubles. And Truesdale . . . he *was* her troubles. Not that she could speak to him if she wanted to, since he seemed to be avoiding her today.

She had no one. She was completely alone.

It was not the first time Marianna had been left to her own company, her own advisement. She'd been by herself a year ago, too. Only things had been much simpler then. Her goal was clear: find a titled husband to love. But that was before she'd discovered she was plain as a post. Before she'd lied to her parents. Before she met True Sin. Everything was complicated now, and Marianna had never felt more alone.

Bells in Heaven, if she did not have anyone to confide

in for the next month, she knew she would go mad. She looked over at Lord Lindenshire, took a deep breath, exhaled forcibly, and filled her lungs again. "There is something you can do for me," she said.

"Name it."

"I . . . need a friend."

As Marianna walked into Trowbridge Manor's parlor, where everyone—except for the viscount and Ophelia, drat them!—were gathering before supper late that evening, she felt the earl's eyes upon her, felt bolstered by his very presence. It had been so easy to unburden herself to him. As soon as she had requested his friendship, the young man had vowed to keep her secrets and offered her comfort and understanding. She needed both tonight.

Her stomach was in knots.

True Sin hadn't shown his face all day, though all of Trowbridge knew he was in attendance. The servants said he was in his bedchamber. She had sent two requests asking to see him in the library, with no result or reply. He and Marianna had been so angry with each other last night, said such ugly things—not that Marianna had not meant every one of them!—that she was afraid of how he might behave when he appeared at last. They were supposed to have announced their betrothal at last night's supper. Of course, that had not happened, and Marianna could only assume the viscount would announce their betrothal this evening instead—unless he were planning to stay in his room until his guests just drifted away for lack of a host.

She thought about stealing up to his bedchamber and trying to discuss things with him, but she rejected the idea. It had been one thing to walk him to his chamber—or hers, by mistake or design, she still wasn't sure which—in the dead of night with no one about. But the manor was full of guests and their servants now. She couldn't risk it.

No. He needed her gems, and for that he needed to fulfill their bargain. That was that. He would show soon. Probably tonight, and probably still in a rage. It would not be a towering rage as it was when she saw him last, but it would be a smoldering one, and Marianna dreaded it just the same. She steeled herself to sit at table with the man, a benign smile upon her face no matter what happened.

It weighed heavily upon her mind that the scene would be the backdrop for her formal introduction to the *ton*. She was not optimistic.

Until her betrothed strolled into the parlor a few minutes before supper was announced.

Instantly, everyone's attention—including Marianna's—fixed upon him. True Sin was gone. In his place stood Truesdale Sinclair, the Viscount Trowbridge. Impeccably dressed from his starched and expertly folded cravat to his formal white stockings and polished shoe buckles, Trowbridge appeared to be the perfect gentleman, complete to a shade. Marianna's eyes grew dry from not blinking as she stared at him.

She soon found it was not just his clothing that had undergone a change, but his manner as well. As he greeted each of his guests, he executed a perfectly crisp formal bow. He uttered correct and courteous welcomes in a voice that was even and soft-spoken, cultured and pleasant.

Marianna stood motionless in the corner as Trowbridge moved clockwise about the room until he finally came to her. All eyes in the room were fixed upon them. She wanted to bolt.

He bent low over her hand. "Your servant, my lady," he intoned.

The footman-turned-newly-appointed-butler announced supper, and Trowbridge offered her his arm. As she allowed him to lead her into dinner, Marianna caught several speculative looks traded among the guests. They couldn't be any more eager to know what would happen next than Marianna herself!

For the first half of the long meal, she waited for True Sin to surface, her heart threatening to beat its way out of her chest. But Trowbridge was the perfect host, never saying or doing anything beyond what was strictly proper. An hour into the meal, Marianna began to relax. For the first time, she actually tasted the excellent dishes set before her.

Her tirade had worked. Trowbridge was bowing to her demand that he behave like a gentleman. This perfect display of manners and conversation told her he would give her no more trouble. Everyone would believe she had reformed him. She would be the talk of the *ton*. The tamer of the sea. The soul of propriety. A proper young lady no true gentleman would hesitate to court.

Tasting nothing but the sweetness of triumph, she popped a bite of fish into her mouth and ventured a glance at Lord Lindenshire. Now, *he* was a true gentleman.

She'd been aware that he was watching her from the time they sat down. Now she threw him a conspiratorial smile, and he returned it reassuringly, adding a surreptitious wink.

Marianna looked up at Trowbridge.

He was staring at Lindenshire, and he was not smiling.

The look he leveled upon the young earl was not one of murderous rage, but it was not exactly amiable—or apathetic. Marianna lost her benign smile. The man was jealous!

She brought her napkin to her mouth to conceal her surprise. Trowbridge *had* been making improper suggestions to her since the moment she had arrived . . . but she wasn't fool enough to think he actually wanted to make good on them. Like a lion who has eaten his fill yet still defends his kill, True Sin did not want her—but he did not want another man to have her, either.

He caught Marianna staring at him and smiled tightly, but she could see that his jaw was still tightly clenched.

Good. She looked down at her plate and took a bite of fish, exultant. The fact that he was jealous of Lindenshire only added to her triumphant pleasure. She beat down a giggle, contenting herself with the barest of smug smiles. She was even feeling a little sorry for poor, downtrodden Truesdale.

But then poor, downtrodden Truesdale turned the conversation toward the brook.

"I was saying to Marianna only a few days ago," he told a dowager countess to his left, "the brook is so vastly refreshing this time of year."

The dowager put down her fork. "Refreshing, Trowbridge? How is that?"

"How? Its waters flow gentle and cool and are so invigorating on a hot summer's day—or even at night." He looked over at Marianna. "Is that not correct, my dear?"

The countess sniffed at her wine goblet. "Have you served us water, Trowbridge?"

"No." Truesdale laughed. "I refer to paddling in the water, not drinking it."

The countess narrowed her corpulent eyes at him. "Do you mean to tell me that you have voluntarily immersed yourself in this . . . this . . ."

"Brook," Truesdale supplied, gazing at Marianna intently.

"—this *brook?*" the dowager echoed as though hearing the word for the first time. She slid a glance at Marianna.

"Oh, yes," the viscount said, his voice well nigh a caress as he steadfastly held Marianna's gaze. He bent toward the countess. "It is quite *exhilarating,* especially when one sheds one's"—someone dropped a knife—"cares," True finished in a whisper anyone could hear, and winked at Marianna.

"My lord!" the countess cried.

"My lord," Marianna said calmly, "you have a spot on your cravat. Here, let me help you with that." Deftly, she scooped her napkin from her lap and brought it to his spotless neckcloth, dragging it in the raspberry sauce on her plate as she did so. She dabbed at the nonexistent spot, which of course only got worse, until Truesdale was forced to excuse himself to change.

Marianna spent the next ten minutes enduring the obvious speculation on the faces of her guests, who were wondering, as he had to have known they would, if she'd been paddling *sans* clothing alone in the brook or if she'd been enjoying True Sin's company there. Marianna avoided so much as a glance in Lord Lindenshire's direction. She didn't think she could bear what *his* expression might hold.

When their host returned, he sat down and said, "Pardon my lengthy absence. What were we discussing? Ah, yes . . . the brook." Their supper guests nearly fell over themselves to change the subject. He let the matter drop, but then he had the audacity to grin at her, his smug expression telling her that he was exacting revenge for the insults she had dealt him last night.

He was enjoying himself, the bounder!

And True Sin wasn't quite finished toying with her yet.

Nine

True heard them before they were even announced. Supper was nearly over when their too-loud voices boomed with an imperiously slow cadence in echoes down the hall. To hear them, one might think they were an elderly and hard-of-hearing duke and his duchess, but True was not fooled. Their unhurried voices did not match the rapidity of their footfalls. As the supper guests traded expectant looks, obviously wondering who the newcomers were, True fixed his eyes on Mary, for she, obviously, recognized the voices well.

She'd gone still as a standing stone. Her face was ashen. It was not the sort of reaction one would expect to see from a loving daughter upon hearing her parents' voices after more than a year's separation. There was nothing of joy in her expression. On the contrary, her mouth had straightened into a grim line, and she held herself tightly upright. To one unaccustomed to Mary, it might have appeared she was unconcerned, but True could feel panic rolling from her in waves.

He put down his napkin. "Ah, there are your parents, darling. Shall we go tell them our good news?" His words were tantamount to an announcement, and every face at the table registered surprise—including Mary's, though she recovered her wits quicker than most.

"As you wish," she murmured. She stood and hastened to precede him out of the room.

In her wake, True addressed the assemblage. "Lovers'

quarrels are soon mended. Best not to mention the brook to her." He smiled broadly, and a round of false laughter heralded his departure. He knew their impending betrothal would be discussed minutely while he and Marianna were absent from the table.

He took his time following Mary to the entry hall. He found her standing erect and still, waiting for the elder Granthams to notice her as they divested themselves of their outerwear twenty paces away. She did not call to them, wave, or approach. Instead, she waited for them to notice her. Behind her, True raised an eyebrow. England was a nation of people known for their restraint, but this was taking things a bit too far. She had not seen her parents in over a year!

He had intended to stand at Mary's side as she greeted them, but now True stepped into a shallow alcove in the darkened hallway, the better to observe the trio.

The first thing he noted was the elder Grantham's clothing. It would have been difficult to miss. Though the night was fine, the weather warm and dry, both of the elder Granthams wore heavy coats trimmed in ermine. And, though their garments were made of the finest cloth and tailored to perfection, something in the way they carried themselves suggested they had once been used to wearing something far different. They fussed over the coats, admonishing True's poor footman to be wary with them—and then they threatened the man with dismissal if the items were damaged in his care. True's eyes narrowed. Mary had never spoken to a servant in such a manner.

Finally, Mr. Grantham looked up.

"Daughter," he said.

"Papa, Mama . . . welcome to England."

"Welcome back, more like," said Mrs. Grantham. She shoved her fur-lined scarf into the arms of the footman without a word and looked her daughter up and down. "You've grown thinner."

"It is the fashion."

"Is it? Well . . . good, then. I suppose that is the way *he* prefers you?"

"Where is he?" her father asked.

True stepped from the shadow of the hall. "Excuse me. I was detained," he lied. He executed a crisp bow. "Truesdale Sinclair, at your service."

"Ah. The butler," Mrs. Grantham said. She addressed True, "Does your man here know how to care for fur?" She motioned at the footman.

"Mama—"

"I hope for your sake that he does, for I daresay those coats cost more than a year of your salary," she said menacingly.

"Mama, this," Mary said, indicating True, "is my—"

"Husband," True supplied on impulse, unable to resist knocking the elder Granthams off balance. They deserved much more, the insufferable twits.

The three said all together, "Husband?"

True smiled fondly down at Mary, who gaped at him. "We eloped. Went to Gretna Green. I could not wait to be her husband." He nearly laughed. For the first time since they'd met, Mary was quite literally speechless. She stared at True as though he'd just turned into a flying octopus or some such, her lips slightly parted and her eyes big. He winked at her, and she blinked. Her lips worked, but she said nothing, silent as a fish—for now.

He knew she would deny his wild assertion as soon as she found her tongue. Would she chalk it up to some made-up bent True had for practical jokery? Or say True had taken a bump to the head and his memory—or sanity—was playing tricks on him? True hooted with laughter. "Did I surprise you, darling? I hope you did not mind my hastening to inform them. As you can see," he said, gesturing at her parents, "they do not object to the match." The statement was absurd enough to make the cat laugh, for the expression on her parents' faces said nothing of the kind. Her father's face was red with fury, while his wife's had gone white as an egg. They both still thought he was the butler.

Mr. Grantham sputtered. "But you—you're nothing but a . . . a—"

"A viscount," True said.

"A viscount! Rubbish. Since when do the nobs hire viscounts as servants? We've been in the West Indies, but things haven't changed *that* much since we left England, that's for certain. Where is your master, you fraud? I'll see you're dismissed, that's what!"

His wife's mind was clearly a bit faster than his own, for Mrs. Grantham suddenly said, "Oh!" and laughed nervously. "Oh, of course!" She turned to her husband. "This is Marianna's *husband,* the *viscount,* Mr. Grantham, not the butler."

Beside True, Marianna made a strangled sound.

"You gave us your Christian name, my lord, leaving off your title, and naturally we thought—Oh, do forgive us." Mrs. Grantham turned back to True and smiled so sweetly that even bees would have been repelled.

Her husband looked startled for a moment, but then a satisfied expression slid over his features. "A viscount, say you?"

The pair of them looked like cats left in the creamery. They quickly offered a graceless bow and curtsy before plying him with a cascade of simultaneous questions that took only seconds to disgorge. Was the estate his, and was it entailed? Had the title been long held by his family? Was Truesdale's father dead? Any elder brothers? How much land was there? Did True own other estates? What other important personages resided in the neighborhood? Did the viscount travel to London soon? Was he able to acquire vouchers for Almack's?

Encroaching mushrooms! True nearly turned from them in disgust.

People like these were the reason the *ton* detested the *parvenu*—and the reason he'd had to work so hard to gain the trust and respect of his sailors and workmen. *Parvenus* such as the Granthams believed their riches made them better than anyone who had less. They treated servants with disdain and paraded their finery. They were thoughtless and cruel and greedy.

These two were delighted to discover they'd just added a title to their list of acquisitions. So intent was their interrogation of True, that they completely forgot about their daughter—until Mrs. Grantham had apparently recovered her wits sufficiently to take notice of Mary once more. And then she did not embrace her daughter, kiss her, or wish her happy. No, instead of behaving like any loving mother would, Mrs. Grantham only offered criticism.

"A Gretna wedding is not entirely respectable. Is it?" she said, sliding a nervous glance in True's direction.

"No," Mary blurted, finally finding her voice. "No . . . no . . . *no!*"

True grinned, anticipating the rest of her denial.

"No?" her father echoed.

"Uh . . ." Marianna faltered, and True realized she hadn't a clue what to say next.

He grinned.

She scowled.

Her parents were looking at her expectantly. He watched as words formed on her lips even before she knew what she was going to say. "Uh . . . Mama is correct. A . . . a Gretna wedding is . . . is not proper. No, not proper at all!"

True almost laughed as her vehement agreement clearly puzzled her parents, who stared at her in bemusement. Their scrutiny only made her appear more nervous, and she stammered out, "Yes . . . in fact . . . in fact, the . . . the ceremony must be—"

"Kept secret!" her mother finished, clapping her hands together. "Quite so, daughter, you are right. That's just the thing. We will tell no one. No one at all."

"No one?" her husband asked. "Ever? Whatever do you mean?"

"Yes, darling," True drawled, and smiled at Marianna. "Whatever do you mean?"

Her chest rose and fell rapidly. She looked from him to her parents and back. "I . . . I mean that . . . that . . ."

"She means," cried her mother, "that a Gretna wedding is not at all the thing. She means to keep the marriage secret so we can hold a grand Society wedding. A capital idea." She clapped her hands together again, clearly savoring thoughts of presiding over her daughter's wedding. "Just perfect. Shall you be married at Westminster?"

"Yes. No!" True and Mary said together.

True laughed again. Mary's mouth was hanging open again, and she was shaking her head. This was clearly not the way she'd wanted the conversation to go, but the outcome suited True just fine. "You must forgive my wife," he said. "She is tired."

"Oh, but we've so much to discuss," her mother said. "We must begin our wedding preparations immediately. I have nothing suitable to wear, and Mr. Grantham and I shall have to buy a fashionable house in Town. . . ."

True turned away. He would waste no more time on these vain and selfish people. "Barrett," he told the footman, "pray see to bringing in Mr. and Mrs. Grantham's belongings. I shall escort them to their chambers myself." The footman departed, and True turned to the Granthams. "You are tired and in need of rest. Supper is over," he lied. "I shall have a tray sent up."

"Indeed!" Mrs. Grantham said. "I am eager to see our lodgings. Are they quite fine?"

True turned on his heel without responding to her. He did not think he could say anything to her without slicing her to shreds.

Poor Mary! Growing up with parents such as these! Now he understood why she was the way she was. Why she was so proper, so concerned with what others thought. He could almost forgive her desire to become a member of the *ton*.

Almost.

Even after having lived in London as a semi-servant, she still thought the only people worth living among were the *beau monde*. She viewed them as the ideal of societal perfection, and she strove to match it.

She'd never have him now that she knew he was not a

pattern card of propriety. She would take someone like Lindenshire. He'd seen them from his window. The cub had been hanging upon her every word. Looking in his crystal ball, True could see the two of them standing in Westminster even now. Hell and blast, they were practically on the steps.

He had to stop them.

It was easy for Perfection to focus on the smallest flaw. But if Perfection herself were flawed . . . True knew Marianna would be more forgiving of his scandals if she were forced to live down a few of her own. He had to give Marianna's shiny surface of perfection a few glaring scuffs. The Gretna lie he'd just told was a bit too easy for her to buff out. He knew Marianna would devise a clever way to explain it away within minutes, probably before they made the top of the stairs. The damage he'd done in the dining room was more lasting, he thought with satisfaction—though even that was not permanent.

He'd led everyone at supper to think he and Marianna might have been paddling naked in the brook—but as soon as they had a chance to observe her for a week, they would know she would never do such a thing. Still, it would be enough for her to taste what it was to live with scandal. She would certainly be more forgiving of his own indiscretions after this.

He led the way up the stairs, wondering how Marianna was going to extricate herself from the Gretna bumblebroth. He could hear her light footfalls behind him as she followed her parents docilely up the stairs.

Docile. That was one quality True hadn't thought Mary had in her. He rolled the word around in his mind and found it vaguely . . . disappointing.

She'd panicked. Marianna berated herself for twelve kinds of fool. She'd said the wrong things. No, she corrected herself, she'd said nothing at all. It was her mother who'd said the wrong things—her mother and True Sin. Marianna had done nothing but stand witlessly by, stammering. She cursed silently as the four of them made their way to her parents' bedchamber. She was so angry with the viscount, she could not speak. First the brook accusation and now this! And the blackguard was enjoying every second of it.

She slanted a glance up at his handsome face. The dim sconce-light accentuated its fine planes and angles. Dressed as he was, he cut a fine figure indeed. Her mother must be prodigiously happy. Her father, too. When they found out she was not yet married to the Viscount Trowbridge after all, they would be so disappointed.

Marianna dreaded telling them.

She would accompany them into their chamber and explain everything. Well . . . she'd lie, actually. She'd say that Truesdale was a great practical humster, that humor was his way of bringing them into his inner circle and making them feel at home. The poor dears would still be bitterly disappointed, but once she told them that she really was engaged to Truesdale—once she lied about being engaged to him, she amended with regret—they would forgive her and be happy. Her mother would throw herself into planning their wedding, her father would throw himself into enjoying the dining room and the card tables, and she would—She would return to the task of choosing which of the bachelors present at Trowbridge would be her husband. After she had delivered a proper, blistering set-down to Trowbridge. Again. She grimaced, remembering the reason she had been so angry with Trowbridge the day before.

If she did not tell them herself, her parents would learn tomorrow of his scandalous past, the same way she had, via the wagging tongues of the Trowbridge houseguests. Her only hope lay in convincing them she had reformed the viscount—and *that* was dependent upon the blackguard keeping up his pretense of being an unaffected, genuine gentleman *comme il faut*.

She almost moaned. He was still angry for the insults she'd delivered last night. His lies and insinuations were clearly meant as retribution. Heaven only knew what the scoundrel would do next.

"Here we are," the scoundrel said. "Your chamber is across from mine."

"You mean 'ours,' don't you, Trowbridge?" her mother asked. "Or does my daughter have her own adjoining chamber?" She eyed the improbable bends in the hallway. Clearly, Truesdale's large, peninsular room had no adjoining chamber.

"Mama," Marianna said, "I have something to discuss with you. Do let us go into your chamber and—"

"No, no! I will not hear of it," Mrs. Grantham said. "It is late, as your husband pointed out, and—"

"But that is what I would like to discuss with you. He is not—"

"I am not accustomed to waiting," Truesdale broke in, and opened his door. "Coming, darling?" His flawed eyebrow rose and his dimples appeared, proclaiming his utter lack of contrition.

At that moment, a servant came down the hall. Unable to speak openly, Marianna stood by helplessly as her mother opened their chamber door and entered, exclaiming over the fine accommodations.

And then something happened that Marianna never could have foreseen. Her father, in an uncharacteristic show of emotion, *touched* her. Touched her lightly on the cheek. "You have done well, daughter. Marianna." He shuffled uncomfortably and lowered his hand.

Marianna couldn't remember the last time her father had touched her, and he never—ever!—called her by her name. It was always "daughter" this or "daughter" that. And on top of that he had praised her. Every part of her wanted to move forward, to step into his embrace, to feel his arms curl about her shoulders. But she knew that was impossible. It was too much to ask. She stood there in utter disbelief, tears of love and longing pricking her eyes. And another miracle occurred. Her father smiled.

"Your mother and I couldn't be happier, Marianna." His

eyes flicked to the viscount's, and he straightened. His face regained some of its grim solemnity. "Go with your husband now," he ordered.

Vaguely, Marianna felt something tugging on her arm, and, wordlessly, she half stumbled and half walked along with it, realizing seconds later that she had just walked into Truesdale's bedchamber!

He shut the door, a boyish expression of delight molding his features. "That worked out better than I could ever have imagined!" he said with a chuckle.

She was stunned. "How could you let things come to this?" She gestured vaguely around her. "Just look at where your lie has landed us now!"

"Mmmm . . ." he practically purred, looking about him. "Yes. Just look at this. The two of us." He looked at her through his thick fringe of lashes, his expression suddenly turned serious. "Alone." He stepped toward her. "In my bedchamber." He slipped his arms through hers and pulled her against him. His eyes focused upon her lips. "Whatever shall we do?" he whispered, and then his mouth made warm, firm contact with hers.

Marianna should have pushed him away. At the very least, she should have frozen in place, like a block of ice, cold and rigid. But the languid kiss melted her resolve, drained away her senses, and she did nothing but kiss him back.

He wound his fingers into her hair. She felt a tug and then the entire mass came down. He kneaded her back and shoulders with his hands as his lips kneaded hers. This kiss was nothing like the last. This one had her tingling from the soles of her feet to the top of her head, had chills racing up and down her spine. She consumed him, as though slaking a thirst long ignored. She was past parched; she was dying of thirst. Heaven help her, she'd wanted to kiss him this way since the first time she'd laid eyes on him. She'd wondered what it would be like. And now she knew. It was heavenly!

She closed her eyes, completely lost in the heady sensations. Their mouths slanted and pressed, opened and delved. Suddenly, her knees went weak, and he wrapped his arm around her and lowered her—saints and sinners!—onto his bed? Saints and sinners, she didn't care! He kissed her as his hands explored her face, her neck, her shoulders. He dragged his mouth away from her lips long enough to kiss her neck, just below her ear. Marianna gave a little cry—though whether it was a cry of pleasure or a protest for the absence of his mouth from hers, she couldn't have said. It was no matter. He returned quickly and began another passionate exploration of her mouth. She moaned her pleasure.

"Marianna!" her mother called.

Marianna jerked her head to the side.

The doorknob turned. "Marianna?"

Pushing away from Truesdale as though burned, Marianna scrabbled to her feet. Her hands flew to her unbound hair, to her swollen lips, to her flushed face. If her mother saw her like this, she would know they'd been kissing! Her parents would think she was no better than a common strumpet! She groped wildly for her hair comb, realizing a split-second later she had no time to twist her hair back into shape. She *could* just pretend the comb had fallen out! Yes, that was it! Jumping up and pulling her fluttering hands down from her crown, she crossed them over her bosom—only to find that somehow the row of tiny buttons down the front of her gown was three-quarters undone.

"Truesdale!" she screeched. The door swung open. *Cover yourself!* her panicked mind yelped. *Cover, cover, cover!* And for the second time that day, Marianna panicked. Abandoning all logic, all reasoned thought, she did the first thing that came into her mind. She grabbed the counterpane and tried to pull it off the bed, but it was tucked in at the foot and would not come free. An alarming glimpse of ostrich feathers coming through the doorway propelled her onto the bed, where she pulled the counterpane to her chin. She realized how foolish that was immediately, of course, but there was no time for anything else.

Violet Grantham strode into the room. "Oh, Marianna, I forgot to ask you if—oh!" She caught sight of Marianna.

"We were in a bit of a rush to get into bed," Truesdale drawled. "The late hour, you know."

"Well then . . . good night," she said with a satisfied smile. "Newlyweds must get their . . . uh, rest."

Truesdale grinned. "Indeed. Good night, madam." Violet Grantham made a hasty exit, and Truesdale closed the door behind her.

Marianna stared at the door in shock. "What have I done?" she whispered.

"You have kissed me, and you have enjoyed it."

She locked gazes with him and said nothing. There was no point in denying it. She *had* enjoyed their kiss. Saints and sinners, she'd done more than enjoy his mouth on hers, she'd worshipped it, reveled in it—and she wanted it again. Now. And the knave knew it.

"I have to get out of here." She threw back the covers and realized her bodice was still immodestly open. Gripped with a sudden anger, she turned her back to him and re-buttoned her gown, unsure who she was more angry with, herself or True Sin.

"You might as well stay."

"Rubbish. What are you talking about?"

He gave her a considering look, a frown lurking about his mouth. "You cannot deny the attraction between us. Marriages have been founded on much less."

"Marriage! What are you saying?"

"I am saying that—for once—I intend to do the honorable thing. The blame for this disaster can be placed squarely upon my shoulders. I was reckless. I should never have lied about our going to Gretna. I should never have pulled you into my bedchamber, and once I got you here, I should never have kissed you. I knew how strong your attraction to me was, even if you did not. I have known from the very first day. You were fascinated with me as soon as you saw me."

"I was not!" she said, holding his gaze unblinkingly. Lies were becoming easier and easier.

He held up his palm. "I do not wish to join issue with you, my dear. It matters not one whit in any case. The damage is done—unless you wish to tell your parents we are not wed—in which case your father would demand a wedding or pistols at dawn. Under the circumstances, honor would demand I delope, and I would rather not die if I can help it. So you see? We have little choice but to wed, and you might as well stay here in my chamber with me. What can it hurt? Your parents already believe we are wed. We can travel to London tomorrow, where I will acquire a special license. We shall return home to Trowbridge Manor with the deed a *fait accompli*. And tonight . . ." He gave her a slow, seductive smile that made her insides flutter. "Tonight, we can explore your attraction, Mary."

"My name is Marianna."

"And my name is True. Come, let me hear you use it." He advanced toward her, reminding her of a predatory cat.

Her heart hammered in her chest. Her head pounded even harder. "Do . . . do you love me?" she asked.

He stopped, looking puzzled for a moment, and then his face hardened. "Love is not necessary to a successful marriage."

He did not love her. She felt herself blanch and turned away, reaching for the bedpost for support, her thoughts swirling like a tempest in her head. Marry True Sin? Marry a man who did not love her? A man who would never love her? It was not what she had wanted for herself, but it was what she had been prepared to do for her parents' sake.

Until now.

There had to be another way. She went to the tall window and looked out upon the lawn. The moon cast its ethereal light over the garden. The shadows in the depths of the trees and in the hollow where the brook ran close to the manor seemed as black as her mood. She lifted her eyes to the hills. They glowed in the distance, seeming to beckon her. For a moment, she lost herself in a fancy. She was running barefoot over those hills in the moonlight, free.

She would rather be anywhere but here. With him.

She sensed Truesdale waiting behind her. He was probably waiting for her answer to his proposal. She tried to turn her attention away from him and focus on her situation, instead. There had to be a logical way out of this coil.

Ten

True watched impatiently. Victory was almost in his grasp. She was almost in his grasp. *Her fortune* was almost in his grasp. All she had to do was say yes and allow him to kiss her once more. He knew with a practiced certainty that if she did, she would be his beyond redemption before the night was through. They would marry, and he would return to the sea knowing the ABC's would be taken care of.

Mary stood motionless at the window for what seemed an eternity and then turned suddenly.

"My mother did not see my state of undress," she said. "I was completely hidden under the counterpane. She did not even see me kissing you like a . . . like a strumpet." She blushed an improbable shade of crimson and looked down at her hands. "We can tell them we were not serious about Gretna. We can say that you are fond of such tricks and that you were just bamming them. We will say funning was your way of bringing them into the family, of bringing them into your inner circle and welcoming them as one of your own. We can pretend that I went along with your Banbury tale to please you."

She was too clever. True's hopes sank. "They will never believe you," he said. "Here you are in my bedchamber. Alone. With your hair down."

She put her fingers to her hair and bit her lip. "You may

be right. They might not believe me. But I have no other choice. I cannot marry you. We would not suit." A desperate note had come into her voice. "We are not in love."

At that moment, True knew he had lost.

"Besides," she continued, "you are not the sort of man my parents wish me to marry. They still know nothing of your reputation. When they hear of your misdeeds, they will be most displeased. They will think I have chosen imprudently. They will believe I am foolish."

The very idea made True angry. "If they believe that, then they are the foolish ones. Why do you care what they think of you?"

"They are my parents!"

"What they are," True shot back, "is vain and selfish."

"Vain? Selfish? How dare you?"

"I dare, because I am no one's slave."

"Are you implying that I am my parents'—"

"I am implying nothing," he said. "I am *telling* you, quite frankly, that your parents control you out of self-interest. I am telling you they do not give a fig about your happiness. I am telling you that what you need is to act spontaneously for once, to defy your parents and to do what your heart tells you to do."

Mary shook with fury. "What I need," she said, "is to adhere to discipline and follow the path my parents have sacrificed everything to clear for me. They are good people. They want only what is best for me. And they love me."

"I do not doubt it," True remarked with studied insolence. "I love my best spaniel bitch, too, and she doesn't mind half as well as you do."

She fisted her hands at her sides, looking like she wished to strike him instead. "If you have a shred of decency left in you," she said, "you shall behave as a gentleman for the rest of the house party. If you cannot do so out of a sense of honor, perhaps you will remember our bargain and do so out of a sense of greed."

* * *

Marianna spun away from him and scooped her hair comb from the bed before unlocking the door and stomping down the hallway and storming into her own chamber. She had to calm down before seeing her parents.

She pulled her hair back into its smooth bun and paced before the fire until her heartbeat had subsided into a more normal pace and then made her way back through the dimly lit halls to her parents' bedchamber. Peeking through the keyhole, she could see no light, and she discerned her father snoring within.

She would have to tell them the "truth"—that it had been all a hum—in the morning. *If* Truesdale corroborated her story, and *if* he continued to act the part of a gentleman, they *might* just believe her.

But they would still be disappointed that she was not married. And they would still discover she'd betrothed herself to an ill-mannered blackguard. The poor darlings.

For the hundredth time that day, she wondered why Ophelia hadn't told her about True Sin's many sins.

It was barely eleven o' the clock. Not late for Town hours, and Ophelia, Marianna knew, kept Town hours. She turned and headed for the Robertsons' chamber. Knocking softly, she lowered her voice to a hiss. "Ophelia?" She waited. "Ophelia, I know you are in there! Let me in. I shan't go away until you do." She knocked again. "Ophelia, please! Please," she said, her voice breaking, her anger giving way to despair. "I need to speak with you!"

"Come," a muffled voice sounded from within.

Marianna entered the room. A single candle burned on the dressing table. Ophelia was sitting on a sofa amid a fluff of orange spangled silk and green feathers.

"My parents have arrived," Marianna said.

"You do not look happy about it."

"And you," Marianna accused, "do not look as though you have a megrim."

"I do not."

"You have been avoiding me."

The old woman nodded her head. "Can you blame me, my dear?"

"No," Marianna conceded, sinking wearily onto the chair opposite Ophelia's. She gave her old friend a piercing gaze. "Why?" she asked. "Why did you not tell me about him?"

"About Truesdale's wicked history?" Marianna nodded, and Ophelia sighed heavily. "I did not tell you," she said, "because you would not have come to Trowbridge Manor if I had."

"But, why Truesdale Sinclair? Why not some other bachelor?"

"Because he was the correct choice. Your only choice."

"There must have been other bachelors in financial straits."

"There were. But I say again," Ophelia said stubbornly, "Truesdale Sinclair was the correct choice."

Marianna shrugged and rubbed her temples. "I do not wish to join issue with you." Not that arguing with Ophelia would ever accomplish anything. "Ophelia, you are my friend, and I believe you were trying to do what was best for me." She sighed and pinched her nose. "I believe I have something that belongs to you."

"What?"

"Your megrim." She tried to smile. "You had no way of knowing how angry my parents will be when they hear of his reputation for scandal."

"Pish, dearling. Your parents will be delighted."

Marianna shook her head. "You are mistaken."

Ophelia tipped her head sagely to one side. "I think not." She picked up the china dragon on the table next to her and tapped it thoughtfully against her palm. "Marianna, True Sin's notoriety makes you an instant object of fascination. His infamous and outrageous behavior has transfixed the *ton*. Where another man may have been scorned and outcast, he has garnered their admiration. When you announce your engagement, you will be one of the most sought-after belles of the *ton*. Everyone will wish to be seen with True Sin's betrothed."

"Perhaps, but soon we shall cry off the engagement, and then where shall I be?"

"Silly gel," Ophelia said, not unkindly, and laughed. "You shall be exactly where you wish to be. You shall have the distinction of being the only lady to have ever brought True Sin up to scratch—and the only one to have subsequently slammed the door in his face. As I said, you shall be an object of fascination. Every gentleman shall want to dance with you, and every lady to invite you to call. The *ton* will be yours."

Marianna bit her lip. "Can it be so easy?"

"Trust me."

"I do. But my parents . . ."

"Not to worry about your parents," Ophelia said. "I will speak to them in the morning and make them understand that an alliance with True Sin means certain acceptance within the *ton*."

Marianna knew she should have been comforted by Ophelia's assurances. And yet, she felt strangely unsettled. Why should the *ton* revere a man such as True Sin?

The *ton* was all that was good and worthy. To be a part of the upper ten-thousand was all that mattered. She had worked her whole life toward it. She had thought she understood the *ton*. But now she found she didn't understand the *ton* as well as she thought. She was at sixes and sevens, unbalanced. Why would the *ton* accept True Sin, much less esteem him? Her head pounded even harder.

"Things are seldom as they seem on the outside," Ophelia said as though guessing her thoughts. "Everyone has hidden motives. Secrets. Even you." Ophelia gave her a pat. "Off with you now. You need your rest, dearling."

Ophelia ushered Marianna from the chamber and then wandered over to the tall window. Moving the gold velvet curtain aside, she stood staring forlornly out at the full moon, deep in thought. Behind her, her beloved John emerged from his connecting room.

"Were you eavesdropping, as usual?" she asked him.

"Aye, you old dragon, that I was." He wrapped his arms around her and gave a loving squeeze. "Why didn't you tell 'er?"

Ophelia sighed and leaned into his embrace. "The time is not right," she answered.

"Maybe the time ain't never goin' to be right. What then?"

"I do not know," Ophelia whispered. "I do not know."

Eleven

The elder Granthams slept until well nigh noon. Marianna thought the poor darlings must have been vastly tired from their journey. She hovered outside their door for two hours, unwilling to wake them, and then, when she heard them rise, she hovered some more, waiting for them to dress.

Finally, she knocked.

"Eh?" her father answered through the thick wooden door. "Come in, come in! What took you so—Oh. It ain't my lazy valet but you, daughter. Or, should I say, Viscountess Trowbridge?"

Marianna winced. "Papa, I need to speak with you."

"Who is it, Gerald?" Her mother's voice stabbed its way out of the dressing room. "Oh," she said, coming out to see for herself. "It's you."

"Says she needs to speak with me."

"With both of you, actually. May I sit down?"

"We do not wish to be late for breakfast," Violet Grantham said.

Marianna eyed the sharp light slanting through the tall window. The sun was already quite high. A week ago, she and the viscount had already breakfasted with the ABC's, been out for a morning ride, and partaken of a short nuncheon by this time of day. It was one of the more pleasant surprises she'd been faced with at Trowbridge Manor. She'd been glad the viscount preferred early hours, as she did.

She turned to her parents and folded her hands in front

of her. "What I have to tell you will not take long," she told them. "Please—" She motioned to the chairs at the fireside, her stomach in knots. "Please sit."

"Marianna, this is most irregular. What could possibly be so important that you delay our introduction to the houseguests downstairs?"

For the first time, Marianna took note of how they were both dressed. They looked more ready for a ball than for breakfast. Her father wore formal black clothes with white silk stockings and silver buckles, while her mother wore a pink flounced gown with a black lace overskirt. Fluffy black ostrich feathers swayed in her hair and long, formal black gloves encased her arms and hands, while at her neck lay a dazzling display of diamonds.

"She don't look well," her father commented. "In faith, she looks a fright. Didn't you sleep last night, daughter?"

Mrs. Grantham rolled her eyes. "They *are* newly wed, Mr. Grantham."

"Eh?" he looked at his wife. "What's that? Oh. Yes. Yes, of course."

Marianna realized with embarrassment what the two of them were thinking. She shook her head. "In truth, I slept exceedingly well all night, in my own bedchamber. Alone," she added. She was about to tell them why, when her father spoke and rendered her speechless.

"Don't tell me you haven't yet allowed him to bed you!"

"No!" Marianna cried.

"Then you have made a mistake, daughter."

"A mistake?" Violet Grantham cried. "You must be suffering from an excess of Spanish coin. What the girl's done is acted stupidly." She turned to Marianna. "Did you give your wits away as alms? You had a perfect opportunity last night."

"Aye. I seen—"

"Saw," his wife corrected him.

"Saw how he looked at you."

"How he looked at me?" Marianna murmured, confused. Her mother turned to Mr. Grantham. "She's blind as well as witless! Good God, Marianna, that man wants to bed you."

"Mama!" Marianna felt as though she'd been struck.

"If you think I'm speaking too plainly, then you'll truly be shocked at what I say next, my girl. Listen well. Gretna weddings are sometimes contested."

"Aye," her father said, "and even with our kind of money the nobs would win at court. They always do. You've got to allow him to bed you. It's the only way to make the marriage stick."

"We are not married!" Marianna blurted. She hadn't known what to expect, but it wasn't the expressions of pure rage that slashed across their features like winter lightning. Marianna rushed on. "What I mean to say is that we are not married *yet*. Trowbridge is a great prankster, you see, and . . ." She recited her carefully rehearsed explanation. She'd had all night to perfect it, and it did what she expected it to do. As she spoke, her parents' faces relaxed into understanding. She chided herself for a fool—something she'd been doing a lot of, lately. Truesdale was wrong. Her parents were not the selfish creatures he imagined them to be. No, they cared about her, loved her. They only wanted the best for her. "And we plan to announce our engagement quite soon."

"When?" her father asked.

"I . . . I am uncertain." It was the truth. After what had happened last night, she was unsure when the announcement might take place. She would have to ask Truesdale. "It should be any day now."

Her parents traded looks, and something seemed to pass between them. Her father walked to the window. "Tell her, Vi."

Violet Grantham leaned closer to her daughter. "Your father and I came to a decision on our journey back to England. We know the ways of the world. We know what is best for you. A gentleman sometimes cries off his engagement. When his first rush of excitement over his bride's fortune wanes and he discovers he is about to be

bound for life to a girl who is less than fetching, he may
get it into his head to run. I am sorry, but there is no
delicate way to say this, Marianna. You are not beautiful.
You never have been. Even though you are not yet married, you must do everything you can to entice the viscount into bed with you."

"Into his bed?"

"His bed, your bed, a bed of hay. Makes no difference.
If he gets you with child, he won't be able to back out of
your engagement, and our place in Society will be assured."

Marianna absorbed her mother's words with shock. She
shook her head. There had to be some misunderstanding.
She looked to her father, but he only stared out the window,
silent. He had to have heard what Mama had said. But that
was impossible, wasn't it? He could not possibly want her
to—"I do not understand."

Her father slashed one angry hand through the air. "Just
do as you are told, daughter. As you should have done last
night."

Mrs. Grantham nodded. "We cannot allow him to break
the engagement."

"But . . ." Marianna murmured, "what if he is not the
one who wants to break the engagement?"

"What? Nonsense!" her father thundered. "After all we
sacrificed! You've got a title in the parson's mousetrap, my
girl. It took you a year to snabble this one. Plain as you
are, it may be the last."

"You would break your engagement?" her mother asked
plaintively. "Do you wish us to hie back to the islands in
disgrace and die in obscurity? Are you so ungrateful?" She
broke a sob.

Marianna bit her lip. She didn't know what to say.

Mr. Grantham tugged at his cravat. "Perhaps the viscount
is still abed. Go to him now."

"Yes, Marianna." Her mother sniffled. "Obey your father
this time, as you should have done last night." She reached
to pat Marianna's hand as Ophelia had done, but her fingers
felt cold, her touch distant, somehow. "It is not as unpleas-

ant as it seems. Only think of all it will bring us. Everything will turn out as it should. Go."

Woodenly, Marianna obeyed the command to leave, but she did not go to Truesdale's bedchamber. Instead, she wandered back to her own room, her footsteps as heavy as her heart.

Her parents' words had hurt, but what hurt even worse was the realization that what Truesdale had said about them was at least partially correct. They loved her, cared for her, but their harsh reactions, bleak pronouncements, and stern orders had proven that they really did care as much for themselves as they did for her.

They actually wanted her to—to give her maidenhood to Truesdale. Before marriage! And they didn't appear to feel any guilt over the notion, either.

The thought of enticing Truesdale into bed with her brought a blush of shame to her cheeks. Her parents would never expect her to do such a thing if they knew she had never had any intention of marrying the viscount. They would not expect her to submit her body to him if they knew there was never a real understanding.

Would they?

She shook herself. Of course not! Their motives were pure. How could she expect them to understand the situation when they were victims of such terrible subterfuge? Especially after what her mother had witnessed last night. Marianna was the one who should feel guilty, not her parents.

Their reactions and demands were perfectly understandable, given their knowledge of the entire maddening mull. Were they not entitled to their happiness? Did they not deserve a respite after years and years of hard work and sacrifice? Of course they did! And that certainly did not mean they cared nothing for their daughter.

She dressed hastily in a white-and-gray-striped walking dress with pretty rose-embroidered ribbons, and quit the house, feeling sorry she had doubted her parents. Drat Truesdale Sinclair for planting a foul seed of mistrust in her mind!

Though she knew she ought to inform Trowbridge she'd told her parents they were not wed and she knew the question of when to announce their betrothal should be settled between them, she steered clear of the stables, the fields, the outbuildings—all of the places he might usually be found. Instead, she struck out through the east woods and tarried under the cover of the green leaves and soft shadow.

It was a relief to be alone there, away from questioning eyes and plaintive expectation. She relaxed a little, letting the cool dampness seep into her rattled soul.

It was a place where she could have taken out her feelings and examined them, but she didn't. Instead, she deliberately kept them locked away and concentrated on the feel of the loamy earth beneath her feet. Taking off her gloves, she sat for a time on a wide, flat rock near the footpath, which had obviously served as a bench for wanderers like herself since time out of mind. She took a deep, soothing breath of the moist air and leaned back to stare up at the forest canopy, which was alive with birdsong on that summer morning. It was easy to lose her thoughts within it for a time, but inevitably her mind came back around to the problems that awaited her, and she found herself wishing she could be happy and carefree like the birds that sang and swooped overhead.

Lucky things. You do not have another fortnight's lies to suffer through.

After a long while, she headed for a pleasant meadow of bluebells lined with birch she'd passed while riding a few days before. Bluebells were her favorites, and yet she hardly looked at them. She was in such a sour mood that she almost missed Lord Lindenshire as well. He was kneeling, examining a fallen log in dense shade near the edge of the wood. Wearing a fashionable coat of bottle-blue superfine trimmed in black velvet, a startlingly white shirt, and gray breeches, he looked like he had just walked off St. James's Street, yet he was hunched over the log like a cobbler fixing a shoe. Peering through a spying glass with all of his concentration, he was oblivious to her presence.

"Is that not the spying glass from the library?" she asked, admiring the fact that her voice did not seem to startle him. Instead, he just calmly lifted his head.

"Guilty," he affirmed, and Marianna could hear the grin in his voice. "Think anyone back at Trowbridge Manor will miss it, Miss Grantham?" He hadn't even seen her yet. He knew her voice.

"Oh, most definitely it will be missed," she said, "for I believe it is every lofty-titled guest's fondest wish to examine a . . ." He turned to her and she nodded toward the fallen log with a question in her eyes.

"A fungus," he supplied.

"To examine a fungus," she finished. "Or, lacking so refined a notion, perhaps they will discover a burning desire to discern the location of the Spey or the Tay."

"Will you expose my crime?"

"Not if you tell me what that fungus is," Marianna said.

The two of them, Marianna and Lord Lindenshire, spent the next half hour roving over the meadow. The air was warm, yet crisp with newly fallen rain, and the birds were singing joyously in the trees. The meadow was so pleasant, seemed so perfect a sanctuary that she was almost able to forget what she had come to escape—until it emerged from the wood.

As Trowbridge emerged from the shade of the trees, the sun limned his head in golden light. The wind blew his curls this way and that, and his gait was easy and relaxed in spite of the width of his shoulders. His penetrating dark eyes swept the meadow. He was obviously searching for someone.

Herself, she concluded, when he caught sight of her. His gaze fixed upon her for a moment before flicking once, twice to Lord Lindenshire. And then True Sin frowned, but the expression was swept from his face almost as soon as it appeared, and he approached.

"There you are, Mary," he said. "And Lindenshire. What a surprise."

"Yes," Marianna said, taking note of his just-slightly-wry

tone. "To me as well. I went for a stroll, but Lord Linden-shire had already laid claim to my favorite meadow."

"She just arrived," the younger man said, though Mari-anna had been there above a half hour. So, she was not the only one who had taken note of Truesdale's jealousy. "Since it is time for tea, perhaps you will escort Miss Grantham back to your magnificent house?"

"What about you?" Marianna asked the earl. "You have been here most of the day. Are you not quite sharp set?"

His face reddened. "I . . . carried a meal with me." He patted his pocket, which bulged slightly. "A cold chicken leg and a biscuit," he said, and gestured to the log. "I had seen these fungi earlier and wanted to get back to them."

Marianna gave him a smile. Eating lunch out of one's pocket was not the proper thing to do, but it *was* an en-dearing thing. She found she liked Lord Lindenshire more and more.

Truesdale coughed and offered her his arm. "Shall we, my dear?"

"You do not have to 'my dear' me in front of Lord Lin-denshire, Trowbridge. He knows our secret." She was sat-isfied to see a scowl blossom on Trowbridge's face and even more satisfied to see the earl straighten his spine and lift his chin slightly, taking a stance that was not quite a chal-lenge but which was definitely not subservient. Marianna stepped around the viscount without looping her arm through his and made for the footpath that led back through the woods to Trowbridge Manor. He fell into step behind her. She could hear the moist leaves crumpling beneath his feet. The woods were fragrant and alive with wildflowers and butterflies and swooping birds. The wind and the light sifted through the canopy of green leaves, turning the woods into the grandest cathedral. Were it not for the Viscount Trowbridge, it could have been a most pleasant walk, but Marianna was all too aware of his presence. He followed her like a shadow, dark and silent, without a single word.

When they'd reached the center of the woods and were

out of ear-and-eyeshot of the meadow, he clamped his hand around her wrist and pulled her to a stop.

She turned. "What do you want now?" she said uncivilly.

"I wish to have a word with you about our guest list. Do you not think it is rather top-heavy with bachelors?"

Marianna cleared her throat. "I thought you did not care a pin who I invited to the house party."

"I suspect it was not *you* who decided whom to invite, but Ophelia. Am I correct?"

Marianna said nothing, and he said, "I thought so. Why did you not tell me what you were up to? Did you think I would not guess you are auditioning the bachelors for the position of husband?"

"I did not know what you would think. Nor did I think you would care."

"Would it matter if I did?"

She shook her head. "Not in the least."

A smile and a frown chased themselves over his features, and his eyes flicked back to the meadow. "Is he your choice?"

"Who, Lord Lindenshire?"

"Do you love him?"

A denial sprang naturally to her lips, but she stopped herself from uttering it. "He is a pleasant and polite fellow," she averred. "When I marry, I will choose someone with an appreciation of the *ton*. Someone with some notion of propriety."

He laughed. "Someone like that cub Lindenshire, I suppose."

"Well . . . yes. He has impeccable manners, and he would never . . . never—"

"Sweep you into his arms and kiss you senseless as I did last night?"

"Lord Lindenshire would never do such an improper thing."

"Of course not. He is predictable."

"Indeed, yes."

"Steady as a rock."

"Yes."

"And well nigh as exciting."

"He is amiable and good-mannered!"

He snorted. "Granted. He is that. *Amiable and good-mannered,*" he muttered.

"Your tone makes those things sound like insults rather than compliments."

Truesdale let go of her wrist. "He is not the sort of man you need."

"Oh, really! What sort of man do I need, exactly?"

Without warning, Trowbridge pulled her to him. "You need a bold man." He slid his arms around her waist and shoulders. "A spontaneous man." He lowered his face to hers until their lips were nearly touching. "A man who will sweep you into his arms and kiss you." He took her mouth in a swirling, sensuous crush. For one insane moment, she began to respond to him, began to kiss him back, but then reason took hold. She wedged her palms between them and shoved away from him, breaking contact.

"Why did you do that?"

"Because you needed me to. You wanted me to."

"You have not the first notion of what I want or need. And you are wrong about Lord Lindenshire." She had a sudden urge to knock him off balance, to see the self-confident smirk on his face crumble. "The earl can be spontaneous and bold, too," she said.

"Oh, certainly," Truesdale said, crossing his arms over his broad chest. "As spontaneous and bold as one of his precious fungi."

"We will see about that." She spun around and stomped back to the meadow, surprising Lord Lindenshire for the second time that morning.

"My lord," she called to him. "Have you an interest in salamanders?"

"Indeed. Lovely creatures."

"The young Misses Trowbridge described to me a spot in the brook they said was positively crowded with salamanders. Would you care to accompany me for an expedition there?"

"I would be pleased to escort you."

She smiled, throwing a triumphant glance at Trowbridge, who had followed her into the clearing. *See? Spontaneous and bold, just like I told you,* her look said.

"What time tomorrow shall I order my tiger and carriage brought 'round?" Lindenshire inquired.

"Tomorrow?" Marianna hadn't thought to go tomorrow, she'd meant right then, without delay, in order to prove to Trowbridge that Lindenshire was spontaneous and bold. She glanced at Trowbridge, whose expression was both amused and derisive.

"Will you be coming along with us, Trowbridge?" asked the earl.

The viscount came forward and shook his head. "Not my area of interest at all." He let his eyes rove over Marianna, leaving little doubt just where his interest lay.

"Well then," Lindenshire said, turning back to Marianna, "we shall leave precisely at eleven o' the clock, and I shall bring my tiger. The proper thing, you know."

"Of course," Marianna murmured.

"Lindenshire, old man," True Sin said, clapping the younger man on the shoulder, "you are all that is dependable and steady." *Like a fungus,* he mouthed to Marianna as Lindenshire bowed, his straight brown hair falling into his eyes.

At that moment, the ABC's scampered into the meadow. Marianna started toward them. "I shall walk the girls back home, my lords. And, as we will no doubt take a circuitous route, there is no need to accompany us."

The three adults took their leave of each other and parted, and Marianna allowed the girls to lead her onto an out-of-the-way path.

"So, my fine young ladies, you've not been naughty with any more salamanders, have you?" she asked. The day the guests arrived, four of them had found a salamander lounging in their clotted cream.

"Nooo . . ." all three girls averred.

Marianna put her hands on her hips and stopped to give them a schoolteacher look that spoke brutal, merciless volumes.

"It was Eleanor's idea!" Beatrice blurted.

"I didn't touch any salamanders!" Eleanor defended herself. "It was a frog this time. An' it was Alyse who put it in there." She pointed her chubby little finger at her eldest sister.

"I have the longest reach," Alyse said, wincing.

"Where did you put the frog?"

"In Lady Allen's reticule."

"She smells funny," Eleanor said.

Beatrice nodded. "And she called Eleanor an impolite little mongrel when Eleanor told her so, too."

Alyse stuck her chin out. "We had to do something to avenge our little sister's honor. It was a matter of chivalry."

"I must stop reading you King Arthur stories at bedtime," she said. The stories had obviously fired Alyse's imagination, for the girl's cords were standing out in indignant lines on her neck. Marianna fought down a chuckle. Even she had to admit that Lady Allen was not the most pleasant person to pass the time with. In fact, the young widow was quite a nasty piece of work.

"Well," Marianna said, "it *was* unkind of Lady Allen to call you names, and I suppose one little frog will not hurt anything."

The ABC's exchanged guilty looks and fixed their gazes on the ground.

"What have you not told me?" Marianna could see their story was all moonshine.

"It wasn't one little frog," Alyse said.

"It was a dozen!" Eleanor said proudly. "An' I know 'cause I counted them all! I counted the grasshoppers, too, and the—"

"Eleanor!" Alyse and Beatrice hissed.

"Grasshoppers?" Marianna groaned, and then set to extracting the entire story from the girls. She knew she would not get at the truth by behaving in an authoritative manner, so she cast herself in the role of co-conspirator. It worked. Apparently, the ABC's were waging a private war on those of the guests they had chosen to dislike, using salamanders, grasshoppers, worms, and whatever else they had at their tender disposal.

She knew better than to think she could stop them, so she did the next best thing: she offered to help them. Logic reasoned that if she were in on their mischief, she could mitigate the damage.

Of course, becoming a full-fledged co-conspirator had its drawbacks. By the time they made it back to the manor, Marianna had been apprised of the ABC's' entire battle plan, and she had a horrible megrim. She retired to her chamber with a promise from the ABC's that there would be no more mischief that night and a promise from Cook to send up a supper tray.

She undressed, pulled the curtains closed, and gratefully slid into her bed—only to remember she had forgotten to ask True Sin when they would announce their betrothal.

Twelve

The next day, the sky was a deep, endless blue; a refreshing breeze rustled the verdant leaves; the green meadows were full of bluebells and foxgloves, yarrow and honeysuckle; the brook tumbled over cool stones; clouds of butterflies floated about in all their painted glory. Marianna was dressed in one of her new gowns, a becoming confection of white muslin sprigged in crimson, and Lord Lindenshire was an appreciative, charming, and intelligent companion. Except for her gloves, which itched, everything was perfect.

She should have been happy.

She was miserable.

While her mind should have been fixed upon Lord Lindenshire's pleasant baritone voice, she could think of little else but Truesdale Sinclair's hard, mocking tone—and of how much worse that was after she'd heard him whisper tender endearments.

While she should have been concentrating on Lord Lindenshire's obvious expertise on salamanders, she was distracted by thoughts of True Sin's obvious expertise on the birds and the bees. Drat the man! He would not leave her alone, even when he was nowhere near. She kicked a round stone in frustration, sending it skipping into the brook and eliciting a concerned look from Lord Lindenshire, who assessed her with his serious brown eyes and frowned.

"I say, Miss Grantham, is anything amiss? Are you fatigued? Do you wish to start back?"

Before she could answer him, he gave a whistle, and his tiger, on duty a discreet yet proper distance away on the other side of the meadow, circled Lindenshire's smart equipage around and started toward them.

"I was up late last evening," she averred. In truth, she was not the least bit tired, but she found herself too out of sorts from her last encounter with Truesdale to continue the outing. She liked Orion Gray, the Earl of Lindenshire, and didn't want him to think she may be a shrew. There was no sense in spoiling their acquaintance with ill humor. "Perhaps we could venture forth another day . . . ?" she suggested.

"By all means, I—"

He never finished his sentence. Something over Marianna's shoulder caught his eyes. They narrowed, betraying a wariness that compelled Marianna to glance backward. A large figure on a huge gray horse approached them, leading an unsaddled white mare. He was dressed in a white, flowing shirt and plain brown waistcoat, with no coat or cravat in sight.

Truesdale Sinclair.

"Good day to you, Trowbridge," Lord Lindenshire called.

"Good day. Thank you for amusing my betrothed while I attended to other matters, Lindenshire." Trowbridge patted his stallion on the neck.

Marianna wrinkled her brow. Trowbridge knew very well that Lindenshire was aware of their ruse. There was no need to refer to her as his betrothed. On the surface, it seemed nothing but a tongue-in-cheek hum—but somehow Marianna sensed it wasn't. She looked from one to the other of them. Both wore pleasant enough expressions, but she had the feeling that neither of them was feeling precisely charitable.

She crooked an eyebrow at Trowbridge. "I thought you had more important matters to attend than watching salamanders, my lord."

The viscount smiled. "I did. I arranged a lovely garden

party out on the front lawn back at the manor. Everyone is assembled, and they should just be finishing their luncheon. I was afraid they would become bored, so I decided to arrange an entertainment."

Bells of warning clanged in Marianna's head. Though Trowbridge sounded sincere, his dimples had deepened and his eyes crinkled at the corners just enough—"What are you up to?" she asked, looking at him through squinted eyes. "Why have you come?"

"I am here to issue a challenge."

"What sort of challenge?" Lindenshire asked, clearly unconcerned at whatever Trowbridge's answer might be. "Hunting? Chess? Cards?"

Pistols at dawn? Marianna thought.

The image panicked her for a split second, until Truesdale answered Lord Lindenshire. "My challenge is not intended for you but for Mary."

"Me?"

"A race. From here to Trowbridge Manor, right now." He tossed her the mare's ribbons. Marianna didn't even attempt to catch them. They fell to the ground, and Dover, the mare she'd been riding since she'd come to Trowbridge Manor, sidled a few steps away and buried her soft nose in a luxuriant patch of fragrant green clover.

"A race!" Marianna scoffed. "Even you cannot think such behavior is proper for a lady, Trowbridge." She shook her head. "And even if it were, I am much too engrossed in Lord Lindenshire's discourse on amphibians to leave now," Marianna said, ignoring the fact that she'd been speaking of leaving a few moments before.

Lord Lindenshire did not correct her.

"My dear Mary," Trowbridge said with a wide smile, "I thought you might be a little hesitant to take up the gauntlet. So . . ." He plunged his hand into his waistcoat and drew forth a blue object. It was fabric, rolled into a tight ball, and as he unfurled it with a wicked gleam in his eye, Marianna heard bells jingling!

Her eyes flew to Truesdale's, and the obvious question

passed between them. *What are you doing with that stocking?*

"What is that?" Lindenshire asked testily, trying not to stare at the improper ladies' undergarment.

"This," Trowbridge answered happily, "is the trophy. If you win the race, Mary, it gets stuffed back into my waistcoat, and no one but Lindenshire here will see it. But if I win, it stays in plain view and I display your stocking triumphantly for everyone to see."

"That *thing* is yours?" Lindenshire asked, incredulous.

"Everyone?" Marianna said weakly.

Truesdale nodded, his dimples showing. "Everyone assembled back on the lawn at Trowbridge Manor, of course. They are all there now, waiting near the fountain to see the finish of the race."

Marianna was incensed. "Oh, no," she began, "I will not be pulled into some mad—"

Truesdale laughed and shrugged. Then, waving the outrageous stocking in the air, he kicked his stallion into a gallop and shot up the brook's embankment to the meadow above. "First one to the fountain!" he shouted.

Marianna didn't think. There was no time. Instead, she leapt aboard the white mare's back and took off after Trowbridge, thanking God for the fullness of her skirts. She was a competent rider, not a circus acrobat, and without a saddle, riding astride was the only hope she had of keeping her seat.

And keep her seat she must!

Trowbridge was already across the wide field, but even from this distance, the stocking's bright, silver-shot brocade and shiny bells announced their presence as they glinted in the sunlight, and jingled even over the hoofbeats and the wind.

Bells in Heaven!

If the assembled company back at the manor saw the highly improper and outrageous stocking, they might begin to believe Truesdale had been telling them the truth about her paddling with no benefit of clothing in the brook—and with Trowbridge waving that stocking, it wouldn't be much of a stretch to believe the part he'd implied, too—that he had been paddling with her.

She either had to get that stocking back or win the race. And since she had no idea how she could get it back without wrestling him for it, she set her mind to winning the race.

The viscount and his gray had a good lead. They flew over the meadow ahead of her, aiming for the bridge over the brook. Fighting her mare, who naturally wanted to follow the other horse, Marianna cut across the meadow and headed for a shallow ford instead. She knew Journey would balk at the water and would have to be taken over the wide bridge, but Dover had no such faults and would go willingly across the ford. Marianna could cut several seconds off her time that way, and if she were lucky, she could beat Trowbridge to the fountain. It was not an honorable way to win the race, but why should she have been concerned with honor?

True Sin certainly wasn't.

She could see him ahead of her and veering off to the side now, still waving that blessed stocking, could hear his laughter echoing through the air.

She bent her head low to Dover's neck and urged her on, digging her gloved fingers into Dover's mane, giving the magnificent white horse full rein and encouragement to perform the needed miracle of speed. They swept over the meadow, splashed across the ford and up the steep, muddy embankment on the opposite side of the brook. Slipping into a little-used lane, Dover gathered speed again, finally galloping into the crossroads leading from the bridge.

She was ahead of Trowbridge!

Once more, she bent her head low and urged the mare forward, calling to her. "If we beat them, I shall give you a dish of sugar. A hot bath. A whole stableful of black-coated stallions!" She winced. If the mare thought as much of stallions as Marianna did of True Sin just then, she'd have done better to have promised the mare a gelding iron instead!

They shot across the last open field with Truesdale and the gray gaining ground all too fast. A tall hill crowned with a thick copse of trees stood before them. Dover surged up the hill with great strides, but the stallion, stronger and larger than the mare, gained even more ground. Marianna reached the top of the hill with Trowbridge only a second or two behind her. The safe thing to do was to slow down as she entered the copse atop the hill.

An image of her parents' faces staring at the stocking dangling from True Sin's fingers assailed her, and she shuddered.

Ophelia would have spoken to them yesterday about True Sin. She would have told them that True Sin's reputation would enhance Marianna's, but that would make little difference. Their anger was inevitable. If she won the race, they would be shocked and put to the blush with embarrassment to see her fly onto the lawn in the lead. And if she did not, how much worse would they feel when they saw her trailing after a man waving the shameful stocking? The wind tore a moan from her mouth, and she clung to Dover's neck, urging the animal to even greater speed, heedless of the rough, dark tree limbs that threatened to sweep her from the horse's broad back.

As she dodged a low limb, the thought occurred that if she were knocked unconscious, at least she would not have to see her parents' faces as Truesdale displayed his "trophy."

She emerged on the other side of the thick copse at the top of the hill having gained a few precious seconds. Trowbridge, taller than she and seated atop a larger mount, had been forced to slow down. Marianna looked down the long, velvety hill. Far below, on the wide lawn in front of the manor, she saw the forms of the muslin-clad ladies and the taller forms of the gentlemen floating slowly over the lawn. Which were her parents?

She galloped recklessly down the hill, making for the last obstacle separating her and the viscount from the fountain in front of Trowbridge Manor—a long, narrow footbridge. Suddenly, Dover swerved, and, unaccustomed to riding bareback astride, Marianna lost her balance. Her heart leapt into her throat as she began to slide off the mare's back. She could hear—and feel—the pounding of Journey's hooves just behind her. And then, somehow, she righted herself at the last possible moment.

As they raced toward the footbridge, someone on the lawn gave a shout, and suddenly everyone was on their feet and turning in her direction. Miraculously, Marianna made it to the bridge a second before Trowbridge.

She beat down a bubble of laughter that threatened to escape.

She slowed Dover to a walk going over the footbridge, knowing full well there was no way for him to pass her. The bridge was too narrow, and he could not cross the brook.

Dover's sides were bunching up as she strained for air, and flecks of foam fell from her soft white mouth. The animal was tired but, as Marianna had thought, she was strong and sound and still bore an eager wildness in her eyes as she pulled against the ribbons, signaling her desire to run.

Thank goodness!

Marianna would need to urge Dover into a last desperate gallop as soon as they were off the bridge, in order to be the first to the fountain.

In the last second before she urged Dover from the stone bridge to the footpath beyond, she glanced back at Trowbridge to gauge the condition of his mount.

The viscount sat his horse at the apex of the long bridge, a satisfied smile sculpting his handsome, angular features. Journey pranced in place beneath him, anxiously eyeing the water below with the whites of his eyes showing, but Trowbridge made no move forward. Marianna's blue stocking was nowhere in sight.

"Where is it?" she demanded, pulling Dover to a stop.

"Safely tucked away," he answered, patting his waistcoat. "I have won, then."

"No, I have, for I have reached my goal."

Marianna wrinkled her brow. "But you are behind me. Everyone can see that. And you have not touched the fountain yet!"

"Touching the fountain was never my goal."

"What do you mean? What trick are you playing, Trowbridge? If you think you can—"

"I wanted you to forget for a moment."

"Forget? Forget what?"

"Rules. Edicts. Mores. Society. I wanted you to experience one moment of pure excitement. One moment of pleasure. And you did."

"I did not! Racing you was a miserable, dangerous, reckless, frightening, maddening . . . disaster." She was acutely aware that even if they hadn't seen the stocking, everyone waiting for them at the fountain would have seen and recognized *her* from this distance. "Look at me," she said in an accusing tone. "I am riding astride!"

He nodded and grinned lazily, allowing his gaze to slide seductively down her heaving bosom and over her hips to settle at the juncture of her thighs where she sat the horse, her legs spread immodestly open.

"Lucky horse," he said, apparently reading her thoughts. "Too bad she's a mare," he said. "I vow a stallion would appreciate you better."

Marianna gave a sound of frustration, but to her dismay it came out sounding more like a moan of passion. She was too angry to speak.

Thirteen

There was nothing more to do but straighten her spine, nudge Dover into a walk, and approach the garden party with as much dignity as she could salvage. She was so busy scanning the crowd for her parents—who, to her considerable relief, were not there!—that she was abreast of the tables set out upon the lawn before she remembered again that she was riding astride.

Saints and sinners!

She pulled on the mare's ribbons and worried about how she was going to dismount without showing too much of her chemise—or other things—but she didn't worry about it for more than a moment before a pair of large hands encircled her waist and pulled her off balance. Marianna gasped as she slid into Trowbridge's warm embrace. His scent—no cologne, just woods, fresh linen, and clean masculine exertion—filled her nostrils. His strong hands lingered, and she danced lightly away from him.

The assembled guests looked upon the two of them with varying expressions of amusement, mild astonishment, and intrigue. Ophelia was there, too, and she hastened forward to congratulate Marianna on winning the race in the bold, brash style that only she could pull off. The others followed suit, murmuring their congratulations with anything from polite regard to openly admiring fascination.

Marianna wasn't quite certain if the race had made her an Original, or if she'd won herself a reputation as a hoyden instead.

She tried to act as self-confident and nonchalant as if she had just been taking tea with the patronesses of Almack's and the royal princesses rather than disgracing herself in front of God and the entire, blessed *ton*. She managed to accept everyone's congratulations with what she hoped was a beatific smile. She even allowed herself to be cajoled into relating the part of the race they had not been able to see: how she had outwitted the viscount by taking a shortcut and then nearly unseated herself in the wood. Trowbridge said almost nothing and kept the stocking hidden away. Everyone listened so attentively and laughed so gaily that before she realized quite what was happening, Marianna was enjoying herself—until something drew her attention from what she was saying and she glanced up at the manor, eyes drawn inexplicably to a high window. There, two figures stood watching her. Her parents. And they were not smiling.

Amid a shower of protestation, she excused herself as quickly as she could and made for the house. Trowbridge appeared beside her and slipped his arm under her hand. She allowed the contact until they were inside the house and out of sight and earshot of the guests. Then she jerked her hand away and stomped toward the stairs.

"Where are you going?" Trowbridge's deep voice echoed off the marble floor and columns.

"To find my parents. I must apologize to them."

Just as Marianna's foot hit the first tread, Trowbridge's hand clamped onto her arm and he tugged her into the library and shut the double doors. Knowing protest would do her no good, Marianna set her jaw and stood mute, refusing to meet his eyes.

"What must you apologize for?"

"You can drag me in here against my will, my lord, but you cannot make me speak." She crossed her arms in front of her to emphasize her point.

Trowbridge mirrored the movement, but then he spoiled the effect by pacing before the fire. "You enjoyed the race. Admit it."

Marianna said nothing.

"You enjoyed the thrill of the chase, the speed, the strategy, the challenge, the danger. And most of all, you enjoyed besting me. I wager that you would do it all over again if you had the chance."

She threw her hands up in exasperation. "You are wrong." She shook her head. "I did only what I had to do. What you forced me to do. I acted only to neutralize the threat you presented. I did *not* enjoy it." Even as she said the words, she knew they were not entirely true. She *had* found the speed exhilarating, the competition invigorating, the applause and excitement of the crowd satisfying. But she certainly would not wish to repeat the experience, and that meant she hadn't enjoyed the race. Didn't it?

Trowbridge rubbed his slightly cleft, shadowy chin. "I wager that all your life you have been told that frivolity, gaiety, and spontaneity are wrong."

"Rubbish," she said, knowing he was right. She hadn't played much as a child. She had spent her days learning to be a lady instead, for that was what had most pleased her parents. She had always tried to be a good daughter. How many times had she watched with a secret longing as the laborers' children played, splashing and laughing and chasing one another on the white sandy beaches, while she stood quietly, itching in her gloves and whalebone stays?

He studied her and then smiled knowingly. "The race was my way of forcing you to taste what it is like to be me. To force you to savor your own wildness. And"—he cocked his head to one side and his dark eyes gleamed— "and perhaps now that you have your own disgraces to live with, you will be more forgiving of mine—especially since, like me, you quite enjoyed your misbehavior."

"I did not!"

"Do you mean to tell me that you are so concerned about what others think of you that you will not even admit to yourself when you're letting go and having fun?"

"Yes. No! Oh . . . ! You know perfectly well what I mean."

"Yes," he said, his flawed eyebrow arching, "I am certain

I do." He raked his roughened hand through his dark, unruly hair. "It seems I was mistaken. It is not that you will not admit you are having fun—"

Marianna gave a sharp satisfied nod. "Humph!"

"—it is that you cannot have fun at all. You do not let go of your proper little false persona. Ever. Not even when you are alone. You, Mary, are so busy worrying about what other people expect of you that you have no real personality, no individuality, and no sense of adventure."

"I do so have a sense of adventure! I became a teacher at a boarding school, did I not? I made up—" She lowered her voice to a whisper. "I made up stories to tell my parents. That was adventurous."

"No," he said, crossing his arms over his broad chest once more. "It was not adventurous, it was cowardly."

"Cowardly!"

"Aye, for instead of deceiving your parents, you could have stood up to them and demanded they give you time to make a love match. Again, you were too concerned with what others would think of you. No, Miss Grantham, the only way you will ever have any real adventure is when it is thrust upon you—and then you will not have the freedom to well and truly enjoy it. You cannot be honest with yourself. You are afraid to really live."

"How dare you?"

"Freely, Miss Grantham. I freely dare anything I please. And that," he said, "is the difference between us."

"I can think of a few more," she said, allowing her voice to vibrate with sarcasm.

Once more, he allowed his gaze to slide seductively down her body and grinned. "So can I."

Marianna scowled and spun away from him, slamming the library doors closed behind her. She had to calm herself before she spoke with her parents.

No amount of inner calm would have helped. Her mama and papa had been playing cards with one of the older couples during the race and might have missed it but for one undisciplined Trowbridge servant who had come whooping into the front hall and calling to the other servants that the Lady Trowbridge-to-be was racing against their master.

Her parents' faces were as red as love apples. They were beyond furious.

"Papa, Mama . . ." she began as soon as she found them alone in the yellow salon.

"Sit!" her father ordered, his expression stormy. "Not one word. Your mother and I witnessed the entire disgraceful incident."

"You have disappointed us again, Marianna," Violet Grantham intoned, her voice as sharp as her husband's.

Marianna endured their hour-long lecture stoically, as usual, staring down at her hands, counting the individual tufts of thread in the thick yellow and cream carpet under her feet, and not daring to tell them that she had raced only to save what was left of her reputation. She knew that would require an explanation about the blue stockings, and there was no escaping the guilt for that transgression. The fact was that if she hadn't fashioned the outrageous stockings in the first place, the race could never have happened.

When they finished scolding her for the race, they began scolding her about having chosen True Sin for a husband. As she'd promised, Ophelia had explained to them the peculiar advantages of being allied to the notorious True Sin, but the house party guests had apparently been regaling the Granthams since early yesterday afternoon with stories of True Sin's infamous exploits.

"Why you would choose to ally us to him is beyond me," her mother said. "The stories we have heard of him are shocking."

Her father had stopped talking at all, a sure measure of his anger.

Marianna looked at her hands and fidgeted. "I did not know about those things when we—when we became engaged."

"Did not know about them?" her mother cried. "Did not

know about them! How could you not know about the man having *offered carte blanche to Lady Jersey in front of the prince at Almack's?* No . . . I do not believe it. You are not stupid. You must be lying."

Marianna remembered her mother saying she *was* stupid two days ago, but she said nothing, of course.

Her mother waved her silver-gloved hand. "And that outlandish woman—what is her name? Delia? Orphea?"

"Mrs. Ophelia Robertson?"

"That's the one. Insufferable woman. Whyever did you choose to stay with her when the duenna we chose for you turned up her toes? She's not even a titled lady! Do you know she married a *servant?"*

"She . . . she is my friend," Marianna said quietly.

"Friend. Hah! Some friend, allowing you to traipse about and become engaged to such a man."

When they finally released her and sent her to her room like a naughty child, Marianna went gladly and stayed.

She curled up on the wide four-poster and buried her head under one of the down pillows, but no matter how fervently she wished to hide from everything, she kept remembering the awful censure in her father's eyes. Though she was quite miserably sharp set after not having eaten any luncheon, her stomach was too upset for her to eat, and she fell into a deep and drugging sleep, missing the evening meal entirely.

She awoke before the sun rose the next morning and sat near her window, watching the world come alive. Her parents were right. The Viscount Trowbridge was most unsuitable for any purpose, and she should have known it. The moment she heard his nickname, True Sin, she should have turned her head and found someone else. She had been foolish and imprudent, and her parents were the ones paying the price. There was no way she could avoid his influence now. No matter whom she married, the *ton* would always connect her name with True Sin, and no amount of assurances from Ophelia could convince her that *that* was a good thing.

She did not want to be an Original. She wanted to be a lady.

It was too late for that, though.

Yesterday's race, coupled with Trowbridge's suggestion that they may have been swimming naked in the brook together at night, would probably already be enough to keep the more respectable bachelors at bay. No *ton* mama would want her son connected to a hoyden, would she?

Marianna's only hope lay in convincing them that she wasn't a hoyden, after all.

From then on, she would be on her best behavior. Whenever any *tonnish* eyes were upon her, she would be the soul of propriety. Not only would she wear her gloves, but she would also not fidget within them, and she wouldn't get a single smudge on them.

She dressed even more carefully than usual, in a plain brown-flowered jaconet gown and demure fringed cream shawl. She pulled her hair into its tight bun, making sure not one curl escaped to mar the smooth outline of her face, and pinned on a simple yet smart chip straw bonnet with brown velvet ribbons. She looked at herself in the cheval glass and gave a satisfied nod.

Proper. Almost elegant.

She was still a plain miss, but she was a well-dressed plain miss who knew how to conduct herself as a lady should. She would marry well, yet. Her parents would be accepted into the *ton* along with her, and they would all live happily ever after, just like in the fairy stories.

A little after sunrise, a knock sounded on her door, and she opened it to a chorus of glum voices: the ABC's.

They were dreadfully put out at not having been allowed to see the race, and they complained bitterly, for she'd had little time with them since the arrival of the guests.

"Even Uncle Sin has abandoned us," Alyse said, and stuck out her lower lip. Marianna noticed that she had at least made an attempt to brush her long, dark hair.

"Yes, he went hunting early this morning, with some of

the men from Town." Beatrice scowled and picked at her fingernail.

Framed in blonde curls, Eleanor's little face was full of concentration as she attempted to copy her sisters. She scowled, picked at her fingernails, and stuck out her bottom lip as she said, "Mr. Montescue said they will not be back till after dark."

"A rat deserting a sinking ship," Marianna muttered. How dare he leave her alone to fend for herself after what he'd done to her yesterday? She could fancy him starting off that morning, leering up at the sleeping house in fiendish delight. He knew very well what a coil he was leaving her to face all alone.

"What ship?" Beatrice asked. "And how did it get so stinky?"

Marianna smiled and ruffled the girl's long, dark curly hair, and then distracted the three sisters by allowing them to open the box sitting on her dressing table.

The four of them shared exclamations of delight when the top came off the box, revealing a breathtakingly lovely gown. The last of the gowns she had ordered, it was fashioned of layers of snowy muslin, with an overskirt of deep blue silk. She examined it along with the girls and decided it was almost too fancy for a country supper. It looked more like a ball gown. Oh, but it would look lovely on her, and she tried to find some pleasure in imagining the compliments she would receive when she wore it. Again, the idea that one of the gentlemen here at Trowbridge would soon be her husband startled her. She tried to fancy what the faceless young lord would say to her when he saw her in the gown, what compliments he might whisper, the forbidden longing she might glimpse in his eyes as he lifted them to hers after bowing over her hand. But the lovely daydream was spoiled, for the only face she could conjure was Truesdale's, wearing the same impudent grin he'd worn after the race.

A sudden thought occurred to her.

If he'd forced her to race in order to taste his way of life for a moment or two, perhaps it was time True Sin got a taste of his own medicine.

"Come, girls," she said. "We have a ball to plan."

"A ball?" the three cried. "Here? When?"

"Tonight," Marianna said with satisfaction.

Fourteen

Darkness stole over the countryside, quieting man and beast.

True was grateful. He was tired. Tired from shouldering his gun all day, tired from walking and riding and crouching, tired from trying to coax some discipline out of his brother's ill-trained hunting dogs. Worst of all, he was tired from having to spend the day with a group of men from the *ton,* eight men who were either trying to best him or deliberately avoiding it so as to endear themselves to him. They were all attempting to become his friend—and to appear to the others as though they already were. It was a deuced nuisance.

All he wanted was a hot bath and eight hours of mind-numbing sleep.

As they turned up the lane toward Trowbridge Manor, a light in the window shone through the tall trees. It was a welcome sight. Then he saw another. And another. His eyes narrowed. As the hunting party neared, the scene resolved into a blaze of candlelight. Every light in the house must be in use.

"What the devil?" he muttered.

The drive was littered with equipages. He recognized several of them. There were Sir Quincy's fine coach and a carriage belonging to a pair of spinsters from the next village. There were Squire Gordon's cabriolet and his sister's ancient phaeton. There were a half dozen other carriages he did not recognize, along with well nigh a dozen smaller wagons and gigs.

True ignored the questions his companions peppered him with and rode to the door in silence. Several grooms and a footman were waiting for them.

"Good evening, my lord," the footman said.

"What is going on here?"

"Why, the ball, my lord." His tone made it clear he thought True knew all about it.

True knew nothing about it. In fact, he was relatively certain no one had known about it when he'd left that morning. A ball took a good deal of preparation, and none of the servants had been doing any extra bustling about that morning as he quit the manor.

One thing was certain: if he *had* known about it, he'd have been sure to put a stop to it.

His empty stomach rumbled.

The footman directed his attention to the rest of the group. "If you will step this way, gentlemen, I will show you to your chambers." The front door was only a few steps away, but the footman did not turn toward it. Instead, he started toward the back of the house, and the men of the hunting party fell into step behind him. Behind their backs, True sneered. *Sheep.* They wouldn't dare be seen in their hunting clothes. They'd all be shown up the back stairs and emerge from their bedchambers washed and pomaded and perfumed and dressed as though they'd been lounging upstairs since noon. He doubted any of them had broken a sweat all day, but they'd certainly all demand a bath at once, nevertheless. The poor servants would be kept busy hauling hot water up the stairs. As though they did not have enough to do with a ball in full swing! Well, True would have none of it. He wasn't going to creep up the back stairs of his own house like a thief in the night. No, he was bloody well going to walk in the front door.

He'd make efficient use of the basin and ewer instead of taking a bath. It wasn't even that much of an inconvenience. He'd certainly made do with less than that aboard ship any number of nights, after days when he'd got dirtier, sweatier, and more tired than he was now. He wasn't going to perfume and dress and parade downstairs with the rest of them. Hell and blast, he wasn't going to attend the ball at all! No, he was going to bed. Mistress Mary would not be happy about his absence, but she should not have sprung a ball on him.

He marched into the front hall—and stopped.

She was there, waiting for him.

"I knew you would not go with the others," she said.

"So," True said, taking off his gloves, "you are here to bar my way?"

She did not bother to deny it. "You cannot go up the main stairs. Everyone in the ballroom would see you."

"Everyone in the ballroom knows I have been out hunting since before dawn this morning. Everyone knows I am dressed in hunting clothes, that I am tired, that I am dirty. If I suddenly appear dressed in black-and-whites, they will know I used the back stairs. Do you not see how ridiculous that is, Mary?" He raked his fingers through his hair. "Can you not see how ridiculous it makes you? I thought you were more . . . more logical than that."

She recoiled from the remark as though struck. "Ridiculous or no, it . . . it is the way of Polite Society."

"Polite Society! Bah! Half of them have not the first idea of what the word 'polite' really means, and the other half does not care."

She stared at him as though he'd grown four extra eyes, and True realized he'd made a grave mistake. Sharp set, weary, and irritable as he was, he had put his foot in it. He'd told her how he felt about her precious *ton*.

He shrugged. In for a penny, he might as well kick for a pound.

"Mary," he said, "the society you aspire to is anything but polite. I just spent the entire day in the company of men who would give their best friends the cut direct just to be seen standing next to me at a ball or a rout. And their wives! Do not ask me what their wives would be willing

to do to be seen with me. Mary, they have not the first idea
what it really means to be polite. They pretend to be polite,
but it is a jolly thin veneer, indeed. I will not go in there
and pretend with them."

"But you are their host!"

"No, I am not. I did not invite them, you did. Without
consulting me. Which means that you shall reap what you
have sown."

Her eyes flashed with angry fire.

She was dressed in a graceful ball gown of white and
deep blue with satin ribbons tied in tiny bows and rows of
lace scallops. Her hair was shot with more of the blue ribbons intertwined with tiny white rosebuds. Her slender arms
were encased in long, white gloves. "You look lovely," he
said, leaning insolently against the door frame. "You should
be angry more often. It makes your eyes sparkle." She
flushed and blustered. "Now," he said, "if you will excuse
me, I am weary, and I'm going to bed." He turned his back
on her and started for the stairs.

She laid a gloved hand lightly on his shoulder, stopping
him. "You cannot," she said quietly. "For the girls' sake,
you *must* not."

"What do you mean?"

She dropped her hand. "What you do tonight will affect
the girls' reputations among the *ton*. You could be playing
host to their future in-laws this evening."

"Unlike some people, I do not aspire to marry my
charges off to titles."

"Then whom do you wish them to marry? Tonight's company isn't made up of just the *ton*. Most of the guests are
from the neighborhood. Most of the families who live
within a half day's ride of Trowbridge Manor are repre-
sented. The ABC's must have somewhere to look for husbands. They have got to find a place in some society, be it
Town or country—unless you wish them to marry one of
your sailors."

He opened his mouth to spit out a terse reply, but there
was nothing to say. She was right.

"That," he said slowly, "is the only argument you could have offered me that would compel me to attend."

"I know," she said simply.

He saw the hint of a triumphant smile ghost across her features and knew instantly that she'd planned the whole thing. "Why have you done this?" he asked.

"My lord," she answered, "yesterday you forced me to experience life from *your* perspective."

"And you are doing the same for me, I suppose?"

She nodded. "Except that instead of forcing you to taste spontaneity and imprudent behavior, I am forcing you to sample responsibility and propriety. I knew you would not let the ABC's down." She smiled beatifically and glided past him. "Do not take long to dress," she said.

Her white-gold hair was piled in curls high atop her head. One errant wisp fell as he watched, trailing down her nape and across her milky shoulder and back. He had a sudden urge to kiss her there, where the shiny curl brushed her skin, to loosen her hair and let it cascade down her back in waves of silk. Dressed as she was in a gown whose color reminded him of the deep blue of the open sea flecked with foam, she was almost beautiful.

And he was almost a lunatic.

He regained his senses as he washed and dressed upstairs. He ruined four cravats trying to tie the blasted things properly. By the time he descended the stairs in his black-and-whites, his neck itched and he was thinking quite clearly again.

Every man in his ballroom had an itchy neck, and yet, contrary to what was reasonable, every man still wore a blasted cravat. And the women! They still wore stockings and garters and drawers and stays and corsets and God only knew what contraptions under their gowns. They blackened their eyelashes with soot, they rubbed arsenic on their white skins.

He shook his head as he came off the stairs. No. Not all of them did such things. Mary was naturally pale. Pale, colorless, and uninteresting, he told himself. A milk-and-water miss. No wonder she was attempting to catch a bachelor's eye here in the country. In London, she would be lost among the crowd. Transparent and unnoticeable.

And yet, somehow, amid the dazzling swirl of rainbow colors in his ballroom, True's eyes found Mary immediately. And True wasn't the only one who had noticed her. She was standing in the center of a cluster of young men. He looked from one face to the other, noting various degrees of fascination, admiration, and . . . and lust.

He tugged his gloves on and moved purposefully through the ballroom. As people noticed him, a wave of silence descended upon the company. As host, he would have to make an opening speech, though the ball had clearly been underway for quite some time. He gained Mary's side and executed a crisp bow, then smiled up at her.

"Good evening, my dear," he said as though they'd not spoken a half hour before. "You look lovely." He straightened and held out his arm. Wordlessly, she took it, and he led her to the dais at the end of the room. Turning, he scanned the crowd. He recognized most of the faces staring back at him. He glimpsed wonder in their expressions. Wonder or skepticism. Most of them had never seen him dressed so formally.

"Ladies and gentlemen," he began, "thank you for attending our little gathering this evening. My apologies for the short notice. It was unavoidable. I wished—*we* wished," he said, gazing down at Mary, "to include as many of you as possible upon this occasion. We wanted to be here at Trowbridge, among those who lived near home, when we announced our betrothal."

The room exploded into applause. For most of the company, it was not an unexpected announcement. The news of Mary's stay at Trowbridge Manor would have traveled from house to country house with the servants, but all of the country folk pretended they'd not had the first inkling until then, anyway. Most of the *tonnish* expressions, however, showed genuine shock, for, in spite of the hint he'd given them several days before, it had not occurred to them that

True Sin would ever really wed anyone. He knew they'd harbored speculation Mary was a kept woman attempting to masquerade as a housekeeper or some such nonsense.

He smiled.

If, where the *ton* was involved, his goal were to do the unexpected thing, True had accomplished that in glorious fashion this evening, for the respectable thing was the last thing the *ton* expected True Sin to do! Mary had unknowingly given him the means by which to nettle the *ton*. He would be a pattern card of respectability and politeness—until his next Town ball! He nearly laughed out loud in anticipation.

He stood politely by Mary's side as they were congratulated and wished happy, and then he fetched her some refreshments before politely requesting the pleasure of a dance. He was satisfied to see more than one set of raised eyebrows, and he chuckled.

They moved onto the floor. The set formed for a country dance, and they went through their figures, weaving in and out of the two long lines of couples until they got to the end and had a moment to talk. "Does my behavior meet with your approval, my dear?"

"You know it does. They all believe I have reformed you."

"Perhaps you have," he said, "for now."

She shook her head, her errant blonde curl swaying over her shoulder. "You cannot fool me. I have only tamed you, my lord. And like any wild creature, you can go back to being wild in the blink of an eye."

"Aye." He bowed and brushed his lips over the back of her gloved hand. "I could, for instance, pull this glove from your hand and kiss your fingers . . . your palm . . . the inside of your wrist. I could sweep you into my arms and devour your mouth like a starving man."

He looked into her eyes and was struck suddenly by their color—a clear, lovely aqua, the color of a tropic sea atop a bed of snowy white coral. It was a deep, pure blue, all the more beautiful when set against the rosy glow of her blushing cheeks. She was certainly not colorless now.

She swallowed reflexively. "You could do those things," she said. "But you will not. Not when the reputations and the welfare of the ABC's are at stake."

"Cunning."

"I beg your pardon?"

"Cunning," he repeated. "I am adding it to my list."

"What list?"

"I keep a short mental list of a person's attributes in my head to keep me from being taken off guard."

"Does it help?"

"In your case," he drawled, "not yet. You keep surprising me. You are a stunningly intelligent woman, Mary." He straightened. "And a beautiful one."

"You lie."

It was time to take their places in the set once more. The steps separated them. True was glad, for a denial had come to his lips unbidden, a denial he did not want to face, much less to utter. For, at that moment, Mary Grantham really had seemed beautiful.

He glanced down the long line of dancers. Her deep blue gown was quite fetching against its snowy relief of white skin, lace, and pearls. But it was not the gown that drew his eyes, it was her face. In the last half hour, he'd seen her wary, angry, proud, defiant, strategizing, pleading, and triumphant, all at once. She seemed different tonight, somehow.

And I must be more weary than I thought.

He stole a glance at her. She was smiling now, genuinely pleased that she had outwitted him. Inexplicably, True felt a bolt of happiness surge through him, too.

He scowled. Why should he feel anything but rancor? He should be thunderously angry with her. But he wasn't. He felt curiously off balance. And the rest of the evening did nothing to help him regain his steadiness.

* * *

Ophelia sat in an odd corner and affected the appearance of being overwarm. Her fan, which she'd had made of a famously expensive silk, was wonderfully transparent when the light was positioned just so. It had been unfurled and in front of her face for most of the evening, and she had been able to stare directly at everyone without anyone knowing. Just then, she had her eyes on Orion Chase, the Earl of Lindenshire.

In spite of his admirable devotion to fashion, Lindenshire was a serious young man, and right then he was serious about Marianna. He'd had mooncalf's eyes for her from the hour they'd met, and unless Ophelia missed her guess, Marianna had confided in him. He was peering at the gel myopically from an alcove near the rather inexpert musicians.

Ophelia rose from her chair in the corner and moved to his side. He didn't even notice her.

"You could see her much better if you used your quizzing glass," she said.

Lindenshire glanced over at Ophelia and then down at his hands. "Am I being that obvious?"

"Yes."

His face registered embarrassment. "Your charge is a fine young lady."

"Come now, we both know Marianna is no more my charge than I am a slave to fashion." She patted her gown, which, except for its high waist, was unlike anything in the Trowbridge ballroom—or any ballroom, for that matter.

He let the first part of her comment slide past, which told her that her guess was correct: Marianna had confided in him.

"Madam," Lindenshire said, "an Original does not have to dress in the first stare of fashion to be considered *au courant*."

"An Original? Is that what they call me?"

He nodded.

She lowered her voice. "Is that what they are calling Marianna now, too?"

He smiled. "Since yesterday's race, I have heard the word seventeen times, from six different mouths."

Ophelia returned his smile. "Good. Just good."

They both returned their attention to the rest of the room. Marianna was sitting amongst a group of ladies—all smiles, Ophelia noted with satisfaction and then sought Truesdale. He was standing in a knot of gentlemen—mostly men from the country, and, for once, not every face was directed at him. This ball was turning out to be a complete success.

"Would you care to dance, Mrs. Robertson?" Lindenshire asked at her elbow.

Startled, Ophelia almost dropped her fan. "Thank you for asking, but I do not like to dance, my lord."

"Thank goodness. Neither do I."

They laughed together, and at that moment Ophelia felt sorry for Orion Chase. Clearly, the dear boy pined for Marianna, but it was Truesdale who had the upper hand.

Truesdale . . . Ophelia gazed at him and smiled a secret smile.

Marianna was just attempting to answer a question concerning her nonexistent wedding plans when she saw a flash of white at the tall, glass terrace door. She thought it was an owl, or perhaps a stray dog, but then she saw another. And another.

One, two, three . . . oh, dear!

Suddenly Alyse's round face popped over the bottom edge of the glass. She looked directly at Marianna and crooked her finger before disappearing once more.

Marianna left the cluster of ladies in haste on the excuse of visiting the ladies' retiring room, but she slipped down the back stairs and out onto the lawn instead. Stealthily, she crept up the terrace steps and peeked over the railing.

Just as she thought.

Three little girls, hiding behind a potted holly, were peering furtively into the ballroom.

"How many people do you think are in there?" Beatrice whispered to her sisters.

Eleanor shrugged. "I cannot count that high."

"Are you certain we have enough, Alyse?" Beatrice asked.

"Certain," her sister confirmed. "A crockful is a good many when they are spread over the floor."

"Think she'll leave?"

Alyse's voice took on a gleeful tone. "Oh, yes! In a minute she shall be dancing so fast, she'll have to go back to London for a month to rest her old bones."

They giggled.

"Whom are we targeting this time?" Marianna said behind them, attempting to infuse her voice with the appropriate interest.

"Smelly old Lady Allen," Eleanor supplied, wrinkling her small nose, but then she brightened. "She doesn't like spiders. She said so!" She clapped happily and pointed to a small earthernware crock right under Marianna's bench. "So we're going to chase her away with those."

"Oh."

Truth to tell, Marianna did not like Lady Allen any more than the girls seemed to. Even less, more like. The young widow had not been invited to stay at the manor, coming along as a surprise guest of another guest. It was bad form, a breach of manners that might have been overlooked, were Lady Allen any more pleasant than she was.

Lady Allen—who did not like spiders, children, or washing, it seemed—complained about everything. Nothing was good enough—most especially the ABC's. Marianna had quite come to dislike her.

"Well," Marianna whispered, bending toward them conspiratorialy, "if you are trying to chase Lady Allen away, I can think of a much better place to deposit the spiders than the ballroom." *Which would be a complete disaster,* Marianna added to herself.

Alyse and Beatrice traded looks.

"Where?" Eleanor asked.

"Come with me," Marianna said, and led the way.

True tried to observe the scene with cool detachment, but as host he could not avoid being drawn into first one cluster and then another. He resisted participating in their conversations and even listening at all, but he found he could not avoid their bibble-babble entirely without appearing rude. Thank goodness they were none of them addressing him, he thought. But then his luck went aground.

"I hear from my housekeeper," Squire Gordon finally said, turning to True, "that you are affecting some changes here at the manor, Trowbridge."

"Indeed," said another, "my man Thomas says to me this morning, 'The master's making everyone toe the mark up to Trowbridge Manor.' I could hardly believe it, but now I see for myself, I am satisfied it is the truth."

True was unaccustomed to such plain speaking outside the docks. It just was not done in Town.

" 'Pon my honor," Squire Gordon agreed, "it is fine to see the place looked after at last."

Sir Quincy coughed. "Is that corn I see from the lane, planted in your north fields, Trowbridge?"

True nodded.

"Ain't it rather risky to plant there instead of on the flats closer down the valley? I should think the crop will wither up where you put it."

"Aye." Squire Gordon nodded. "I mind your father's steward putting in a crop there that would not grow. Sickly plants. Leggy and pale. A total loss."

True nodded. "I had my brook damned. Diverted a small flow of its water to that field. And my steward suggested the addition of burnt seashell and seaweed." True explained about how the soil was prepared.

"Seashells in the soil?" Sir Quincy said, fingering his

snuffbox thoughtfully. "Your steward is rather young, ain't he?"

True nodded. "He has just finished his education."

"Education?"

"Mr. Montescue went to university in Edinburgh."

Bringing any outsider into the neighborhood was bad enough, but a Scot? True waited for the inevitable protest to erupt but was pleasantly surprised. The only remark was made by Squire Gordon, who did not see how a university education qualified a man to manage crops.

"Still," the squire's nephew commented, "the Trowbridge corn is bushy and green, and you cannot find fault with results like that." ·

Murmurs of agreement and congratulation accompanied nods and a firm handshake or two. True couldn't help feeling a stab of pride for their esteem. He *had* been putting a great deal of work into the estate, and it felt good to be recognized for it.

But there was something else True found himself enjoying as the conversation went on and the men plied him with questions. They were not just asking his advice about how to bed women, as men usually did. No. They talked of planting, shearing, market conditions, and the proper way to handle squabbles between servants. And they were actually asking True's opinion on these things.

Him! *True Sin.*

More than once, he glanced up to see Mary gazing in his direction. Invariably, she gave a little smile before looking away. He had to admit that what she'd done had worked. He was surprised at the reaction his modified behavior and dress elicited from his guests—and at how their unaccustomed deference made him feel. Throughout his life, the people surrounding him had always regarded him with horrified fascination, never with respect.

Then again, he had never acted respectably before now.

Mary had to have known he would be thunderously angry when he found she'd cornered him, forced him to partake of the ball. And yet she'd lain in wait for him at the front door and faced him down like a leopardess.

He didn't know whether to add "courageous" or "reckless" or "vengeful" to his list first, so he added all three. He glanced up for another look at her, but she was no longer in the same spot. *Where is she?* He looked about the ballroom, but she was not there. He asked a servant to locate her, and the footman came back with the report that she had been seen slipping out the back door.

True strode outside with narrowed eyes. What the devil was she doing outside at this time of night, during a ball? His eyes lit upon the stable yard. John hadn't shown his face at the ball and was probably hiding out in the stables. True imagined she was probably paying the old man a visit.

But no, she wasn't there.

True had just turned to go back to the ballroom, when he caught sight of a faint light in an upstairs window. Far below, the ABC's were attempting to hide in the bushes with little success.

True took the back stairs four at a time.

He knocked softly on the door of the appropriate chamber. There was no answer. "Mary?" he whispered. "Mary, I know you are there."

The door opened at once, and she emerged, her finger to her lips. In her hand she had a small earthen jar. She scurried toward the back stairs and motioned for him to follow, but she stopped before going outside. "Spiders," she whispered, pointing to the crock. "The ABC's were going to use them to chase Lady Allen away, so I put them in her closet drawers."

"You what?" he said incredulously.

"Shhhh . . . !" She warned him and grimaced. "Believe me, it was better than their original plan."

"Which was?"

"To release the spiders into the ballroom."

"But you discovered the plot in time to stop them."

She nodded.

"Then why," he asked, "did you not simply banish the spiders to the wood and the ABC's to their beds?"

She answered him with a question of her own: "Would you prefer to know about their nefarious plans before they execute them or after?"

He softened his expression and then crooked into a deliberately wry smile. "Your logic is impeccable."

"I must say," she said with a laugh, "I am relieved you agree. Now . . . I must herd the ABC's to bed before anyone discovers them awake, and you," she told him sternly, "must return to your guests."

"Are we wunning away?" Eleanor asked the next morning as Marianna ushered her and her older sisters out of the house in the predawn stillness.

"No, silly," Alyse answered her. "We're going to go build a house. Right, Marianna?"

"Quite so, darling."

"But we don't know how to build a house," Beatrice said with a yawn, "and I want to go back to sleep."

Marianna hugged the girl. "Sleep will be the furthest thing from your mind when we get to the Smith cottage." The Smiths were a farming family whose cottage had burned to the ground the week before. Last night she'd learned the poorest folk from all around, all the world and his wife, would converge on the Smiths' place to help them raise a new cottage this day. Marianna thought it a wonderful opportunity for the ABC's to meet some of the local children and to practice their new manners. "There will be other children to play with and lots of good things to eat," she said, patting the large basket she carried. "I have here fruit pies, meat pies, cheese, and bread." The girls looked hungrily at the basket, all three licking their lips, and Marianna smiled.

They walked along companionably, the girls exploring here and there, but never ranging too far away from Marianna, until she noticed that they were lagging quite far be-

hind her. When she looked back to check on them, the three
had their heads together. It appeared as though Alyse were
whispering something, and, as Marianna watched, Beatrice
and Eleanor both flicked furtive glances in her direction.
Beatrice nudged Alyse, who looked up and smiled. All three
girls ran to catch up with Marianna.

Beatrice, easily the boldest of the three sisters, laid a
hand on Marianna's sleeve. "Marianna, we—"

"*Miss* Marianna," Alyse corrected her.

"Miss Marianna . . . we want to tell you about our
names now. About why C and D are missing."

"Very well," Marianna said.

Beatrice held Alyse's hand and Alyse took Eleanor's.
Then Beatrice said, "We had two more sisters, Cassandra
and Delilah. Baby sisters. Twins. But they died."

Alyse's gaze dropped to the dry, rocky lane. "We did it.
Made them die."

Beatrice refused to drop her gaze and looked Marianna
steadily in the eye, but her chin quivered as she said, "We
wanted the babies to be boys, and we asked our mother to
give them back to the angels. We wanted her to trade them
for two boy babies."

"But all they got was me," Eleanor said miserably. "I'm
s'posed to be two boys!" She began to cry. "They did not
want me!"

Alyse and Beatrice exchanged guilty looks and then they
began to cry, too. Marianna knelt and gathered the three of
them into her arms. "Oh, my poor beauties . . . !" She
rocked them together in her lap, right there in the middle
of the lane, tears cascading down their cheeks. "Alyse and
Beatrice, darlings, you had nothing to do with your sisters'
deaths." Gently, she reassured them. "And, Eleanor, dearest,
your sisters love you. They would not trade you for a dozen
fine boys now." Alyse and Beatrice wailed their agreement
and continued to cry.

Marianna held the girls as they sobbed into her bodice
and skirt. According to Truesdale, they hadn't cried when
their parents died. Certainly they hadn't mentioned it to her,

not once. But now that the floodgates of their tears had opened, their anguish seemed to come from a deep place, a hidden well of sorrow, and she suspected it had more to do with the loss of their parents than it did their baby sisters. Whatever the reason, Marianna made no attempt to stanch their tears. She held them, stroking their hair and crooning softly to them, inventing a lullaby about all five ABC's playing together in Dreamland.

In truth, she felt tears pricking her own eyes. She would exit the girls' lives very soon. She had become attached to them quickly, and she'd been attempting to console herself with the thought that she would help them all she could while she was there—and with the idea that perhaps they would not slip from her life forever. One or all of them might still marry within the *ton*. If that happened, then Marianna could renew her acquaintance with the sisters. But that would be years from now, and Marianna was all too aware that her time with them *as children* was coming to an end. It saddened her, and as the girls quieted and she kissed them and cleaned their faces, she pondered why it should. After all, she had not formed such an attachment to any of her charges at Lady Marchman's School for Young Ladies. Certainly she had cared for them, but she did not mourn their absence from her life as she knew she would the ABC's.' What was it about these children that was different? She did not know.

As the sun rose, its rays turned the dewy spiderwebs that dotted the lane into festoons of diamonds. Beatrice soon complained of her feet growing tired. The Smiths' place was halfway to the next village, perhaps a league's distance and quite a trek for the little ones, but Marianna soon turned it into a game and a lesson at the same time, challenging the girls to see how many different sorts of spiders they could spot. They were soon absorbed in the game and ambled happily along, picking wildflowers and chattering about playing with the other children, apparently quite carefree. Marianna wished she could be as unconcerned as they.

In truth, she was apprehensive over how the four of them

might be received at the Smiths' place. Marianna was an outsider, even if everyone did think she would soon be mistress of Trowbridge Manor. And the ABC's . . . well, they were still the ABC's. Their reputation for mischief was not restricted to the Trowbridge staff. What if the other children shunned them? Or—worse—were not allowed to play with the girls at all?

Then the thought occurred to Marianna that their parents might shun her, too. They were not of the *ton,* after all. They had no hope of ever attaining that level of social status. Would they be jealous of Marianna? Would they feel her so far above their social station that they would not interact with her at all? She had already decided that she would fold up her sleeves and help wherever she could, but would they let her? Would she be welcome? Or would she find herself walking back home the same hour she had arrived? And how would she explain that to the ABC's? Poor darlings! As up in the boughs as they were with the prospect of playing with other children, they would be crushed.

She needn't have worried.

While she did receive several curious and several more incredulous glances upon her arrival, an hour later she had already kneaded bread, sliced apples, plucked chickens, and scoured a kettle. Many families had come to help. The children played while the men worked on the cottage and the women worked to prepare a grand meal. By the time the first course of the cottage walls was built, Marianna was hard at work watching the children, who with their rambunctious cavorting had already caused several accidents even before she arrived with the ABC's. Soon, Marianna had them sorted into teams of five, and she organized a day of contests, both physical and mental. The ABC's were quick to suggest a spider identification contest. Marianna laughed and agreed, sharing a covert smile with the ABC's, who hastened to let their new teammates in on their secret.

Everyone was having a grand time.

Until True Sin showed up.

Fifteen

"My lord," called a stout woman not much older than True. She wiped her floury hands on her napkin and nervously tucked back an errant wisp of brown hair as she hurried up the lane to greet him. " 'Tis a pleasure to receive you, though I am afraid we're not ready for such company. We've been living in our barn since the fire, and it's not fit for—for entertaining company." The woman was clearly distressed.

True slid from his saddle and looked more carefully at her. "Eliza? Eliza Church?"

Her raised eyebrows declared her surprise. "You remember my name, my lord? It's been so long. Why, the last time you saw me, you weren't nothing but a—"

"A spoiled and cruel whelp?"

" 'Upon my word!"

"Well . . . it is true, is it not?"

She looked at him with suspicion. "I'm Mrs. Smith now. Married Thomas the year before you left."

"Thomas, the boy my father whipped on more than one occasion for stealing apples from the Trowbridge orchards?"

"That's the one. But he's changed!" she blurted.

"So have I," True said earnestly.

"That's what I heard, but—"

"But you did not believe it?"

She looked down at her hands, clearly unwilling to answer him. "Is there something you need, my lord? Something I can help you with?"

"I was hoping there was something I could help you with, Mrs. Smith." He took from his saddlebag a hammer and hefted it experimentally. "I've never built a house, but I've seven years of repairing ships behind me, and I'm no stranger to wood. Do you think your husband could use another pair of hands?"

Her eyes grew round before she smiled back at him and said, "Yes, my lord, I do believe he could, at that."

True pulled his brown felt hat from his pocket and placed it on his head. As usual, he wasn't wearing a coat. He followed Mrs. Smith up the lane toward the new homesite.

She clucked to herself, "My, my! If this ain't the day for surprises!"

"Surprises?" True asked.

"Beggin' your lordship's pardon, but . . . but first her and now you? Well . . . none of us would have fancied it, never."

"Her?"

"Your lady, my lord." Mrs. Smith pointed toward the west meadow, where True was amazed to see Marianna herding a score of children about like a loving sheepdog. He squinted. Were those the ABC's in one of the little groups clustered about her? It was difficult to tell, for the children were all giggling at something Marianna was saying, clutching each other for support.

"She's good with 'em," Mrs. Smith said, following his gaze. "Kept 'em out of our bonnets and happy all mornin'. She showed up here with your little'uns while the dew was still wet on the grass. Announced she was here to help. And then she tucks her skirts up into her belt and tries to help, sure as I'm standing here."

Something in her tone alerted True. *"Tries* to help?"

Mrs. Smith turned a pained and apologetic expression up to him. "Ladies like her ain't supposed to be good at such things. Nobody blames her. She didn't mean a lick of it. We all know she meant to help."

Uh-oh. "What did she do?"

"Sliced the apples."

"That doesn't sound so bad."

"Before we'd had a chance to peel 'em, my lord."

"Oh."

"Then she beat the bread dough like it'd been naughty."

"Beat it?"

"Yes, my lord. 'Twas how she thought kneading should be done. She ruined three loaves before we stopped her. They'll be hard as a rock, fit only for the pigs. But that wasn't the worst of it."

"It wasn't?"

"No, my lord. The last thing she did before we shooed her off to watch the children was to pluck a chicken."

"And?"

A chuckle escaped Mrs. Smith as she said, "It was a live chicken."

True hooted with laughter. *"She tried to pluck a live chicken?"*

Inexplicably, Mrs. Smith scowled at him. Her eyes flicked toward the house and barn. Only then did True notice that his arrival and subsequent hoot of laughter had brought all activity in the wide clearing to a stop. As he glanced their way, the men all took off their caps, the women all dropped a curtsy, and the children just stood and stared.

His laughter wasn't the only sound that had carried. Apparently, his remark about Mary's ineptitude with the chicken had carried over the calm summer morning air as well, for she was the only one moving. And she was moving in the opposite direction. Stomping in the opposite direction, rather.

True flashed a rueful smile at Mrs. Smith. "It seems I have something else to repair before I turn my attention to your new house. Pray inform your husband I will be back as soon as I am able." And True sprinted after Mary, leaving a wake of open mouths behind him. Apparently, viscounts were not supposed to know how to swing a hammer *or* run.

Mary had gained the cover of a copse of trees before he caught up with her in a pleasant little dell. "Mary," he began, "I must apologize. I did not mean to—" Only then did he notice she was weeping. She was turned away from him, but her shoulders heaved and she dashed away a tear.

"Mary. I am sorry," he said.

"They all think I am st-stupid."

"No," he said, taking hold of her shoulders and turning her about.

She shook her head violently. "They think I am the veriest ninny. I tried to help, but I sliced the apples before they were pared and—"

"Mary."

"—and I do not know what I did wrong with the bread, but—"

"Marianna!" True said.

She gaped at him. "That is the first time you have ever used my whole name."

"Do not get used to it," he said with a grin. "Marianna, the people here are glad of your help with the children. Mrs. Smith said so. She said she thinks you are 'plummy good with them.' "

"She did?" She dabbed at her nose with a handkerchief.

"Yes. Your skill with the children surprised everyone. But the biggest shock to them was that you came to help at all."

"Of course I came!" She sounded insulted. "Is it not my duty and obligation as your betrothed to help these people wherever I am able?"

"Indeed," he said with a nod. "Except that no one expects a lady of the *ton* to be able to help at all. Not with any practical matters. They might have expected you to send a servant with a hamper of food—"

"I brought it myself. It was not heavy."

"—or a basket of flowers—"

"Rubbish! What need have they of flowers?"

"—or something equally useless. But they never expected you to help them prepare a meal."

"I did not help them," she said miserably. "I created more work than I saved."

"No. But you tried to help. And that is all that matters to them." A strand of her white-gold hair had fallen from its tight bun. He tucked it behind her ear. "I suspect you have made some friends today, Marianna. I suspect you have impressed and surprised them with your generosity, with your willingness to help." He tipped her chin up with his fingertip. "I know you have surprised me. Again." He gave her a quick kiss on the cheek before turning and striding away from her. He did not want to leave her side. Hell and blast, what he wanted was to lower her to the soft grass of the dell and ravish her delicate mouth until she was aching with the same desire as he was.

"Where are you going?" she said behind him.

"I brought my hammer," he said. "I intend to surprise them, too."

"Well?" Marianna asked, falling into step beside Truesdale as they walked home early that evening. "Do you think you surprised them?"

"Well," he echoed, grinning down at her impishly, "not as much as you did when you tried to pluck that chicken, but . . . aye. I do believe I surprised them." He was leading Journey, and she was leading Farmer Smith's pony, with the girls tucked snugly inside a little two-wheeled cart behind.

Truesdale stretched out his hammer arm and attempted to rub the soreness from it with his other hand, but the ribbons he held hampered him.

"Here, let me take him for you," Marianna said. "Come now, Journey." She took the ribbons and patted the horse's neck, and the huge animal fell into step beside the pony. "How considerate it was of Mr. and Mrs. Smith to insist we borrow their pony and trap. The ABC's were so tired, I was afraid they were going to fall off Journey's back on the way home."

Truesdale looked back at his nieces and Marianna followed his gaze. The three little girls were already asleep, snuggled together with smooth, angelic expressions.

"Amazing," Truesdale said, following her gaze. "I've never seen them so still."

"They played hard today."

"They had a marvelous time. It was wonderful of you to bring them."

"I am so proud of them," she said, glancing down at the girls. "I am certain they surprised a few people today, too. They used their best manners."

"Manners you taught them," he said.

She looked down at her hands and fingered the ribbons. A denial faded on her lips. He was right. The girls hadn't any manners before she'd arrived at Trowbridge. She was proud of them. They had come so far in such a short time. Even Eleanor's speech had improved. "Do you know they had never even met any of the neighborhood children, my lord?"

An angry muscle flexed in his jaw. "Yes. My brother was not the sort to encourage the gentry. Whenever he was in the country, he filled the manor with guests from Town. Their behavior was less than . . . well, it was shocking—to the country folk anyway." He said more quietly, "I am certain they did not want their children mixing with the ABC's, but now"—Truesdale smiled tenderly as he looked at them and then turned back to the lane—"now they have changed."

Something about him looked different today, but she couldn't quite fathom what it was. She studied him, watching as he stretched his arms over his head, the white linen of his shirt binding across his massive shoulders and down his back, where it dove into his breeches. A tiny frisson of feminine awareness made her avert her gaze for a moment, but her stubborn eyes soon found him again. He was splendidly made, from his fine hands to his muscled legs encased in their close-fitting brown breeches. His sleeves were rolled to his elbows, and the setting sun glistened on the dark hair that covered his arms. He'd drawn water from the well and washed before they departed to a chorus of thanks and good-byes, and his hair was still slightly damp. She resisted an urge to pull curls from where they clung to his neck. Unbidden, the memory of that last kiss came to her, and it was as though she could still feel his soft lips against her cheek. It hadn't been a kiss of conquest or desire or deception. It had been a kiss of friendship, of comfort freely given and freely accepted.

"You surprised me today, too," she said.

He turned to her, a question in his expression. "Oh?"

"Your behavior today was incongruous with your past, my lord. I cannot reconcile your scandalous reputation with the man who was sweating and laughing atop the walls of that cottage today. I am not sure I know you at all."

It was true. He didn't just look different, he was behaving differently, too. It had been as though he'd been another man that day.

After the first ripples of his arrival had settled, he had blended into the group of men working on the cottage and become one of them. He had worked as hard as any of them. Harder, even. And he had been good at it. Even she could see that. At first, she'd been expecting him to show the same sort of ineptitude she herself had shown, but he had not. He seemed to have an innate knowledge of mortise and tenon, of how to swing his hammer or hatchet just right to set a pin or trim an edge. The wood was his to command, and command he did.

The men were his to command, too, yet he did not. In what was perhaps the greatest shock of all, Truesdale Sinclair had taken his place as a member of the team, not as its leader. And he'd looked like he was having fun.

In a private moment, she'd explained that she'd told her parents they were not married. She'd told him that they seemed to accept her explanation about his Gretna tale. He'd nodded, and then neither of them had spoken of it the rest of the day. They seemed to have an unspoken truce, one that neither of them was willing to spoil.

At lunchtime, he had come up behind her and grasped her waist, whirling her into the air. She'd braced her hands against his shoulders and thrown her head back, and they had laughed together. It was a rare, unguarded moment, and she'd been sorry when it was over.

She met his gaze once more and let down her guard again. "You know so much about me, but after today I feel I hardly know you. You were a different person out there today. You seem to have three different personas. I know the least about True Sin. Please, Truesdale, tell me something about him."

His eyes consumed hers for a moment, and then he seemed to come to a decision. Taking Journey's ribbons back from her, he sighed. "Where to begin?"

The bees buzzed lazily among the cat's-ears and daisies dotting the fringes of the lane. The shadows slanted over the stone walls and through the hedges and trees, gilding everything a golden pink. The birds had gone to roost and were silent, but the brook, which ran next to the road, flowed over its rocky bed, and a cooling breeze sifted the leaves, creating a pleasant music.

She waited patiently, and finally he spoke.

"For as long as anyone can remember, the men of my family have been known as the Sins," he began. "They ruined serving maids and laughed at the poor. They gambled away vast sums while their tenants went without fuel and food. A few, like my brother, spent money they did not have. Every one of them dallied with any cooperative woman who happened along, as well as some who were not cooperative. Married or not. Outside of their own social circles, their recklessness and cruelty knew know boundaries. They were even cruel to their animals. Journey's hoof was caught when my brother, to satisfy a wager, blinded both himself and his mount and rode the beast through the brook at speed."

"Oh, no . . ."

"That is only one small incident. There were hundreds of others. . . ." He raked his fingers through his hair. "Suffice it to say that the Sins indulged in every vice, and I followed their example."

He stared off into the distance and went on with his story, explaining to Marianna that he had become a sensuous rake, a breakneck rider, a daring gambler. But as the youngest Sin matured, he had discovered one significant difference between himself and the rest of the Sins: a conscience. "I learned to despise the Sins' behavior and the society that fostered it."

"The society? You must mean the *ton*. Surely you do not blame the *ton* for the Sins' transgressions!"

"Mary, the *ton* celebrates such behavior. Celebrates it, fosters it, even demands it." He shook his head and sneered. "Why else would I have spent thirteen years proving to the *ton* that I am not one of them. Look at me," he said. "Do I dress like any gentleman you have ever seen?"

She shook her head. "No."

He sighed. "I wear my hair long and dress more like one of my sailors than a lord. I've escorted ladies no better than they ought to be to the most exclusive balls. I publicly disdain everything the *ton* admires: Almack's, Brummell, Bath, and the prince—nothing is sacred—and still I am invited to every blasted ball, musicale, rout, supper party, and picnic. In distancing myself so infamously, I have succeeded only in fixing the *ton*'s hypocritical fascination. They all want to be seen with me, talking or dancing, but behind my back they still revile me."

Ophelia's words came back to Marianna: *His infamous outrageous behavior has transfixed the* ton. *Where another man may have been scorned and outcast, he has garnered their admiration. . . . Everyone will wish to be seen with True Sin's betrothed.*

And then Marianna remembered the conversation she'd overheard between Lord and Lady Wilkinton, who had been disdainful of Truesdale even as they expressed their delight at being invited to Trowbridge Manor.

"The more outrageous my behavior," Truesdale said, "the more invitations I receive. The *ton* hangs upon my every move. I grow tired of it. Were it not for the ABC's, I would let the vultures descend upon the estate to carry away all they are owed and settle my brother's debts that way. I would leave the empty hulk of Trowbridge Manor to rot or give it over to the servants to do as they wished with it. But I cannot. I cannot allow the ABC's to be sundered from the only home they've ever known. They have already lost too much."

He fell silent for a time.

She shook her head. "I thought you needed money because you had spent extravagantly or gambled too deeply. I am . . . I am sorry. I should not have assumed the worst of you."

"Why not?" he asked wryly. "Everyone else does."

"I do not. Not anymore. You may be quite a wicked sinner, but where it comes to those three little girls, Truesdale, you are a saint."

He flashed her a grateful smile.

"If you could leave Trowbridge Manor," she asked, "where would you go? What would you do? Would you settle somewhere and marry?"

"I would go back to the sea."

"You are a navy man?" she asked, surprised.

He laughed softly. "I can see I was somewhat neglectful of your education. No, I am not a navy man. I own ships."

"Ships?"

He nodded. "The one achievement I am proud of, the one thing the *ton* cannot forgive me for. Seven ships. Six now. One sank with my brother and his wife aboard."

"Dear God."

Truesdale shrugged. "We were not close, as I have said. He was much older than I. Close on twenty years. I must have been quite a surprise to my parents."

"Indeed."

He kicked a stone, sending it skipping across the lane. "When I first broke away from my family, my father pulled all support. I spent time working on a cargo ship. Then my mother died, leaving me a small sum, and I bought my first ship. I worked alongside my men for a couple of years."

He smiled. "That's when I got my first taste of shocking the *ton.* I found it satisfying."

The navy would have been the accepted thing for a second son, but Truesdale hadn't been interested in doing the acceptable thing. He strove for the unacceptable. Dabbling in commerce was distasteful in the eyes of the *ton,* and the more successful he became, the better, to his way of thinking. He'd been shockingly successful, increasing his fleet to seven ships in only a few years. And, while it started off as little more than a way to feed himself while displeasing the *ton,* the business soon became something he was proud of.

"It is something I have done all on my own," he said, "and it keeps many families clothed and fed."

"My father is proud of what he has accomplished as well. It is a shame that it is not quite respectable, is it not?"

"The *beau monde* rewards artifice, sloth, and bigotry rather than honesty, hard work, and cooperation. Is *that* respectable?"

"Are you saying you would turn your back on all good society?"

"My God, Mary. Do you hear yourself? Do you believe that the only society worth aspiring to is the *ton?* How can you have spent the day in the company of these good country folk, how can you have worked and eaten and laughed beside them all day ...nd still believe that the only society worthy of your admiration is the upper ten thousand?"

That wasn't what she meant. Was it? She was at sixes and sevens. "Before I came to London, before I'd worked at Lady Marchman's School or come to Trowbridge or met any of the common folk in Town or here in the country, I did believe . . ." Her voice trailed off as she realized how shallow it sounded. "I did believe the *ton* were inherently superior to everyone else. But no longer."

She paused, carefully constructing her next sentence. "I know my parents are too interested in wealth and position, as you say, but you are wrong about their motive. Their hearts are pure." She held up her palm before he could say anything. "My happiness is paramount to them. They truly do believe the *ton* is superior to everyone else, and they only want the best for me. I will not disappoint them."

"Which means you are still determined to marry a title?" His mouth hardened into a grim line.

"Yes. I seek a titled husband." And then, remembering her refusal of his proposal, she added, "A *tonnish* husband."

They walked the rest of the way home in silence. Marianna felt her last words had opened a rift between them, and she wished she knew how to repair it. She wished the ABC's were not fast asleep in the cart; their chatter would have been a welcome diversion from the ominous silence.

As they neared the house, True tugged the pony's ribbons from her hand. "I will take the trap to the stables and ask John to help me carry the girls to their beds."

"Yes. Well . . . I had best go wash and then see my parents. I made the decision to go to the Smiths' place without telling them. They may be worried at my absence."

"They will not be worried, they will be annoyed."

She scowled at him. "Whatever do you mean by that?"

"I mean just what I have said before. Your parents control you, Mary. You dare no spontaneity. You are a timid flower in a field of thorns, afraid to raise your head lest you be noticed, afraid to assert your own desires. You deny your true nature, your capacity for spontaneity so vehemently that you cannot enjoy a genuine moment of true spontaneity even if you are by yourself with no one to witness it."

"Really!"

Suddenly, he pulled her into his arms, and she found herself being kissed—not by the Viscount Trowbridge, or even by Truesdale Sinclair, but by True Sin. The kiss was unmistakably sensuous and impossibly demanding. When she did not respond, he broke the kiss.

"See?" he said. "You have proved my point."

Sixteen

Marianna was unsure if it was hunger or uneasy dreams that drove her out of bed before dawn the next day. She'd been angry all night, lying awake and thinking of what Trowbridge had said, or falling asleep and hearing his words in her dreams, mixed with her parents chanting the words "duty," and "disloyalty" and "disappointment" over and over and over again.

Just as the first rays of the sun glowed on the horizon, she quit her bed, dressed in haste, and, after a breakfast of cold biscuits and fresh milk pilfered from the kitchen, she escaped the house where True Sin slept. He was not in her bed, not in her chamber, not even in her wing of the house, but he still seemed too near.

The grounds and gardens were little better. They were *his* grounds, his gardens. She thought about taking Dover in order to put more distance between herself and Trowbridge, but she decided against it. Dover belonged to him, too. Instead, her feet led her farther and farther away from the manor. She wandered over fields and through several pleasant copses, following the gentle slope of the valley so as not to get lost. The sun rose higher, and the shadows told her it was well nigh ten in the morning when she came to the brook at the bottom of a wooded dell. She was thirsty, and thinking to take a drink before she started back, she took off her shoes and stockings and waded a few steps into the brook. The cool water was soothing against her tired feet. With the trees crowding the banks, and arching overhead to lace their branches together over the water, the brook was a shady tunnel, wonderfully cool and humid. She bent to take a drink and then straightened, pulling uncomfortably at her damp clothing, which stuck to her skin. All at once, she thought how lovely it would be to submerge herself in the water, but she discarded the notion immediately. Her clothes would become sodden, and she could not return to Trowbridge Manor in such a state.

The obvious solution came to mind unbidden. She could disrobe. She hadn't seen a soul since she'd come away from the estate, and there was no dwelling nearby. No one would see.

Ah, but she couldn't. She shook her head. She just couldn't.

She stepped back up onto the bank and struggled to pull her stockings back on over her wet feet. They itched her immediately.

Unbidden, Trowbridge's words flashed into her mind. He'd said she worried so much about what people thought of her that she denied her own desires even when no one was there to witness it. He said she wasn't honest with herself. That she was timid. That she was afraid.

His words still stung. He'd said them with such conviction. He actually believed the things he was saying.

But he was wrong.

In a moment, Marianna's clothes were draped over the branches near the bank, and she was paddling in the water dressed only in her chemise. But the material chafed at her skin, and she thought of discarding it. Truesdale already had the guests certain she made a regular practice of swimming *sans* clothing. And they weren't there to see her anyway. Not that she cared, she thought defiantly as she undid the buttons of the chemise and yanked the white material from her body. She tossed the garment over another branch and dove self-consciously into the cover of the deep water. She was completely naked now. The water flowed sinuously over her body as she glided through the clear brook. She surfaced and looked around her nervously. Nothing moved.

She chided herself. There was no one around. She was completely alone.

She relaxed and struck out up the brook against the gentle current. The exertion felt good, and she swam for quite a distance before she subsided and let the current float her back to her starting place. If only True Sin could see her now! He would take back every word he'd said about her. She had half a mind to tell him about her adventure in the brook, not that he would believe her. He thought she was some timid flower with no personality, no will of her own.

Why was she even thinking of him? She should be enjoying herself, and here she was, thinking of True Sin. She pushed him from her mind. She wouldn't let him spoil her adventure. No. She wouldn't think of him at all. She would have an adventure and it wouldn't involve him. She grasped an overhanging branch and floated, letting the cool water flow past her, feeling her long hair fan over her back like a mermaid's. She blinked at the sky over the brook, where the sun sparkled through the thick canopy of tree branches overhead, and her eyes followed the sweep of one of them, which leaned so close to the water that she could sit on it if she wanted to.

On impulse, Marianna pulled herself up onto it and walked it, arcing high over the water. She knew what she was going to do before she got to the top. She was going to jump. She was going to stand naked in the top of a tree and then plunge into the water with a glorious splash.

"Who has a lack of a personality now, Trowbridge? Who has no sense of adventure?" she asked. She was poised to jump into the clear, deep water below, when she heard a high-pitched *yip,* and a small fox leapt into the air from high up on the far bank. She watched, amazed, as the animal landed and scrambled down the grassy bank and into the shade of the trees at the bottom of the hollow before crossing the brook almost directly beneath her. It must have sensed her presence, because, wet and dripping, it didn't even bother to shake its fur dry before it disappeared up

the near bank. She was still staring after it when she heard
another sound and froze.

Dogs.

And hoofbeats.

And suddenly a hunting party thundered over the brink
of the hollow!

Down the grassy bank they came, down to the water's
edge, where the dogs cast back and forth along the bank
for the scent of the fox, and the group of mounted riders
all gaped at the sight of Marianna's clothing—wet chemise
and all—draped over the bushes.

Seventeen

She considered climbing higher into the tree. She considered jumping into the water. She considered staying quiet and hoping no one would spot her. She considered grabbing a tree branch and trying to cover herself as best she could.

She considered curling up and dying.

In the end, she didn't have to make a choice. One of the hounds spotted her and gave a yelp, and in a moment the entire pack was baying and jumping at the base of the tree.

"I am not a fox, you stupid dogs! Go away!" she cried, though her voice was lost in the cacophony. A moment later, they did as she requested. One hound caught the scent of the fox and bounded across the water and up the bank after him. The rest followed.

Unfortunately, not one of the riders moved off. No. They were all staring, openmouthed, at Marianna. She felt faint and clutched a branch to keep herself from falling with one hand even as she attempted to cover her ample breasts with the other. As though in a fog, she recognized several faces. The hunting party was from Trowbridge, of course.

"I say," a man intoned as though bored, "where is the Viscount Trowbridge?" Marianna recognized him as the tulip who had harassed her the day the guests arrived. "I should have thought he would be here," he said. "Stroking the swells, perhaps?"

A few of the party had the grace not to laugh at the quip, but many more didn't even make the attempt.

"What are you looking at, Raymond?" a lady at the back

of the pack asked, though everyone knew very well that Marianna was visible to the entire group.

"Nothing, my dear," her husband said, and turned his mount. The rest seemed to gather their wits about them, and most wheeled away and galloped over the hill—though several of the bachelors' gazes lingered a bit longer. Marianna marked them all off her list of possible husbands.

She might as well mark them *all* off, she realized. It was no use attempting to winnow her list of bachelors. She'd be lucky now if *any* of them would take her. This disgrace was the final nail in her social coffin. She would never find a place among the *ton* now. She climbed down from the tree and dressed, tears flowing from her eyes so that she found it difficult to see.

Everything was ruined. *She* was ruined.

It wasn't just that a score of the *ton* had seen her naked, swimming *sans* clothing in the brook. Now the suspicion True Sin had planted in their minds, the idea that he and Marianna had been swimming naked *together,* was all but confirmed.

She made the long walk back to Trowbridge, dreading her arrival. Her heart hammered in her chest as she entered the manor and climbed the stairs to her chamber. On the way, she passed two servants and six houseguests. The servants both averted their gazes. Obviously, the news had already reached them, and they were uncertain what to say or do, or even where to look. The houseguests, however, suffered from no such malady. Their smiles were large and falsely gay, their voices cheerful. They engaged her in conversation, but their eyes, flicking from one side to the other, told her they had more interest in being seen with her than in talking to her. She was True Sin's betrothed. And now *she* had a notorious past, too.

She held no hope that her parents would remain ignorant of the matter. She was certain they already knew of her disgrace. The houseguests would have rushed to be the first to tell them, just as they had rushed to Marianna's side to tell her of True Sin's many disgraces. She could imagine their eagerness as they told her poor mama and papa how they'd happened upon their daughter naked in a tree.

She could imagine how they'd laughed together as they'd ridden back to the manor. How they'd scorned her even as they planned to pursue her acquaintance for their own social gain. She was nauseated, humiliated. And utterly disillusioned.

Is this how it felt to be True Sin?

Is this what he was trying to make her see?

She was angry, but not at Truesdale. She was angry with the *ton.*

How could she explain that to her parents? Would they understand? Would they listen to her when she told them what she'd learned about the *ton?* Would they believe that Polite Society wasn't so vastly polite after all?

Had she any right to tell them?

They had worked their whole lives so she could take her place among the *bon ton,* the Good Society. How disappointed they would be to discover the Society they sought to propel her into wasn't the pure goodness they thought it was!

How could she do that to them?

The answer was simple: she couldn't.

There were good people among the *ton,* just as there were bad people outside of it. Marianna would still marry within the *ton,* but she would marry a good man, a sensible man, a fair man, an honest man.

An image of Lord Lindenshire sprang into her mind and, along with it, a pain so sharp that she gasped. He was a very proper gentleman. He was a very fashionable gentleman. Young women who swam naked, raced astride, and consorted with True Sin were not proper or fashionable. Lindenshire knew the truth about her, but the rest of the *ton* did not. By all reports, he stood proudly at the very pinnacle of Society. He would never ally himself with her now.

No proper gentleman would. Unless they needed money

very desperately indeed. Debtors' prison or Marianna Grantham—the choice might not be very clear.

Her heart ached at the thought of facing her parents.

She changed her clothes, donning a modestly cut, soft gray cotton day dress, and added a brown shawl and crocheted gloves. Her hair had dried on the long walk back with no benefit of comb. It curled about her temples now. She gathered it, pulled the curl out as best she could, and pinned it once more into a tight bun at her crown.

Her reflection stared out at her from the cheval glass. She did not look different. She looked as though nothing had happened, as though nothing had changed. Yet she knew everything had changed. *She* had changed.

A knock sounded on her door. She opened it to a servant, who brought word that her parents desired the "pleasure" of her company in the winter parlor.

The white and gold room was an apt setting for their meeting. The Granthams' frosty demeanor was evident as soon as she was shown into the room. Her mother sat on a chair, her back rigid and her expression hard, while her father stared out a window. Neither of them bothered to turn to her when she was led into the room and announced. Without being asked to do so, the servant retreated from the room and closed the double doors behind him.

Marianna sat opposite her mother. "Mama, I—"

"Do not speak to me."

Marianna blinked back a tear. She looked down at her hands. "I am sorry," she said.

"You are stupid, that's what!" her father said, rounding on her.

Her mother nodded. "Your reputation is in tatters, and we are being laughed at." She waved her hand in the air, her fingers clutched around a delicate lace-edged handkerchief and shaking with fury. "It was a mistake to send you alone to London. We should have known you were too silly to pull it off all by yourself. First that race, and now you're caught parading about the countryside with nary a stitch on."

Her father stepped up behind his wife. "Daughter, you have sealed your reputation as a hoyden . . . a hussy . . . a . . . a . . ." He cast about for another word.

"A slut," her mother supplied.

Her father's face hardened into a sneer. "Yes. A slut!"

Marianna shook her head, her eyes filling with tears.

"That ruffian you have betrothed yourself to has no reputation to speak of either, but I would not be surprised if you are too much even for him to stomach. If he decides you are too much of a hoyden to marry, then you will be utterly ruined, and we will have sacrificed all for nothing."

A fat tear fell into her mother's lap. Marianna stared at it.

She should have been feeling sympathy for them. She should have been feeling guilt. But she did not. A curious numbness had taken hold of her, and she sat in silence, saying—and feeling—nothing at all as her parents heaped the violence of their words upon her, weighing her down with their disgust and their broken dreams and their angry disappointment.

She remained silent as they castigated her, their words seeming to slur and blend into each other until they were no longer discernible as anything but a droning dirge of pain. She crawled down into a deep well of guilt and shame.

And then, suddenly, her mind fixed upon one word. *Sin.* Her attention resurfaced.

"*True Sin,*" her father seethed. "Do you know he is almost a pauper, daughter?"

Mrs. Grantham nodded. "He owes more than he has. Without us, he would have to sell this house and all he has in it to settle his debts. A title is all we are likely to acquire from the marriage, but he did not tell you that, did he? The blackguard! No. He pretends to love you because he wants our money. That libertine doesn't give a fig about you. He just needed someone brainless enough to marry him."

Gerald Grantham hooked his thumb in Marianna's direction. "They are a good match for each other, I say, since he cannot be quite bright if he wants to chain himself to a gel as witless as that one." He made a rude noise. "He'll likely throw the blunt away on light-skirts or dice. I hear his father and gaffer were just the same. Wasted all they had—two fortunes in the father's case, for he married twice. Heard both of them was the same as you. Heiresses, wed for their money. Neither had more than one child. Both boys. Probably ruined their insides, the evil brats."

"That's enough." Marianna's voice was hardly more than a whisper, and she wasn't sure she'd said anything at all.

Her father hadn't heard her. "I knew he was a dissembler the moment I laid eyes on him. He dresses like a Sunday sailor, the miserable toad."

"That's enough!" Marianna roared, molten anger hardening into a granite resolve. Her parents turned to her, their pinched faces caricatures of shocked silence. She had never dared speak to them with that tone of voice.

She shook off the remaining vestiges of docility as though it were water streaming over her face, and she looked around her, seeing her parents clearly for the first time. "I can bear your spiteful words. Bells in Heaven, I even agree with you about me. I have acted foolishly, imprudently. But when you launch your ire against Truesdale Sinclair, I will oppose you." Indeed, something inside her had broken loose from its moorings.

She stood and lifted her chin. "Truesdale is a good man, a wise man. He is a loving guardian to his nieces and a kind and reasonable master over the servants, and nothing, *nothing* you can say will ever change my opinion of him. He has told me nothing but the truth, while you"—she felt bile rising in her throat—"you have told me nothing but lies."

Her father blustered. "Preposterous! What? What lies have we told you?"

"From the cradle, you made me believe the *ton* was the only segment of society worth being a part. You instilled in me an innate contempt for all other people. I am just like you. And I am ashamed of myself."

"He has poisoned you," her mother said. "That man has been filling you with nonsense."

"He has set me free."

She meant it.

Truesdale was right; she had been enslaved. She'd never tasted freedom before coming to London. Freedom of will, freedom of movement, freedom of choice. Even freedom of thought. Now that she knew what real freedom was, she was unwilling to go back under their yoke. She could not. She *would* not.

In the face of her parents' anger, Marianna was filled with a strange calm. Suddenly, she knew what she had to do. Telling her parents would unleash their fury, not that it mattered. Not anymore.

She looked at her parents and set her jaw before she spoke what she knew would be her final words to them.

True had been up on the slope in the cornfield with the steward. As soon as he heard the news of Mary's disaster, he galloped his horse down to the manor. Throwing his ribbons to a groom, he had run into the house and taken the stairs four at a time. Poor Mary. He knew she would be like a ship on the rocks. He expected to find her huddled on her bed or hearth, sobbing.

He knew it was at least partially his fault, too. He should never have suggested she'd been swimming naked in the first place. And he should never have provoked her. He'd claimed she was timid, that she was unadventurous and un-spontaneous and without a personality of her own. And all the time he knew none of it was true. He should have anticipated she might do something like this. Because of him, because of his foolish provocation, she was ruined—unless he could still talk her into marrying him.

He ran down the hall to her chamber and walked into her room without knocking. He did not care. Propriety be damned! Mary needed protection, needed comfort, and he would be the one to give it no matter the circumstances.

Her chamber was empty. He stilled. Where else would she be?

Blast it to bloody hell and back!

He bounded out of the room and down the stairs. "Where is Miss Grantham?!" he demanded of a surprised servant.

"The winter parlor, my lord. With her parents," he added, but True was already gone, heading for Mary's side. She was in there, and he could guess what she was going through.

She was good and kind and intelligent and spirited. She deserved so much more than she had. She deserved a love match. She deserved a husband who would cherish her for the lovely person she was, a husband who would recognize her special gifts and her inner beauty.

A man like himself, he realized.

The truth hit him like a wild hurricane. He loved her. He wanted her. And he would defend her. He opened the door and surged through it ready to do just that. More than that. He opened the door ready to kneel before her and ask for her hand—not because he needed her gems, but because he, True Sin, had finally found the one thing he could not live without, the one thing he could not scorn. His Mary.

He yanked open the door. She was speaking. Her parents sat staring at her, clearly angry, but just as clearly hanging on every syllable.

True stopped in his tracks and listened, too, for, to his shock, Mary's tone was defiant, matching the burning anger in her eyes.

"Trowbridge and I are not betrothed," she said. "We never were."

Her parents opened their mouths, but she raised her voice. "I will never marry him!" she said, her voice hard. "And even if you can still find some title desperate enough for funds to take me, I will refuse. I will return to the school forthwith and teach to support myself. I will never be forced to wed."

True's heart thudded to a stop.

What a fool he had been! He had thought to charge in

and rescue the fair damsel, when the fair damsel was already rescuing herself—from him. Her words were clear. She would rather face a life of near-poverty and subservience than marry him.

Guilt washed over him. She obviously despised him. And he did not blame her. His seduction of her had ended in her utter ruination. He looked at her, standing so proudly erect before her stony, angry parents.

She had changed.

And, he realized, she was not the only one.

Before she had come into his life, True Sin wouldn't have looked upon her present circumstances with any amount of sympathy. He had believed that the *ton* was flawed and that anyone who aspired to it was beneath him.

The moment stretched into a brittle silence. His heart ached, for he knew she would never accept him. He had been as rigid and as narrow-brained as her parents. He didn't deserve her.

Even though she'd said she would never accept him, True didn't withdraw from the scene. He knew her parents were too cruel or too obtuse—or both—to give Marianna her freedom. She was going to have to fight for it, and, for all her courage, she would need True there.

He was right.

"Where is our jewelry?" her father demanded.

"Your jewelry?" Marianna asked. "Is it not in your chamber?"

"Do not be stupid, girl," Mrs. Grantham snapped. "He means the jewelry we sent with you to London. It was a large fortune, and you have not worn a bit of it. Did you sell it?"

"Where is the blunt?" Her father curled his lip. "Or have you spent it already? Hand it over—or whatever goods you bought with it—or I swear, by God, that I will call the magistrate and have you taken to Ludgate for theft!"

True stepped into the room. All three looked at him in surprise.

"You," he said, looking from Gerald to Violet Grantham,

"will both leave Trowbridge. Now. Or I will personally see to it that you are *never* received in Polite Society. Ever."

"No one has that kind of power," Mrs. Grantham said. "Not even the prince."

True leaned insolently against the back of the sofa. "Try me. Believe me, I would enjoy the sport."

"Oh, so would I!" Ophelia's voice sang from the doorway. She smiled slyly. She sat across from Mrs. Grantham and smiled at her. "Do test it, won't you?"

Mrs. Grantham opened her mouth as though to say something, but shut it again. She flicked a glance at her husband, but got back nothing but a frown. They were outnumbered and outgunned. They clearly did not know how to proceed, what to say. So they said nothing at all.

Marianna looked from True to Ophelia. She could see they were both ready to do battle for her, and she was filled with a strange elation. Tears formed in her eyes. "How could I have ever thought either of you disloyal?" she murmured.

"Because we were," True answered her, his clear, strong voice steady and warm. "Mary . . . Marianna . . . I have something to confess. And, unless I miss my guess, Ophelia does, too." He turned to her and she nodded.

Ophelia's expression was grim, but her eyes seemed to be dancing, and Marianna wondered what she would say. The old woman turned her attention back to the elder Granthams. The pair looked uncertain, and they seemed smaller of a sudden, as though they had shrunk.

Truesdale gave them a look of distaste and then, appearing to come to some sort of grim decision, drew her father aside and spoke—too softly for Marianna to hear.

"What is he saying, Gerald?" her mother asked sharply.

Ignoring his wife and still listening to Truesdale, Mr. Grantham's eyes went wide. A smile split his features, and he turned to his wife. "Take off your jewels."

Mrs. Grantham's hand went to her throat. "What?"

"Take them off. Now. Give them to the viscount here."

"I will not!" she sputtered. "What can you possibly

mean by this, Mr. Grantham? What did that vile creature say to you? How can you ask me to—"

"Take them off, wife, or so help me I will strike you!"

Mrs. Grantham's mouth dropped open, and she sputtered—but she took off the heavy emerald necklace she wore and laid it on the end table.

"All of it," Truesdale said.

"Do it," Mr. Grantham ordered.

She complied with a growl. Three rings, two bracelets, a brooch, and ear drops joined the necklace on the table, and without a word, Mr. Grantham pushed his sputtering wife through the doorway. To Marianna's astonishment, they didn't go upstairs, but walked right out the front door and down the lane.

Marianna turned to Truesdale to ask what he had said to her father, but Ophelia already had his attention.

"Would you like to offer your confession first, or shall I?" she asked.

Truesdale bowed low. "Forgive me, Mrs. Robertson, but what I have to say to Marianna should be offered privately."

Ophelia inclined her head. "Very well, Trowbridge. I shall speak first, but what I have to say should be said in front of both of you." She gave a tremulous smile, and her hands fluttered nervously. She patted the sofa next to her, and Marianna sat.

Ophelia sighed. "I do not know how to say this without being direct." She chuckled. "I do not know how to say *anything* without being direct, it seems." Her eyes held each of theirs for a long moment before she spoke at last.

"I did not marry Mr. Robertson this past spring, as most of the *ton* thinks I did." She smoothed one parchment hand over her pink feathered gown. "No, I married him thirty years ago. I . . . was with child." She looked down at her hands. "Though the babe was not his, Mr. Robertson gallantly offered to marry me. Foolishly, I agreed and soon discovered that Mr. Robertson and I did not suit." She looked down at her lap and a tear rolled down her cheek. She did not bother to wipe it away. "We parted company.

I gave my babe to a woman who could have no more children, and then I worked as a companion to a lady who—as all the *ton* knows—left her entire fortune to me. I was rich beyond my dreams. I lived grandly, and for a time I thought I was happy, but the novelty of riches wore thin soon enough. The time came when I realized I could never wed again. I had lost my only child and alienated my husband. I paid dearly for my foolishness!

"As my position in Society solidified, I was able to make limited contact with my babe's new mother. She and I even became friends. She needed a friend. Her husband was cruel to her—when he bothered to pay her any attention at all, that is. He was always racing about Town or country with his high-flying set, and he wasn't in attendance at the birth of their baby. He never knew it had died. She'd been too afraid to tell him for fear of his blame and cruelty. She was able to keep the poor babe's death a secret—a fact I was then grateful for, for my own infant was accepted without a wrinkle, and I thought everything would turn out well. I even thought I might have some contact with my child, since his new mother and I had become quite close, but it was not to be, for my friend died, and I was cut off from all contact with the child. When next I saw him, he was grown close to manhood, and I was sick at heart because he had become just like his father and the other men in his family."

"You speak of me," Truesdale whispered. "My God. I am your son."

She nodded, misery in her eyes. Tears flowed freely down her face now. "You'd grown up so wild. And then I watched you reject the *ton*—of which I was so firmly a part—I was certain you would reject me, too. I could see the anger in your beautiful eyes. I was afraid to tell you. Afraid of how you would react."

"Ophelia . . . Mother, I—"

Ophelia held up her hand, interrupting him. "Let me finish—while I can." Truesdale subsided with a nod of acquiescence, and Ophelia went on. "You have made no secret of your determination never to wed."

He sat heavily. "I did not want any children. I thought . . . ."

"You thought your wickedness was in your blood."

He nodded. "I was determined that True Sin would be the last Sin."

"I am afraid your particular flavor of wildness did not come from the Sinclairs, but from me, my boy. You can now rid yourself of the notion that you are a Sin."

"I emulated my father's example brilliantly enough," True said and gave a bitter laugh.

"For a time," Ophelia agreed. "Even better than his own true son, I daresay. Yet you always felt different, somehow, did you not?"

True nodded.

"I know. I watched you grow more and more apart from your family, more and more apart from the *ton*. And I ached for you, my boy." She closed her eyes. *"My boy,"* she whispered, her voice catching. "You deserved more than I had. You deserved a loving wife, a family." She shook her head. "And then I met Marianna . . . ." She bit her lip. "Please. Can you forgive me? Can you both forgive me?"

Truesdale didn't hesitate. He walked to Ophelia, knelt, and embraced her. Ophelia sobbed into his shoulder.

Marianna dashed tears from her eyes and glided soundlessly toward the door, intending to leave mother and son to their reunion, but Truesdale stopped her. "Please, Marianna, wait. Ophelia . . . Mother," he said, "pray wait here. I will return."

Ophelia nodded her understanding and smiled tremulously. "I know."

Truesdale ushered Marianna into the library, where she had first met him. That seemed like a lifetime ago now. "What did you tell my father?" she asked.

"It does not signify."

He was right. It did not matter. She would likely never see her father again. She felt a profound sadness, but she also felt an equally profound relief. She stuffed such emotions away. She would take them out to examine them later. "What do you wish to say to me, my lord?"

His broad chest rose and fell. She could see his pulse beating at the side of his neck.

True looked into her wondering eyes and fought to keep himself from falling to his knees before her and begging her to marry him.

He knew she loved the ABC's. He knew she would do anything to save the girls from losing their home. He knew she would offer him her fortune in jewels, and he knew she would do anything to keep him from refusing her offer— including marrying a man she could only pretend to love. She would sacrifice her own security, her own dreams, for the ABC's. And, as much as he loved her, as much as he wished to be her husband, True would not let her. He had to make her leave Trowbridge Manor willingly, with her jewels, and without delay.

He had to lie to her once again.

"Marianna," he began, "I have deceived you. I attempted to seduce you to secure your fortune. I needed the money to rescue my ships and thus the ABC's. But I no longer need your gems. When I left here a week ago, I went to London to gamble. Luck was with me, and I have word this morning that my shipping business has more than recovered. I am before the wind and well on my way to being free of debt. I do not need you anymore."

He smiled. "I release you from our bargain. Your parents' gems—all of them—are yours to keep." He hesitated for a moment and then kissed her cheek and walked from the library and out of her life. He did not look back.

Eighteen

Marianna was on her own. She was free.

Isn't that what she wanted?

She retired to her chamber to pack but soon heard the guests beginning to take their leave. Unwilling to interact with any of them, she stayed in her room all day as the exodus proceeded. She slept off and on, took meals in her room—which Cook delivered herself with a worried smile and a pat on the shoulder. She half expected Orion Chase, Earl of Lindenshire, to ask to speak with her, and she didn't know whether to hope for it or to dread it, but in the end she needn't have fretted either way, for she received no such request. No one else came to speak with her, either. Not True Sin, Ophelia, John, or even the ABC's.

As the sun's rays slanted low over the verdant hills surrounding Trowbridge Manor, Marianna realized she was an outsider here now.

She would leave at first light, return to London, and get on with her life—wherever that might be.

Truesdale would keep their bargain secret, she was certain. He had proved today that she could trust him to protect her as much as he was able. To Society he would convey that they'd cried off their engagement amicably. She shook her head, silently imagining the expressions of intrigued speculation the *on-dits* would elicit among the *ton,* and then an image of Farmer Smith's wife's kind face filled her mind. Marianna sighed.

Unlike the ladies of the *ton,* Eliza Smith would not find

anything amusing about a broken engagement. No, she and the other women of Trowbridge village would feel nothing but dismay when they heard Marianna was not to be the new viscountess after all. They had all been so kind to her on the day of the cottage raising. They'd wished her happy so earnestly that Marianna knew they truly meant it in spite of all the trouble she'd caused them. She'd thought their hearts truly glad for her and the Viscount Trowbridge.

A pang of regret suffused Marianna with sadness. She would never see the women of Trowbridge village again. The memory of the day she spent in their company would fade in time, along with everything else that had happened there, like a pleasant dream, yet she would never forget what they taught her.

One short afternoon had changed Marianna into a person quite different from the one who had come to Trowbridge Manor. Without them—and Truesdale—she might always have had a distorted image of the *ton's* worth. She might have thought being a part of the *ton* the only way to be happy. She knew now that the *ton* was not the only good society, nor even the best society. She knew now that the *ton's* image of respectability and decorum was only a veneer.

But logic also told her that if there were people among the *ton* like Orion Chase, Ophelia, John, and their niece and nephew, Lord and Lady Blackshire, then there must be more people like them. All societies had their good and bad aspects. There were no absolutes.

She awakened frequently all through the night and kept a candle burning. She had only a few hours at Trowbridge Manor left to her; she could not bear to lose them to the obscurity of darkness, even if all she had to look at was her own chamber.

Sometime before dawn, she looked over at her mother's emeralds, which lay gleaming in the candlelight on the dressing table along with the rest of the jewels her mother had abandoned. Sent by Trowbridge to Marianna's chamber around evensong the previous day, the jewels were not a vast fortune, but they would be enough to live well on. Or, she realized, they would make a tidy dowry—though they likely would not be enough of a dowry to compel any of the Trowbridge bachelors to marry her, not after her disgrace at the brook. They were all titled, wealthy, young, and handsome—and Marianna no longer had a vast fortune to inherit, for she had no doubt her parents would cut her out of their will as neatly as she had cut them out of her life.

Still, not all of the gentlemen of the *ton* were titled. If she were willing to settle for a man of meager means and fewer prospects, then she might yet marry into the *ton* in spite of her infamous past. After all, True Sin was a part of the *ton* in spite of his own scandalous exploits. And so was his natural mother in spite of her equally outrageous behavior. Perhaps Marianna could be like them. Still very much a part of the *ton,* yet . . . different.

She inhaled deeply and stretched her arms above her head. She could go where she wished, do as she wished, think, act, and feel as she wished. She should have been bounding about the room in paroxysms of joy. Instead, she was miserable, and as the first rays of the sun painted the sky blue, she at last recognized why. The prospect of achieving a respectable, unremarkable, highly placed and titled social position held little appeal for her now. She didn't want to be a duchess. She didn't want to be a regular patron of Almack's. She didn't want to spend her time hurrying from one ball to another in smoky, crowded London.

What she wanted was Truesdale Sinclair.

What nonsense! She chided herself. True Sin was a libertine, a reckless gambler, a fortune hunter. Had he not admitted to attempting to seduce her for her fortune? Had he not abandoned her in order to hie off to London to gamble money he did not have—her money? And when fortune smiled upon him so that he did not need her anymore, had he not set their bargain to naught and then walked away without a backward glance?

And yet . . . and yet he had said he'd sought her hand in marriage not for himself, but for his nieces' sake. And he had behaved quite gallantly yesterday and as a friend might, all along. He had forced her to see the truth even when it was difficult, even when *she* was difficult, calling him callous and cruel. He had been kind to Ophelia and John, to the servants and to the ABC's. And even to Marianna.

And—oh!—he had kissed her with passion. Passion and tenderness. She brushed the backs of her fingers against her cheek, where he had kissed her yesterday, and closed her eyes. She could not believe he felt nothing for her. She did not want to believe it.

The logical thing to do was to go and ask him, but for once Marianna tossed logic willingly aside. She needed to talk with someone, all right, but what she needed was a mama—something, she understood now, she'd never really had. She tugged on her nightrail and stole into the hall, seeking the next best thing: Ophelia. She knocked on the door softly as the clocks chimed five o' the clock.

"Enter," Ophelia called.

Marianna peeked inside. "It is I, Marianna."

"Come in, dearling." Ophelia sat upright in her bed. A single candle illumined the room. "I have been waiting for you."

"Where is John?"

"The stables, as is usual for him at this ungodly hour. Sit, child, and warm your feet." She patted the pillow beside her, and Marianna curled up against her shoulder. Ophelia pulled a blanket over her and tucked it in. "Tell me," she said, "have you forgiven him?"

"For deceiving me?"

Ophelia nodded. "For lying, for intending to seduce you into marriage from the start."

"You knew?"

"I have known from the first day. I knew very well your bottle of gems was not enough to satisfy his debts. I knew he would have a go at luring you into marriage. Can you forgive him?"

Marianna stared at the candle. "He deceived me in order to provide for the ABC's. He was in danger of losing his ships and Trowbridge Manor. He did not want the girls to be torn away from the only home they have ever known. He said they have lost too much. How could I not forgive so noble a purpose?"

Ophelia closed her eyes, and a smile softened the lines around her mouth. "Indeed." Her eyes opened and fixed upon Marianna. "Do you love him?" she asked.

Marianna hesitated. Did she? Could she really have given her heart to such a rogue? "It would not matter if I did," she averred, "for he clearly does not love me. He said he does not need me or my fortune and has released me from our bargain."

"He has?"

Marianna nodded.

"But what about his ships?"

"What about them?"

"They are still impounded. He stands to lose everything unless he can find a buyer."

"A buyer?"

"Did he not tell you? He has put his remaining ships up for sale. It is the only way he can save Trowbridge Manor. He refuses to take any money from me, though I know he needs the blunt quite urgently. He shall need every last farthing the ships can bring. Why, one of his solicitors came to dun him here at Trowbridge just today. Nasty little man. He said he would be just the first of a mob of creditors who will be descending upon Trowbridge this week. He loudly demanded immediate payment and then threatened the boy with imprisonment!" She thumped the counterpane angrily. "Can you imagine? I am one of the richest ladies in London. Wait until they find out he is my son! Wait until they realize I could—Marianna?" she said, her voice filled with concern, for Marianna's eyes were brimming with unshed tears. "Marianna, whatever is wrong, dearest?"

"He has lied to me again." Her words tumbled out as she repeated Truesdale's parting words to her. "He told me he was almost out of debt and that his shipping business was safe. Why?"

Ophelia laid one hand aside of her wrinkled cheek. "I do not know."

"Come now, dear friend, we both know there can be only one conclusion. He does not want me. After coming to know me, he has decided he would rather sell his beloved ships than be forced to marry me."

"No, Marianna. There must be some other explanation," Ophelia reasoned.

But Marianna shook her head. "Can you think of one?" she asked.

Ophelia bit her lip and frowned. "I wish I could," she said finally.

Marianna kissed Ophelia's withered cheek. "Thank you, dear lady, for everything." She rose. "And pray thank John for me."

"Where are you going?"

"To my chamber to pack my things."

"Oh . . . Marianna! Dearling, you are welcome at our house in Grosvenor Square. Why, you may stay as long as you like. Forever. I have come to think of you as my daughter, and I will treat you as such in spite of my witless son's lack of a proposal."

Marianna smiled sadly. "Thank you, dear lady, but I believe I shall return to Lady Marchman's School—at least for a time. It seems I have a talent for handling children, and I might do some good there." *And if I am busy at the school, I will not have as much time to pine away for True Sin.*

Marianna knew in her heart she would avoid Ophelia and John's grand mansion, even for a visit. She was sure that Truesdale and the ABC's would be spending time there from now on, and seeing them would be too painful for her. It would be a reminder of all she had lost. A reminder of all she never had—and of all she never would have. No, she would never go there.

"I had so hoped . . ." Ophelia smiled sadly. "You will visit us, won't you? John is excessively fond of you. We both are."

Marianna smiled sadly and kissed Ophelia, then slipped from the room at last. As the door clicked shut, she heard a soft intake of air and then a forlorn sob from within. She fled down the hall.

Returning to her bedchamber, Marianna blindly stuffed her new clothing and other belongings into her trunk, thinking to leave as soon as possible. Saying good-bye to Ophelia was horrible enough, but a moan escaped her at the thought of saying good-bye to the ABC's. Why hadn't they come to see her? She was sure they'd been purposely kept away. If they saw her before she departed Trowbridge, they would ask when they would see her again. Marianna knew it would be a very long time—or never.

It would be kinder to the girls if she just let their memories of her fade into the obscurity of their pasts. It would be kinder to them this morning if she were simply to slip away into the thick morning fog.

She took the time to write a carefully worded letter to them and then dressed in a faded blue-flowered calico that reminded her of her meadow of bluebells. She would never see that meadow again. With a last look around, she quit her chamber, a small portmanteau in hand. She would leave Trowbridge Manor immediately and send for her trunk later.

She walked down the stairs to the grand entry hall for the last time. There would be other meadows, she told herself, and other little girls. But she did not believe it.

There was only one thing left to do. She ducked into the parlor and, taking down the little porcelain box from the mantel, replaced the Trowbridge ruby, the ring Truesdale's adoptive mother had worn, the ring that would never be hers. She put the box back onto the mantel. She had only

to walk out the front door and down the lane now, and her
time at Trowbridge—no, her entire youth, she realized—
would be done with. Her hand lingered upon the box, upon
her past, for a few last, precious seconds, and she stood
there, remembering how tenderly Truesdale had held her
hand when he'd placed the ring on her finger.

And then a movement reflected in the gleaming surface
of the box caught her eye. A figure entered the room behind
her. A man. Her heart pounded and her knees went weak,
and she chided herself for such a reaction. There was no
reason for her to feel that way. She did not love him, after
all. She *would not* love him. What did it matter that he was
here to witness her leave-taking? He would wish her well.
Perhaps he would shake her hand. He certainly would not
sweep her into his arms and kiss her as he had done before.
There was no need for that now. He'd been deceiving her
then, trying to make her think he truly wanted her. He'd
been bent upon seduction. But no longer.

She affected a pleasant smile and turned to face him.

It was Lord Lindenshire.

"My—my lord!" she stammered.

"Did I frighten you?"

She nodded. "I did not expect—"

"I have been waiting for you to come downstairs," he
interrupted her and nodded toward her portmanteau. "Are
you leaving now?"

She nodded.

"May I have a word with you first. In private?"

"Certainly."

Lindenshire turned to close the parlor doors, and mild
shock coursed through Marianna. What could he have to
say to her that required such an impropriety? She willed
her heart to stop beating so fast.

It was easy to see why she had mistaken him for Truesdale. Lindenshire was well nigh the same size as True Sin,
and he was dressed much as Truesdale had been the previous morning, in buff-colored trousers and brown coat. But
Lindenshire was wearing a perfectly tied cravat, a bang-up-

to-the-mark striped and embroidered black satin waistcoat buttoned all the way, and black Hessians that were polished to a shine, while a pair of spectacles sat atop the bridge of his nose and curled over his ears.

"I did not know you wore spectacles."

"I do not, if I can get away with it. I detest the blasted things, and I wear them as little as possible. But a quizzing glass, while quite fashionable," he said, lifting the single lens that hung from a cord fastened to his coat, "is not the best at helping one see clearly. Did you not wonder at my seeming fascination with the library spyglass? Pray, sit," he said, not waiting for an answer to his question, and Marianna took a place on the sofa.

Lindenshire sat in the adjacent wing chair. "Miss Grantham, Lord Trowbridge sought me out last evening. He told me what had transpired between you and your parents. He told me everything, in fact."

"Did he tell you what he said in private to my father?"

Lindenshire nodded. "He did. And that is what I wish to speak to you about."

"Oh?"

"He told your father that I wished to marry you."

"Bells in Heaven!" Marianna could feel her face heat as she blushed crimson.

"He told your father that if he and your mother did not leave Trowbridge Manor immediately, he would stand in the way of our betrothal, but that if they left without further argument, he would do everything in his power to see that we were married as soon as possible."

The cold bite of mortification stung Marianna most savagely. "Pray accept my apologies, my lord. Oh . . . ! I should never have unburdened myself to you. If I had not, Trowbridge would not have drawn you into this horrible coil." Looking down at her lap, she fiddled with the handle of her portmanteau, unwilling to meet his eyes. "I am sorry."

"I am not." Lindenshire knelt in front of her. "Miss Grantham, I am not sorry at all." He tipped her chin up.

He was peering at her earnestly through the thick lenses of his spectacles. "Miss Grantham . . . Marianna, I . . . I love you, and I have been trying to find words fine enough to ask you to marry me since Trowbridge told me he would not stand in my way. He knew my feelings ran deep."

"Lord Lindenshire, I—"

"My name is Orion. I give you leave to use it, but please . . . for now, just hear me out," he said. "Marianna, I do not care that you are no longer an heiress. You are a lovely young woman. Intelligent, sensible, well-mannered. Certainly, you have had one or two . . . misadventures, here at Trowbridge, but the *ton* will soon forgive you, especially if you are married to me. As you know, I am more interested in insects than I am in the latest *on-dits,* and the rest of London knows it, too. I am too busy with my studies to get into the sorts of scrapes True Sin gets into. I am known for my steadiness. Truth to tell, they all think me quite uninteresting." He matched her fingers with his own. "Marry me, Marianna. My coach awaits. It will take us to London. We shall marry, settle down into a life of scholarship, and the *ton* will forget your indiscretions. Please . . . I love you . . . will you marry me, dear heart?"

Marianna looked into his liquid brown eyes. His sincerity gripped her heart. He loved her! She felt tears prick her eyes, and a warmth like a summer's day suffused her consciousness.

Orion Chase, the Earl of Lindenshire, was everything Marianna had ever wished for in a husband. He was steady. Polite. Intelligent. Wealthy. Titled. A catch. He had been a good friend to her these last days, and she felt certain that she could grow to love him. True love, she thought, grew from seeds of friendship. And a part of her loved him already. He was far from uninteresting. Life with him would be filled with pleasant companionship and intellectual fulfillment. He did not need her fortune. He did not give a pin about her reputation or lack of a title. Bells in Heaven, he even thought her beautiful!

A lock of his brown hair had fallen across his eyes, and

Marianna lifted her hand to brush it aside. He kissed the palm, closing his eyes as he did so, and then he waited patiently for her answer, his soulful brown eyes vulnerable with hope and longing.

Nineteen

True kicked at a stone, sending it skipping into the brook. It landed on a wide, flat, dry rock out in the middle of the water, skittered to the edge, and gave a little wobble before finally falling with a splashing *thunk* into the water and sinking to the bottom.

How ironic. This whole miserable portion of his life had begun with one sinking, and it was ending with another.

He knew Lindenshire was proposing to Marianna at that very moment. He'd sprinted from the library, where Lindenshire had been waiting for her, just as Marianna had come down the stairs. He hadn't wanted to get in the man's way.

Lindenshire's carriage was waiting on the curved drive, waiting to carry the two of them away to London, should Marianna say yes.

Truesdale hoped she would.

Lindenshire was a good man. Although a member of the *ton,* and at the pinnacle of fashion, he was too studious, too serious to run in the fastest circles. In point of fact he was considered rather dull, but True knew that was far from the truth. Lindenshire simply cared too much for his fungi and his salamanders to be concerned with who was and was not admitted to Almack's. He was well-heeled and well-respected. And he had fallen arse over instep for Marianna Grantham. Any fool could see that.

True wanted desperately for her to be happy, and if she

could not love him, then perhaps she could love Lindenshire. She had seemed to enjoy the young earl's company.

And then there was that fact that Lindenshire had not lied to her, attempted to seduce her, or deliberately and methodically disgraced her.

True swore.

He sat on a wide, flat rock that jutted out into the brook, unwilling to go back to the manor until Lindenshire's carriage was gone. He would not see it roll past from where he was. He had come down the embankment to the edge of the brook purposely to avoid catching a glimpse of her as the coach rolled past. The rock had been a favorite spot as a boy, a place of refuge where no one thought to look for him. As it had on many other cool mornings, the music of the brook mixed with the buzzing wings of the bees and the occasional bird singing in the trees at the edge of the clearing above him.

"There you are."

True froze. It was the voice he dreaded hearing, the voice he longed to hear. Mary. He turned. She was working her way down the slope toward him. She was wearing a proper little blue flowered dress and a pair of proper white gloves. Her brilliant blue eyes shone against their backdrop of pale cheeks kissed with a light, rosy blush and her white-blond hair, which she had pulled back into its tight little bun.

"I have come to say thank-you for everything and to give you this." She stopped when she got within a few feet of him and held out her hand. "I am leaving for London without delay."

Shock coursed through him. She had accepted Lindenshire's proposal. He stood, unsure whether his legs would hold him.

She held his mother's ring out to him, the ruby winking in the sun. "I was going to leave it for you in the parlor, but, under the circumstances, I thought it the honorable thing to hand it back to you personally."

He reached out to take the ring. She dropped it into his

palm from her gloved hand, and his fingers closed around it. It still held her warmth. He felt a sudden urge to drop it into the water of the brook, to let it reside there with his memories, for all time, but he did not. He did not wish to overset her.

"Lord Lindenshire proposed to me, as you knew he would," she said. "I wanted to thank you before I left, for everything you have done."

"Surely not for everything," he said with a deliberately wry grin.

Her eyes crinkled at the corners. "Yes," she said with an emphatic nod. "Everything."

"Having you here was a pleasure."

"Was it?"

He looked into her eyes. "Marianna, if you had not accepted Lindenshire's proposal, I would have offered for you myself, though I knew you would not have accepted me after what I had done."

Her eyes grew big and round. "You would?"

He nodded. "Yes," he said, and smiled at her tenderly. "I would."

"I refused Lindenshire."

True's heart thudded to a stop. "You did *what?*" Didn't the silly chit know she was unlikely to receive a better offer? Didn't she realize what a good man Lindenshire was?

"I told him I could not wed him," she said. She took off one glove. "You were right, Truesdale. Lindenshire is not at all the sort of man I need or want. He is too controlled, too disciplined, too conservative. I need a man who will not be shocked, who will not balk at my spontaneous, willful, and wild impulses." She crooked one blonde brow at him and pointedly pulled off her other glove.

What the devil was she up to? "Which impulses do you mean, precisely?"

She showed him, surging into his arms and pushing him off balance. They splashed into the brook and the water flowed over them. She didn't let go but kissed him—soundly, playfully, passionately—the scent of her mixing with the sweet water and the wildflowers to produce a perfume to rival any that came from a bottle.

True kissed her back with all the joy his broken heart had longed could be his, then, finally, he pushed her away and held her at arm's length, allowing a tone of mock concern to color his voice as he exclaimed, "Miss Grantham! Such behavior will ruin my upstanding reputation!"

"What upstanding reputation?" she said, droplets of water shining on her cheeks and dripping from her lips and ears and pale eyelashes.

He answered her with a sudden seriousness. "The one I am attempting to acquire. I confess that I am selling my ships so that I can settle down here at Trowbridge and rear the ABC's properly."

"That is not very roguish," she remarked with equal seriousness, but then she grinned impishly. "In fact, it is quite sickeningly respectable."

He nodded. "You are right. I say, Miss Grantham, if we wed, do you think you could find it in your heart to forgive me an occasional lapse into respectability?" He held out his mother's ring to Mary once more.

She regarded the ring thoughtfully for a moment. True's heart formed a hard, hot lump in his throat. And then, finally, Mary slipped her finger into it.

"I might manage to forgive you," she said, *"if* you can find it in your heart to forgive me my own occasional madcap behavior."

True chuckled. "That must be the most unorthodox proposal of marriage a man has ever offered."

"And the most unorthodox acceptance."

They stared into each other's eyes and laughed deeply. True could feel the currents of relief and love flowing between them. He pulled from his coat pocket a sodden folded paper.

"What is that?" she asked, curiosity filling her beautiful eyes.

"It is a special license to marry. I obtained it when I went away that day."

"You mean when you disappeared without telling me where you were going or when you would be back."

"Were you worried?" he asked.

"You know I was. Pray say you will never do that again."

"Hmmm . . . I think I shall have to add 'termagant' or 'nag' or 'shrew' to my list."

"If you add any of them, then you should probably also add 'dangerous' and 'unpredictable.' "

He smiled and kissed a droplet from the tip of her nose. "We could marry today, right now. It is a lovely walk to the church. Or we could wait if you wish. I have not the fortune to give you a grand cathedral wedding, but we could arrange a lovely wedding right here in Trowbridge."

"That sounds lovely, but . . ."

"Hmm?" He hugged her to him.

"But I think a Gretna wedding would be so much more romantic."

Epilogue

The coach lumbered along the rocky coastline in the quiet sunshine of the late summer afternoon. Autumn's chill nipped the air, and Marianna sighed. They were homeward bound. Home to Trowbridge Manor, where their family— the ABC's, Ophelia, and John—would be waiting for them.

Family.

She smiled. Family was whoever truly cared about what happened to you. They were the people who mattered in life. No one else, not the *ton,* not one's adoptive family, not even one's true parents mattered if they didn't care. She was eager to get back home. They would be welcomed with genuine pleasure. Marianna hugged herself. It felt good to truly belong.

She and True had been gone for almost a month. There had been one delay after another. The road back from Gretna had been blocked by a rock slide, the road to London wet. Once there, the negotiations for the sale of her jewels and the payment of their debts had taken longer than they'd anticipated. And then they'd had to journey to Portsmouth and wait there an extra two days in order to settle True's lost cargo and free his ships from impoundment.

In spite of the delays, however, they had not been bored or unhappy for even a second. Newlyweds, they had found, did not suffer for lack of diversion.

Marianna looked over at True, twirled one long, loose curl in her bare gloveless fingers, and smiled.

He smiled lazily back.

She reached under her the hem of her gown.

His flawed eyebrow rose.

Slowly, she pulled off one of the blue stockings. They had been a gift from her friend Lady Marchman, who had paid a surprise visit to Trowbridge Manor, arriving just before they'd left for Gretna. Marianna had given her the outrageous stockings, but Agnes insisted that they were perfect for Marianna's "something blue" and that she must keep them for her trip to Gretna.

She reached slowly under her gown for the second stocking, knowing she had True's full attention now. A stocking in each hand, she shook the tiny silver bells, which jingled merrily, and then she tossed one stocking out the window of the coach and looked at True, mirroring his raised eyebrow.

"Here?" he asked. "Will you not be cold?"

She shook her head and laughed, gaily tossed the second stocking out the window. "True Sin will keep me warm." She curled onto his lap and, filling her lungs with the cool, crisp air, Marianna Sinclair, the Viscountess Trowbridge, began singing "Greensleeves."

About the Author

MELYNDA BETH SKINNER was born in 1963 in Florida, where she still lives with her husband of eleven years and their charming hellions, two little girls who could easily be mistaken for an A and a B both hoping for a C. She enjoys hearing from readers. Write to her at: 7259 Aloma Avenue, Suite 2, Box 31, Winter Park, FL 32792. Please enclose an SASE if you wish a reply. Or visit her online at *www.melyndabethskinner.com* where you can send her an e-mail or maybe even chat with her real time!

If you enjoyed this story, you may also enjoy the author's next novel, *Lord Logic and the Wedding Wish*. It's a tale of the logical and ultra-fashionable Lord Lindenshire and the stubborn, exasperating and irresistible Gypsy who insists it's their destiny to wed. The outrageous blue stockings play a part in their story, too, and you haven't heard the last from clever Ophelia Robertson!

More Zebra Regency Romances